JADED

JADED: Book One of The Jaded Duology
Copyright © 2017 by K.M. Robinson.

Published by Crescent Sea Publishing.
www.crescentseapublishing.com

Cover designed by Reading Transforms.
Image copyright © K.M. Robinson Photography.
Interior graphics by Millennium Genesis.

JADED

K.M. ROBINSON

Crescent Sea
PUBLISHING

DEDICATION

To all the brave people who have the courage to do what is right, even when it costs you. You are the world changers. Don't give up.

The consequence for my father trying to overthrow the commander and failing is my life. I am no longer my own. I belong to the Commander's son...as his wife. I can't see my father or my family. I am alone and trapped in a marriage I never wanted. My husband seems kind, but there's something there I can't quite explain. My father warned me that my life is in danger...and I think he might be right. Can I trust the man I married to protect me from his father or will I have to survive them both on my own?

CHAPTER 1
JADE

 have always been warned to stay away from Roan Diamond. He is the enemy. He is dangerous.

But today I will marry him.

And it's not my choice.

When I was five years old, my father challenged the Commander. He tried to overthrow him and take power over the country, if you can call this a country. It's more like a large city, but the Commander's father, being the power-hungry man that he was, wanted to call it a country. So a country it is called.

After the war, the real country split into sections, each adopting a name, rules, and borders. The problem was that Aloysius Diamond was less of a leader and more of a dictator. His son, Robert, adopted his policies and today we find ourselves in a precarious state of survival.

My father, a politician and leader, tried to overthrow the Commander to help set up a democracy, something none of our broken pieces of the country have seen in a long time. My father failed.

But there would be far too much of an uproar if the Commander had killed my father, even if it seemed like an accident. No, my father's life was safe. Mine, however, was fair game.

So now I stand before a mirror, my long dress swishing around my feet, waiting to be summoned. Brides wear white. *I* used tea to stain mine an *off-white* color. I refuse to be the bride they say I should be.

We all have to get married at some point, and usually we aren't given much of a choice as to whom it is we marry. I have *no* choice; Roan Diamond will be coming for me any moment.

I answer the knock at the door to find not Roan, but my father. This may be the last time I see him.

His face is washed with concern and he's fighting back tears.

"Jade," he says, enveloping me in his arms. "I'm so, so sorry, my baby girl."

His voice is muffled against my swept-up hair.

"I'll be all right, Daddy," I try to soothe him, hugging him tighter.

"Remember what we talked about."

I'm sure we're being monitored, so we can't speak freely.

I've been preparing for this moment since the minute

it was decided over ten years ago. I know that the Commander is going to try to hurt me. I know his son will be a part of it. I know my death will probably look accidental. And I know it is my job to survive: my father cannot help me once I walk through those doors.

I am prepared for the monster I am about to marry, for the prison I am about to live in, and for the killer who will be known as my father-in-law. I will not go down without a fight.

My father slips away and I want to cling to him as if I am five again. If only he hadn't been so motivated to protect everyone else, he could have protected me.

A knock sounds almost immediately and I rush back, thinking it must be my father returning. Instead I look into the green eyes of the man who is stealing my life.

My breath catches in my throat and I force myself to hold his gaze for a moment.

"You look very nice, Jade," Roan appraises me.

"Thank you," I say, casting my eyes down to prevent him from seeing my true feelings. I cannot bear to look at him.

He offers me his hand and turns slightly to lead me away. I hesitate and can't keep the look of disgust off my face. I know he notices it, but he doesn't flinch. I reach out and take his open hand and he leads me toward my sentencing. I am the most lovely convicted woman on Death Row ever.

The ceremony is simple, led by the Commander. Ordinarily this would be an honor, to have our country's leader officiate a wedding. A few times a year, he does just that, surprising a few happy couples. Personally, I'd rather be locked in a cage with a rabid dog. It's a funny comparison, because at the moment, the Commander actually *looks* a bit like a rabid dog. Flecks of foam spit from his mouth as he speaks. I can feel the pent-up rage threaten to bite and latch on to me. But there is also something there that a rabid animal does not have, and *that* is the overwhelming sense of victory. He knows in this moment *that he has won.*

My father shows no emotion, nor do I. He may have won, but we will not lend ourselves to his victory. He shall have no satisfaction from our reactions. And in that moment, I know what I must do.

I glance to my father and his eyes are trained on me.

I am changing the plan on him. I have to make him understand.

I smile; a forced smile at first, but I let it morph into

the smile he has known my entire life. He squints a touch before straightening his face.

When I turn back to Roan, I lean in. My hands are in his and I let my excited energy flow through them to his hands. I catch his eye and let mine sparkle.

Today is my wedding day and I love this man.

And I will make him believe it. He will know I am in love with him, for that is how I will survive.

Roan's eyes widen when he sees me lean in. His smile seems so genuine. I know it's nothing; it can't be. I will fight him with the very thing he isn't expecting: adoration.

We say our vows and I clutch his hands in mine. When we turn, I loop my arm through his to leave. I catch my father's expression; his eyes narrow ever so slightly. If I hadn't spent years studying his face, I wouldn't have noticed it.

I lean toward my new husband, moving my head to lean toward his arm.

I can see the plan click in my father's mind and he nods once in approval. I know he understands.

Roan raises his free hand to rest on my hands, which are wrapped around his arm. My first instinct is to pull away, but I fight the urge and smile up at him. I will win him over if it's the last thing I do...and it *will* be the last thing I do, should my plan fail.

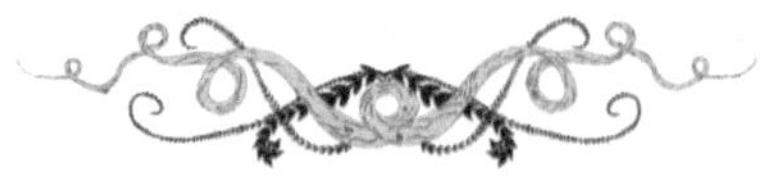

My new home is large—much larger than the home I lived in as a politician's daughter. I had no say in it; my new family-in-law designed it. This is as far from my taste as possible and I have a feeling it was planned that way. I am *supposed* to feel alien in my new home.

"Are you hungry?" Roan asks.

"No," I reply, eyes wandering the room. Then, I think better of it. "Actually, do you want me to make us something?"

"I can do it," he says kindly. "Come sit with me."

He motions me over to the barstool in front of the island in the kitchen.

I sit and carefully arrange my skirt around me. He works quietly for a few minutes, pans clinking together the only noise in the room.

"You looked very nice today," he says quietly, avoiding eye contact.

"Thank you." I cast my eyes down and blush. "So did you."

He smiles at me and I return it. His eyes linger for a moment too long and suddenly I realize: we are alone...and married.

"I..." I start but the words stick in my throat. "Roan...I...I'd like to take this slow...get to know each other. Can we do that?" *Please, please, let us do that. Please don't force me into anything.*

"Jade, of course. I would never push you into anything. We don't know each other; I know that. We'll take our time. There is no pressure."

He reaches for my hand, but instinctively I pull back from his touch. He flinches as I withdraw from him.

"Thank you," I say with breathless relief. Even if this is part of the trap to gain my trust, I don't care. He won't touch me tonight.

"Of course, Jade. I want you to feel comfortable here. I know this was never your idea, and I'm sorry you got forced into this, but we're here now and we need to learn to get along. I know it takes time."

"You're very rational," I say as he slides a plate toward me. I pick up a fork and start moving the food around in front of me while resting my chin in my free hand.

"You seem pretty practical, too."

"I guess we are a good match. Who knew?" I joke, looking up through my eyelashes at him.

His eyes sparkle as he watches me. I might actually be able to pull this off.

"So anyway," he says after he swallows, "I'll take the spare bedroom. You can have the master. I've already got my things in the guest room."

I nod.

"We may have to act like we're a couple out there"—he jerks his head toward the outside—"but in here, we can learn to be friends first."

"I think that's a good idea," I reply. "So tell me, what are *you* like, Roan?

"I'm...just me," he says thoughtfully. "I don't know... what do you want to know?"

"Well..." I think for a moment. *What could I possibly use to my advantage here?* "You're nineteen, right? And I'm eighteen. So we're one year apart. What's one thing you've learned in the extra year that could help me?"

"Wow." He looks impressed. "Going for the deep stuff right away, huh?"

I shrug. "Might as well. We're going to be here awhile, so why waste time on small talk."

"All right then," he smirks. For a moment, he is lost deep in thought, but then his eyes flick back to me and catch my gaze.

"In my extra year, I have learned that other people

will always make plans about your life and there's nothing you can do about it but try to survive."

He smiles at me but my blood runs cold. *What does he mean?*

"Like my father, with this marriage. He decided this for us, not us. But we're going to get through it…together."

I hope that's all he means.

"That's a good realization, Roan. We can't control others, but we can control ourselves."

"Exactly," he breathes, relieved I understand. "I've also learned that if you don't eat fast enough, you lose your food."

His fork lashes out and snatches the food from my plate. He pops it into his mouth and grins at me, wild-eyed. My jaw drops open and I try to speak but it only comes out as a squeak.

He darts for his second mouthful, but I rap his hand with my own fork.

"Oww!" he cries, shaking out his knuckles. "Hey, *wife.* Play nice."

"Mind your *own* manners, *husband,*" I chastise playfully.

He goes back to eating off of his own plate and I finish my own food. If this is what it will be like for a while, I can survive it.

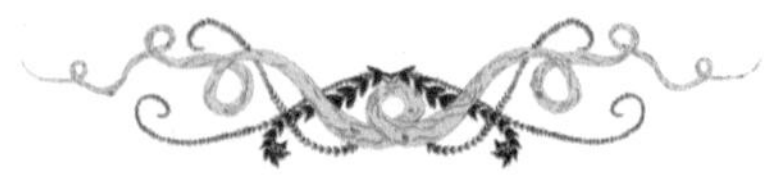

True to his word, Roan takes the guest room. I convince myself not to put a chair in front of my room door. I have to play the part. I can't show I was scared. Despite my nervousness, I manage to get a few hours of sleep.

Morning comes quickly, and being an early riser, I am the first to step into the common living space.

I move around the couch and wander over to the kitchen. I should cook for him…try to make an effort. Searching the room, I locate where everything has been stored and set to work making something edible.

"Good morning, Bird," Roan greets me as he steps into the kitchen.

"Bird?" I question.

"Early bird, you know…since you're up early. Are you always up this early?" He rubs his eyes.

"Oh." I giggle. "Yeah, I'm a morning person. I take it you're not?"

"No, I am…just not as early as you," he corrects me. "Notice how the sun is just starting to come up? That's what we call the *actual* start of the day."

I guess I did get up earlier than usual.

"Are you hungry?" I ask, setting a plate on the counter.

"Thanks." He slides into a seat and I stand behind the

island where he was standing the night before. "Mmm… you're a pretty good cook."

"Thanks. My dad taught me." Thinking of him causes my ribcage to tighten around me.

"You miss him?" Roan drops his voice and looks down, focusing on his plate.

"Yeah. I know it's silly, it's only been a day…"

"But that day changed our entire lives. I get it, Jade." He looks back up at me. "I know everything is complicated, but we'll figure it out."

I nod.

"So, what are we doing today?" he asks.

The Command gives all newlyweds a week off from work after their wedding days as a sort of honeymoon. Some take the time to get to know their new spouse… others take the time to *really* get to know them.

"I don't know. I'm not used to *not* working. I've never really had a lot of free time."

The Command expects all people to begin work at age sixteen. We are given three months to find a job, or one is assigned to us. That's not something you ever want. So I found a job. I was willing to take anything, but as it turns out, I was offered my pick of several.

Many people who were quietly sympathetic to my father's actions quickly stepped in to offer me placement. In public I was treated like any employee, but in private I was provided with special care. We made it look like I had done all the work to get the job and had convinced them to hire me so that they wouldn't be targeted. I would have felt terrible if Mr. Eroh had been hurt because of me.

Mr. Eroh's shop had been in the middle of my town. It was an eclectic shop, full of pawned items and tinkered trinkets. When something broke, the people would bring it to him to fix. He would often trade his services for those who could not afford his help. It was in his shop I learned many of the skills I could not learn publicly with my father.

"Do you have any plans for today?" I ask.

He gives me the strangest look. "Well, I think we need to stay together, Jade. We *did* just get married. We can't exactly go wandering off on our own."

"Oh. Good point." And it *is*. "Maybe we could… rearrange the furniture?" I suggest.

"Not exactly your style, huh?"

"Not really." I give him a half smile and shrug.

"Yeah, that's fine. We can start after breakfast."

"Okay, great." At least we're cooperating.

We spend the next hour changing the room. I almost laugh to myself when I finally decide I have the living room set up in a way that I'm positive his parents will hate.

"Happy?" he asks, hands playfully resting on his hips.

"Yes, this is better." I give him a smile.

"So now what?" Roan asks, walking toward me.

"Now… I think I should unpack." I step toward my room. "Your parents may have had you already moved in, but I just got here, remember?"

"You didn't bring much with you?" he comments, frowning slightly.

"I only brought what I needed. If I need anything else I can send for it. And besides, I had a few trunks brought over yesterday while we were at the ceremony."

"All right. I guess I'll take a break then." He lies down on the couch and kicks his feet up over the armrest. Placing one hand on his stomach and the other resting on his forehead, he closes his eyes for a nap.

I could do it right now, kill him and escape.

But, of course, I can't.

The illusive safety of my room beckons me and I gladly slip away to hide.

CHAPTER 2
JADE

he outside of my new home is lush with greenery. There are plants and flowers everywhere. The garden must have been another part of the plan, since I'm allergic to flowers.

There is a hammock in the backyard, a high fence blocking it from view of the neighbors. We even have a few trees, including an apple tree that just might be the only thing I like about the house.

The steps off the back porch were recently reconstructed, the wood brand new. Checking over my shoulder to be sure I'm alone, I inspect every inch of the yard, hoping I'm not being too obvious. I'll need to know every inch of the place if I'm going to survive.

"Want some lemonade?" Roan asks as he walks down the steps, holding two big glasses.

I hold in my gasp as I turn to him. I was so focused that I had nearly forgotten to listen and only heard his approach a few seconds before he stepped outside. I had just enough time to make it look like I was watering the flowers on the far side of the steps.

"Sure, thanks," I say, setting down the watering can and reaching for the glass. "Did you have a nice nap?"

"Did you have a nice time watering the plants?" he counters.

"Not especially. Flowers and I don't exactly get along." I scrunch my nose up and shake my head.

"Then why water them?"

"Your parents were so kind to give us such a lovely home, I didn't want to let the flowers die. I really want to make a good impression on your parents, and I have a feeling killing their plants might offend them."

"You care about impressions?"

"Honestly? I don't really care what your parents think of me. I *do* care what *you* think of me, and I know you respect their opinion. Therefore, make *them* happy, make *you* happy, and my plan is a success."

"I'm impressed. Most people wouldn't think of that."

"Well, like we keep saying, we're married now; we have to make the effort to make this work. If that means suffering through allergies, I'll do it."

"Well, I don't want you dying on me now, so how about I'll handle the yard work and you handle a few things inside the house that I'd rather pass on?"

"Deal," I say, a bit surprised.

This guy's good. Loving husband, caring friend…he really knows how to play a girl. If I didn't know better, I'd fall for it.

"I think tomorrow I might go to town, make sure my job is still available for me."

"You're going back?"

"You don't expect me to sit around all day, do you?"

"No, I just didn't think you'd be going back to…where you worked before."

"I like it there. *I know,*" I say thoughtfully, "maybe tomorrow we could go for a walk and show each other important places from our childhood."

I wait for him to smile back at me. When he catches my gaze, he does, agreeing with a slight nod.

"Yeah, that might be nice."

"Great. Then it's a plan," I say, finalizing the details.

"And speaking of plans, my parents invited us for lunch tomorrow. Maybe we can go for our walk after that, so it doesn't get cut short."

I'm a bit taken aback by the invitation. I hadn't expected to have to see the Commander again so soon.

"Sure." I try to smile, but I know it must look as forced as it feels.

"Oh, come on now, Jade. They aren't *that* scary." Roan laughs. "You'll like them once you get to know them."

He pauses a moment before adding, "They won't bite. Promise."

Something flickers in his eyes and I know in that moment I can't trust this man.

"I'm sure they're wonderful. Meeting the in-laws can just be a little... *intimidating*. Think of how you would feel if you had to face my dad less than seventy-two hours after marrying his little girl."

"I guess I can see your point." His smile doesn't quite reach his eyes.

Maybe it would be easier to read him than I thought.

Suddenly his whole face brightens and he stands to his feet, stretching a hand down to help me up.

On second thought, if he can flip switches that quickly, maybe I *will* have trouble reading him.

"What are we doing?" I ask, standing next to him. I watch him walk inside.

When he doesn't answer, I follow.

Once inside the house, it takes a minute for my eyes to adjust to the difference in light. Just as the world is coming back into focus, something pointy hits me in the stomach.

For a moment, I panic, thinking I let my guard down and he struck. I clutch at the object and force myself to hold back my sigh of relief as I realize he had thrown a notebook at me.

"Clearly you have some trouble catching." He laughs. "Think you can handle this?"

Roan waves a pen in the air. He tosses it to me and I

make a show of batting it into the air a few times before finally catching it. There's no need for him to know my skills of catching and blocking oncoming objects.

"Graceful, I see," he comments.

"Let's see *you* catch it," I say, throwing it back at him.

Effortlessly, his hand flies out and catches it. He grins victoriously and saunters over to me. With a flick of his wrist, he holds the pen out to me. As I reach for it, he pulls it back, just out of reach.

"Just keeping you on your toes, *wife,*" he grins.

"Thank you," I attempt to say graciously. I refuse to take the bait. "So just *what* exactly are we writing down?

"A list." He crosses over to the table and takes a seat. "Places to take each other tomorrow. We can compare and make a game plan for the day."

"Oh," I say, a little surprised. "That's actually a good idea."

"I *have* been known to have a few of those." He smirks again, peeking up from where he's already bent over his paper, scribbling away.

If he weren't so deadly, I could actually see myself being friends with this guy.

CHAPTER 3
ROAN

 keep a close eye on her as we're making our lists. She has no idea that our little venture tomorrow serves more than one purpose.

I think she's starting to trust me, which is good. It will make all of this a lot easier. I've been training for this for most of my life, but it doesn't mean I like the idea of hurting her any more than I did when my father first told me about it.

Still, her father needs to pay for what he has done. James Jareau took far too many lives to be let off the hook. And if I must be the one to hold him accountable, so be it.

CHAPTER 4
JADE

"How long will it take you to get ready?" Roan asks the next morning.

I look down at my clothing, wondering if I messed up my shirt during breakfast. When I find nothing out of place, I look back up.

"I'm ready. When do we need to leave?"

His eyebrows shoot up.

"Jade, you look nice, but you can't wear that to lunch at my parents. You have to wear a dress or something."

He genuinely looks shocked that that thought hadn't occurred naturally to me.

I am wearing a pretty lace top and nice shorts. By all accounts, I look rather good. Apparently, when dining with royalty—*or wannabe royalty*—one must look more sophisticated.

"Oh. Okay." I nod, still not sure what to do. "What time are we leaving?"

"They want us there by noon, which means we should be there by eleven thirty. So…an hour?"

"Okay, well that's manageable."

"Great." He stands there, as if waiting for me to get up and go to my room to get ready.

"So I've got some time then…" I say slowly, hinting that I don't take that long to get ready.

He looks like he wants to say something.

I glance back up and raise an eyebrow at him.

"Maybe we should look at your options?"

I'm dumbfounded that he wants to approve my outfit choice as if I have no style of my own or ability to dress myself. But I must play along.

I walk to my room and he follows me, *actually follows me*, into my closet. Turning, I put a hand on his chest, and push him out into the bedroom. Spinning around, I pull out a few of my dresses.

He examines each one as I hold them up.

"Maybe you should try them on," he suggests.

"Like a fashion show?" I ask, surprised. "Are you really going to sit through me trying on all my dresses?"

"Well, not all, but maybe *some*."

I sigh and toss the dresses on the bed next to him. "Get out."

He obliges, taking a seat on the couch in the living room. I shut the door and pull a light blue, tea length dress from the pile and slip into it. Walking out into the living room, I give him an exasperated huff.

He looks appreciatively at the dress and then motions for me to spin. All I want to do is deck him, but I have to play the game, and right now, that's being an obedient little wife.

"That one is nice," he finally says. "What else do you have?"

I march back into the room and force myself not to slam the door. I find a maroon-colored flowy dress and put it on next. This time when I enter the living room, I pause for a moment, and then spin, holding the skirt in my hands and dipping my shoulders in a silly motion as I twirl, making him laugh.

"That one is nice, too. Have anything in purple?"

I think for a moment, and then run back into my room.

My lavender dress is one of my favorites. I only wear it on special occasions and I have no desire to wear it to the Diamond house this afternoon, but I don't mind wearing it for a few moments in the house.

"Wow." His words reach me before I even step across the threshold of my room.

"This is one of my favorites. It's special occasions only, but a few minutes right now won't hurt anything."

"You can wear that around the house every day if you like," he says, making me blush.

"I have a nice black one that might work," I reply, changing the subject.

"Don't you think black is a little formal?" he asks. When I shrug, he adds, "Go try it on."

I dart back in and come out with a high neck, straight black dress that silhouettes my body.

"Stunning," he says. I curtsy.

"Too much?" I ask.

"I *really* want to say no, but yeah," he sighs regretfully.

"All right, I've got one this time."

When I step back into the room, I'm wearing a flowy mint green chiffon dress that stops at my knees. It's simple, but elegant. I added a darker green shrug to it, dressing it down a bit.

"Perfect," Roan says. "And look at that…almost time to go. I should get dressed."

"What, no fashion show for me?" I ask innocently.

He laughs. "Not today, woman."

"Fine, but I expect to play dress-up-my-new-husband at some point this week," I yell as he walks down the hall to his room. He waves his hand at me without turning to look.

I walk over to the kitchen and open the bottom cabinet. When Roan returns, he finds me perched against the island, a fresh blueberry pie in my hands. I bat my eyelashes at him, my elbows propped on the island and ankles crossed on the foot bar of my barstool chair.

"What…?" he asks.

"Blueberry pie." I smile, wishing I could smack the surprised look right off his face. "I thought we should take something to your parent's house today, so I made a dessert."

"When…?"

"Last night." I can't help but smirk. I like messing with his head like this. He never had any idea I was up most of the night cooking.

"Incredible." He shakes his head and jokes, "You know, I'll expect freshly made things for breakfast from now on."

"You're not nearly as important to impress as your parents are, *sweetheart*," I say, though I know the opposite to be true. Roan is *the most* important one to impress.

"Something about this just isn't fair," he gripes as we walk to the door.

"Well, give me a reason to get up in the middle of the night and bake for you, and maybe I will." I drop my voice a bit, suddenly slipping into flirtation mode.

"Well, maybe I'll just have to do that," he says quietly back.

The Diamonds live just ten minutes down the road from us. I'm grateful for the distance. If I ever needed to run, it would be a short sprint to get home.

It's funny how I'm starting to call my cage "*home*" now.

"You ready for this?" Roan asks as we approach the large house.

I note several security guards standing around the property, trying not to be too easily noticed. Large gates stand open, ready to receive visitors, but able to be snapped shut in an instant should the need arise. Flowers fill the yard, much like they did at my own home, though these are far more lavish.

A woman greets us at the door.

"Hello, Maybelle," Roan greets the woman warmly.

"Hello, Roan." She places her hands on his shoulders and leans in for the stiffest of hugs, giving me the feeling that despite her love for him, she tries to keep a line of professionalism drawn. I imagine that's part of the Commander's rules. She turns to me. "And this must be your lovely wife. Hello, Jade. I'm Maybelle. I've worked for the Diamonds since Roan was a child. Don't mind me, but I think of the Diamonds as family."

She gives me a small, embarrassed smile as she explains away the hug.

"And we think of you as family too, Maybelle." Roan grins.

"Thank you, Love." She takes his chin in her hand and gives him a quick squeeze. "And I hope one day you'll feel the same, Jade."

"I think there's a very good chance of that, Maybelle," I say, grinning.

I really liked this woman. If only the rest of the house could be so kind. I'm positive she has no idea of the Commander's plans; no one is that good of an actress.

"Roan, is that you?" another female voice calls from within the house.

"Yes, Mom, we're here."

"You're early," Alice Diamond says, rounding the corner. Her smile fades the moment she sees me, but she rushes to her son and embraces him. "I'm so glad you're here. Come, come."

"Jade brought a blueberry pie she made herself, Mom." Roan motions to me, bringing me back into the conversation.

Alice turns to me and forces a smile. "How lovely. Thank you, Jade. That was very thoughtful of you. Maybelle..."

She motions for her maid to take the dish from me. Maybelle scurries off, and I wish I could follow her.

"Your father will be home any minute now. He had to run to work for a bit this morning." Alice guides us into the living room. Their house is triple the size of mine.

It's, perhaps, the grandest thing I've ever seen, including the old library and church in town.

"Your home is lovely," I say, tearing my gaze away from the intricate ceiling.

"Thank you," Alice says. She turns and engages Roan in a conversation clearly not meant for me. I take the opportunity to take stock of the room.

The colors are magnificent; everything is rich and clear, as if the colors had only been created yesterday. While the rest of the country used whatever was left over from before the Command took charge, it appears Robert Diamond had a team of painters, carpenters, and sculptors visit his home every other week. The colors vibrated off every surface. It was disgusting.

"Roan!" a voice boomed, echoing through the room, catching me off guard.

The Commander.

"Good to see you, son. How's married life?" He hugs his son, clapping him on the back in typical male greeting.

"It's good. Jade and I are great."

He motions for me to join him.

It's all I can do to stand to my feet and slip against his side. I tuck my arm around his back and he holds my hip, pulling me to him.

I hadn't been made aware that we were supposed to

appear close for his parent's sake, but I got the message loud and clear.

"Hello, Jade," the Commander starts. His eyes betray him, flashing menacingly. "It's so nice to have you here. Are you liking your new house?"

His hand still rests on his son's shoulder, forcing us into an uncomfortably close triangle of a conversation. I wish I could step closer to Roan, but that really wouldn't give me any more security than where I was already.

"Yes, it's lovely." I turn to face Alice. "Mrs. Diamond, you must be responsible for those lovely flowers in our garden. Thank you so much. Roan and I are greatly enjoying spending time out in the yard, aren't we Roan?"

I squeeze his hip as I redirect the question to him.

"Yes, very much. In fact, just yesterday I woke up from a nap and found Jade outside watering them. We even enjoyed some lemonade out on the back steps. It's a lovely place to spend time, Mom, thanks."

"I'm glad you like it, Roan," she says, completely ignoring me.

"Come, let's eat," the Commander says, pulling away.

We sit down at a large table. Roan is to my right, his father at the head of the table to Roan's right. Alice is seated across from Roan, leaving me slightly outside of their little group.

Alice, Roan and the Commander chat quietly for a few minutes. I remark on the food, but mostly keep quiet.

"So, Jade…" the Commander says loud enough to get my attention. "How's married life?"

I put on my easiest smile, "It's an adjustment, sir, though I'm sure you're well aware. We're getting along, so I think we'll be just fine figuring things out. You've raised a very fine man, Mr. and Mrs. Diamond. A true gentleman."

The Commander raises an eyebrow at his son, but doesn't say whatever it is he's thinking.

"So, you're adjusting well then?" he continues, returning his gaze to me. "Not missing home, or anything?"

Now I see his game. He means to taunt me.

"Right now, I'm just trying to find my new place here, with your son. I'm sure there will be time to think of the past another day."

"Well good then, Son. It looks like your bride doesn't plan on running away anytime soon." He laughs as if he's joking.

I laugh with him; my high, light laugh.

"No. No, of course not, sir. I'm quite committed, I assure you."

Committed to not dying. Possibly committed to taking you out. But, I don't say that out loud.

"Commitment is a good thing. But only when it's not *misguided.*" His voice slips a little, and his good-natured tone falters just enough to let in an icy edge.

"One can only be misguided if one is allowed to have thoughts," I say quietly with a smile.

I can see him turn a shade of red.

"But of course, the Command is so good at caring for us, who really needs to think for themselves? If one follows the rules, everything will work out, isn't that right, Commander?"

"Of course, *my dear*," he answers curtly.

If I could put my fork through his eye for addressing me so personally, I would.

Roan takes my hand under the table. He tries to redirect the conversation, but his father has other ideas. Just as the Commander starts to speak, Roan jumps up from his chair.

"Father, may I see you in the study?"

The Commander fumes, but follows his son out of the room.

After a moment of strange silence, I ask to use the bathroom. Maybelle leads the way before returning to the kitchen.

CHAPTER 5
ROAN

hat are you doing?* You can't *bait* her like that!" I shout as soon as the study door is closed.

"This is *my* house and… "

"And this is *your* plan. You want to get back at James Jareau for what he did? *This* is your only chance. If you upset her… If she figures this out, it's all over!"

I'm furious. We've worked so hard for so many years to bring all of this together, and my father tries to undo it all with one lunch conversation.

"You're right. She's just so…*infuriating*." My father grimaces. "But she'll pay. This will all work out. We'll make the world think we love her and no one will suspect a thing when she dies."

"Even Maybelle loves her already."

"Jade is good, I'll give you that," Father runs his hands through his hair, pacing around the room. "She's got the whole good-girl act down. No one would believe she's got her father's blood in her."

My father starts to snarl as he moves around the room.

"For now, we make him suffer. We keep him away from her. We parade her around so that he can see her, but can't have her. We make her into one of us and turn her away from him. And then we take her from him. Permanently."

"Yes, Father, I know the plan," I say reluctantly. "But… maybe we don't have to kill her. Maybe we can turn her against him. Wouldn't that be a fate worse than death? She's still here, but she's lost to him."

"Yes, I suppose that would be a good idea, Roan…*but no*. Someone must die for this. Someone must pay the price, and if it can't be James Jareau, than it's going to be his daughter!"

CHAPTER 6
JADE

 back away from the door. My blood is pounding in my ears.

I had been right all along. Everything my father told me would happen is happening. If I hadn't snooped, I never would have known for sure, but now there is no denying it: Roan Diamond is trying to kill me.

I hurry back to the bathroom and splash some water on my face. I must keep calm. And I have to get out of this house.

I make it back to the table before Roan and his father finish their conversation. Alice is picking at her food in an effort to avoid talking to me. At least *she* isn't putting up a front.

"Well, ladies, have you missed us?" the Command addresses us calmly as he and his son walk back into the room.

"You shouldn't have been gone so long, dear," Alice chastises him playfully, pushing his arm as he sits.

I might have actually mistaken them for a loving family for a moment if the Commander's searing eyes hadn't found mine.

"The food is delicious," I say, taking a bite of whatever is in front of me. I chew for an obnoxiously long time to avoid having to speak.

The conversation picks back up and I try to add a few things in here or there. The Commander finds ways to include me—clearly part of his plan to win over my trust and make the country think they accept me.

"We'll have a party for you both, a sort of...welcome-to-the-Neighborhood party," the Commander suggests. "Won't that be nice, dear?" he asks his wife.

"Yes, lovely," Alice says.

Immediately she starts to plan, setting a date in two weeks. I agree with everything she says, never questioning, nor adding my own thoughts. I must be the perfect daughter-in-law if I want them to think I'm buying this nonsense.

"And of course, you'll come to the office party this weekend," the Commander says.

"The office party?" I ask, realizing I suddenly need more information.

"It's a party Dad hosts for all the people in his office. I usually attend when I can; this time, you'll come too.

That way I can show you off to all of Dad's friends," he smiles and squeezes my hand. I try not to pull back.

"It will be nice to meet the people you work with, Commander," I say as graciously as I can.

"I'm sure they're all eager to meet you, too," he says, his smile dangerously close to becoming a sneer, "and of course, you'll both be at the Command party next month."

The Command party. I had nearly forgotten. Each year the Commander throws an elaborate party for all of the government officials. I had never been allowed to attend; my father kept me as far from the Commander as possible growing up, but each year, he'd get dressed up and go to the party. The light at the end of my tunnel had arrived in the form of a ball gown-filled party where I might finally be able to see my father again.

"Of course," Roan agrees, trying to describe it to me as if I don't know what it is. "I think you'll really enjoy it, Jade."

"I'm sure. It's sounds lovely."

"Well, we should probably head out," Roan announces. "Jade and I have plans this afternoon. Mom, Dad, thanks for having us over. It was great seeing you." He hugs both of his parents goodbye and escorts me to the door.

"We'll be seeing you soon, Jade, I'm sure," the Commander threatens, a hint of a growl creeping into his voice.

"It's been a pleasure, sir." I nod and duck out of the door under Roan's arm. He lets the door fall closed behind him and catches up with me part way to the front gate.

"That went well," he says.

"Yes. I learned quite a bit about your family today, I think we're all going to get along just *wonderfully*."

"Did you really lose your first tooth *here*?" I ask, giggling at the thought of a young Roan Diamond pulling out his first baby tooth at the barber's.

"Right there in that turtle chair," he says, pointing at the faded old toy. "Mr. Q was cutting my hair and I just reached inside and pulled it out. Blood everywhere. And you know old Mr. Q, blind as a bat almost; he couldn't tell where the blood was coming from and he thought he had stabbed me with the scissors."

Roan could barely speak he was laughing so hard.

"Unbelievable!" I laugh. "We make lists of important places to go see, and you make your first stop *here*."

"Hey! I told you I had a good list!" He runs his hands

through his blond hair as he turns away from the store window. "Now come on, where's *your* first stop?"

He makes it look so effortless. He just slips into this persona of being kind and thoughtful. Sometimes it seems like we're actually friends. I don't know how he does it so... flawlessly. If I didn't know to look for it, I'd never have guessed what he really has planned for me.

But then, he has no idea what I have in store for him either.

I know one thing for sure: if he's going to kill me, I'm going to do everything in my power to make him feel guilty about it. If my first stop doesn't do it, my second surely will.

We have each picked five stops along our route. We have to go through Roan's first three before we make our way to my side of town. The barbershop was first on his list. We also visit the park he used to spend time at as a child. We pause for a bit to play on the empty swings. He even spins me on the merry-go-round, though only for a moment because I refuse to lose my equilibrium around him.

His third stop is the school he attended. We watch the children run around outside for a few minutes before continuing. Roan tells me his favorite subjects were math and science because they were so predictable and constant. I counter with my appreciation for reading and language classes.

We make our way over the hill that separated our towns to my first stop: the bakery.

"Jade!" a chorus of voices fills the room the moment I walk inside.

Two little girls dart over to me, wrapping their skinny little arms around my waist. A little boy toddles over and hugs my leg.

"Well now, if it isn't our little bride." Annie grins at me as she walks over to the table I guide us to. She sets down two cups and pours me some tea.

"Tea?" I ask Roan as he sits beside me. He nods politely to Annie.

"Now tell me, darling, how is married life?" she asks loudly as she pours Roan's tea. Annie has never had any volume control.

She reaches up and tucks a stray hair back into the handkerchief she's wearing on her head. Two short pigtails poke out the back. If she weren't so mature, she'd look like a teenager instead of a full-grown woman.

"Is this one treating you all right, darling?" she asks me. She swings toward Roan, adding, "Because if he's not,

we'll take him out, and I don't care whose son you are."
She winks at him, keeping it good-natured, but I know
she is more than serious.

Roan holds his hands up in mock surrender. "I promise, I'm taking good care of her." He smiles reassuringly.

"What will you have?' she asks. "Muffin?"

I nod. Annie knows me so well.

"Apple cinnamon, fresh from the oven." She tries to
entice Roan, nodding to the counter where the muffins
sit in a glass dome.

"They're amazing," I add.

"Well, I can't miss out on amazing fresh-baked
muffins, now can I?" Roan asks.

Just then the door swings open and a group of
teenagers walk in. When they see me, they freeze.

"Jade! You're back!" they chorus.

Surrounding us, they pull up chairs and sit with their
elbows on their knees, leaning forward to hear whatever
story I'm about to tell them.

Roan seems surprised that I'm getting so much attention, but I'm reveling in it. I launch into details about my
new house, and how I just came from lunch with the
Commander and how lovely his house is. I tell them
about how wonderfully Roan and I are getting along and
that he's great at cooking, which makes a few of the girls
giggle.

I actually expect them to fawn over Roan a bit more

than they do. But at this point, most of them know why I'm in the situation I'm in and most of my town is mortified for my safety. It shouldn't surprise me that they are wary of him.

"Jade. How lovely to see you," a loud voice says only seconds after the tiny bell above the door rings.

Mr. Zuckerman stands in the doorway for only a moment before coming over and scooping up my hand. It's a bit of a task working his way through the sea of teenagers surrounding us, but he manages. The men who arrived with him take a seat at a far table.

He smiles and shakes my hand. "You seem to be doing well."

Mr. Zuckerman works with my father. He quietly supported my father's rebellion, keeping just far enough away that he wasn't caught when my father was. It was all part of the plan to bring the rebellion about. He's going to run right to my father after this, I'm sure.

"Well, hello, Roan. Nice to see you again." Mr. Zuckerman shakes Roan's hand.

"Hello, Mr. Zuckerman, nice to see you as well."

"How's everything? Fine?" he asks.

"Yes, Mr. Zuckerman, thanks for asking," I reply.

I can't give anything away with Roan so close, but I'll be able to let Mr. Eroh know later that I found out the truth. He and I have developed a way of reading each other over the years.

"Very good. Well, you two enjoy your muffins."

He takes his place by two other men at a table and Annie brings them coffee. One of the men catches my eye before frowning deeply and quickly turning away, his dark hair falling over his eye as his hand grips his mug more tightly. The second man nods and gives me a small smile, a shocking comparison to his rude coworker. He must be working with Mr. Zuckerman on my father's behalf. Or maybe he's just friendly.

The more I look around me, the more I realize I'm not alone.

Everyone here, all of these people, are pulling for me to make it out of this alive.

I just hope I *can*.

CHAPTER 7
ROAN

e only spend a few more minutes in the bakery after Mr. Zuckerman, one of the men that works as a politician for The Command, greets us. I've always known him to be a good, loyal man. Dad will be pleased he saw us on our outing.

The more people that see me with Jade, *and having an enjoyable time*, the better.

I've never seen anything like the display at the bakery. From the moment we walked in, Jade has been surrounded. Everyone seems to know her...love her even.

For someone with such a corrupt past, she sure has a lot of people who want to be near her.

CHAPTER 8
JADE

 have to practically pull the girls off of me as I leave. I wave goodbye one last time as Roan steps outside, and I see a wave of fear fall over every face. A moment later it is replaced by happy smiles and waves. I turn to find Roan has turned to wait for me.

If the adoration of my friends and neighbors hasn't won me any sympathy points, my next stop will.

We take the dirt road through the field and down over the hill.

"Jade, where are we?" Roan asks, confusion in his voice.

Before us stands a massive field, with grass cut short. Stones fill the place and as we draw closer I can see him working it out.

"We've come to see my mother," I say softly.

I make my way through the cemetery plots until I

come to the one with her name on it. Elizabeth Donnelly Jareau.

I kneel next to the stone and fold my legs under me. Tracing the letters with my fingers, I breathe in. For a moment, it's just me and her.

Roan sits down and interrupts my moment.

"Hello, Mrs. Jareau," he says softly. He gives me a small smile and I realize how desperately I want to hurt him.

"I was three when she died. I really don't remember her. Actually, I only have one memory of her at all."

"What's that?" he asks, as if he cares.

But I can't. I can't give up the one piece of my mom that I have. Not to *him.*

"That's between me and her," I say softly, tracing the letters again.

"Hi, Mom, it's me. I've brought Roan with me. I'm sorry I didn't come sooner. The wedding has kept me pretty busy. You'd like Roan; he's been a gentleman, just like you always wanted for me."

I can feel Roan watching me, so I look up.

"She wrote me letters when I was a baby, just in case anything should happen to her. It's like she knew..." I trail off.

"And my dad told me things. So I know stuff about her. I just... was little, so most of what I know is what I was told, not what I remember."

"Do you still have the letters?" he asks.

Suddenly I feel worried. I don't want him anywhere near those letters.

"No," I say, letting tears edge their way into my voice. "They've been gone for quite some time now."

It's not a lie. They *have* been gone from me for quite some time… if by quite some time, I mean since the day I was pulled away from my home due to my wedding.

He lets it go, not wanting to deal with an emotional girl. I'm grateful, both for him dropping it, and for now knowing to use tears to avoid situations when necessary.

"I promise I'll take good care of your daughter, Mrs. Jareau," he says, shocking me into silence. His blatant lie makes me sorry I ever brought him here. I should have kept this place to myself.

But we're here now, and it's time to make him pay for lying to my mother.

"My beautiful Jade," I begin, quoting one of my mother's letters, *"I want only the best for you in this world. I know it has so little to offer you and you have so much to give, so give with all your heart, even when the world is cold to you. My prayer for you is that you'll grow to be a strong woman who puts others first, and in return, you find someone to care for and treasure you the way your father and I do.*

"If you're reading this, my darling Jade, it means I can no longer be there to guide you through this life. I'm so sorry I

have left you. Please know it was never my intention to be apart from you.

"Be gracious in all that you do, for grace is what separates us from others. It is what you have to offer the world. Be kind and honest.

"One day, I hope you find love, a love so deep and true that you could never consider what life was like before it. I know there is a man for you, waiting to love you and honor you. I wish that I could see the day when you marry this man, to see the love in his eyes as he takes you as his wife.

"Be good to your husband, Jade. Care for him and love him. Let him see the true you. Hold nothing back and love fiercely.

"You deserve only the best in life, Jade, and I know the man you marry will be just that; the most trustworthy, loyal, kind, honest man you could ever dream to meet. Cherish him the way I know he will cherish you.

I love you, my baby girl, my Jade. I love you, I love you, I love you." I trail off, tears sliding down my cheeks.

I can see the tears forming in his eyes and I fight the urge to smile.

I won this round.

"She really loved you," he finally says.

"And she had a lot of faith in *you*," I add, driving my point home. I drop my voice to a whisper. "Try not to disappoint her."

Tracing the letters one more time, I stand before he can speak.

"Bye, Mom," I say quietly and start to walk away.

He lingers a moment before running to catch up with me. He doesn't speak, and I'm grateful for the silence. He gives me a curious look when I pull off to the left, but he stays by my side, eyes still slightly red from where the tears had welled up in them.

"A church?" he asks.

I nod. "I grew up in this church."

It's a small building, but the inside is glorious. The colors are all faded and the paint is cracked, but it stands just as lovely as the Diamond household.

I run my hands along the edges of the pews, making my way down to the front. Colors dance on the floor as the sunlight siphons through the stained glass. There has always been a dusty tinge to the scent of the air, but I've always loved it.

I stand at the front of the tiny church and wait. After a few minutes, I turn to Roan and look him in the eyes.

"Roan"—I look down, as if nervous—"do you think… do you think… you could ever love me?"

I dart a glance up at him through my lashes and he is visibly taken aback.

I dare him to lie to me.

"I…" He falters. "I… think that love would be *possible*, Jade."

Would? Does that mean he could see us together if he weren't on a mission to end my life?

"But *will* you love me?" I ask, forcing him into a corner.

He sighs. "I don't know Jade, I don't think either of us can know that. We're both so...new at this. We're just getting to know each other."

I look away, as if I'm upset by his words.

"But I know I'd like to try," he says quickly.

What does that mean? It's my turn to be surprised.

I smile a bit and nod my head, looking away again.

"I'm glad you'll try."

CHAPTER 9
ROAN

t's a good thing I can think quickly. She had me cornered. I try very hard not to lie to her, but rather say truthful things, skillfully worded.

And it's true. In another time and place, if she wasn't who she was, I could see myself trying with her.

She is smarter than I expected. She is even pretty fun to be around. And she is beautiful, so much more than I thought she would be. Even when she isn't in any of those soft, girly dresses she tried on for me only this morning, she's stunning; to the point where I almost let her wear those shorts to lunch.

But I can't think like that. I can't afford to let her get in my head. I have a job and I have to see it through. It won't help to get attached to her.

Her taking me by the hand and leading me away from the church doesn't help matters.

CHAPTER 10
JADE

e flinches when I take his hand, but I don't let go. I'm far too excited to get to our next stop.

Mr. Eroh looks up as the bell chimes over the shop door. The look on his face bounces between shock and elation.

I can tell he wants to run over and hug me, to make sure that I'm truly safe, but he holds himself back.

"Well, look who's back. I thought you weren't coming back to work for a bit. And what's this? You brought me a new worker? Are you looking to cut your salary in half, young lady? I bet this one will draw in quite the young female crowd. I might get some new business," he jokes playfully.

"Feel free to wander, my boy, Jade and I need to catch up." He pats the cushioned stool next to him.

I take a seat and Roan stays by my side. Mr. Eroh

waves his hand toward a box crate in the corner, indicating Roan should pull it over and have a seat.

The moment his back is turned, I make sure my hair covers my face and mouth "He's going to kill me," to Mr. Eroh, confirming every suspicion we've been operating under since the day I was committed to marrying Roan as a child.

He smiles, turning his attention to Roan as he returns. He's upset, but he covers it well.

"So, our Jade is quite the cook, I hear. Has she made you many good meals?" he asks Roan.

"A few, yes, sir."

"Good, good." Mr. Eroh rocks back and forth. Taking his glasses off, he wipes them clean with the hem of his shirt.

Mr. Eroh has always appeared like a kindly old man to the public for as long as I've known him. It's only when he's certain no outside eyes are on him that his true character comes out. He is a crafty and incredibly skilled man with a talent for deception. Not even my father knew just how capable he was until I started working there.

"And what do you do, young man? That is, how are you supporting your young bride?" he questions Roan like a loving grandfather might.

"I work with my father, sir. He's..."

"The Commander, yes, I know," Mr. Eroh interrupts. "But what do you *do*?"

"Right now, a lot of paperwork." Roan laughs and waits for me to join in. I do, but it's a second too late, just enough to make it awkward.

"But really, sir, right now I'm working on a project to help further community gardens. The more we can support ourselves, the more we can grow as a community."

"I see. So you're feeding people, then?"

"Yes, sir," Roan replies.

"I suppose you're *both* good with food then."

"I suppose so." Roan looks like he's actually having a good time.

"Take a look at this, young man," Mr. Eroh instructs, pulling out a small wind up device. "This is a project I've been working on this week. It's a handmade toy, completely self-contained, and powered by this windup piece here.

"The pin broke, and it took two days to get the shell apart so I could get inside and fix it. But I kept tinkering and now watch."

He gives the pin a few twists and sets it down. The toy toddles across the counter, teetering on the edge. Somehow it realizes it's about to fall, and moves in reverse, changing its trajectory.

"It knows when something bad is coming," he says. "It

can sense it, a lot like people. It then has a choice to make. Let the worst happen and see if it survives, or try a new course. What do you think, young man? Do we all have choices or is our life decided for us?"

Even I wasn't prepared to be confronted with the deep reality of the situation we were in. It was just like Mr. Eroh to use something he tinkered with to make a life altering point.

"I'm not sure I know," Roan replies.

"Why don't you take this then, and think about it?" Mr. Eroh places the wind-up toy in his hand and wraps Roan's fingers around it. Patting his hand, he releases it and stands.

"Well, I expect I'll be seeing you next week then, Jade; the usual time, please."

He escorts us to the door and thanks us for stopping by.

Outside, Roan opens his hand and looks at the toy. It's an odd shape, more of an obscure oval with feet than anything else. It's green, almost gem-like.

"What is it?" I ask.

"I don't know. It almost looks like… a jewel with feet?" He stares at it, trying to decipher it.

But I understand it. Green. Jewel-like. It's jade: a not-so-subtle reminder of me.

I grab it and hold it up next to my face, hoping I'm

forcing the point without actually saying it. "I think it's cute."

I shrug one shoulder flirtatiously at him before handing it back.

"Ready for stop four?" I ask.

"A library?" Roan asks. Apparently, I've shocked him again.

"Mhmm," I answer, sweeping my fingers across shelves of books. "Reading is one of my favorite things. I especially like books from *before*. Do you like reading?"

"I've been known to enjoy a good book."

I bury myself in the shelves, feeling at ease in the stacks of pages. Even when things were hard growing up, I could always escape into a good book. I loved learning, but *exploring* was my favorite.

I show Roan around, pointing out the different sections. I stare for a moment too long at the children's area, glancing up at him, hoping to make him think of having a family with me. I'll try *anything* to get him to think of me as a person, not a target. Sighing, I continue on.

He wanders off, looking through a book about architecture or something. I look for something to take home with me; *anything* to bring his mind back to this day and these moments. If I can personalize the house and bring in objects that remind him of our time together, my chances of winning him over are strengthened.

That's when I see her. She slips around the corner of a stack, giving me just enough time to notice her. I wait a moment before following.

Tucked into the spines of the books is a tiny paper. It stands out just enough that I can see it.

"Confirmed?" it reads.

I tuck the paper back into the books, moving it two bindings down, indicating that it is confirmed. I trail down the aisle, as if searching through the titles. At the end, I find a second missive.

"Safe?" Now that she knows I have confirmed the Commander's plan, she needs to know how much danger I'm in.

I crumple the paper quietly and drop it at my feet before moving on, letting my aunt know that I am not safe.

I catch another glimpse of her as I stroll away. Worry flashes across her face as she notices the paper on the ground.

My Aunt Sophie must have seen me enter the library with Roan. She was always a lover of books, so it wouldn't be unreasonable to find her here, even this time of day.

We hadn't planned on communicating. None of us ever thought I'd make it back to my town for anything other than work, if I were lucky. Now that I was here, we were all trying to take advantage of the time and use it to communicate. With Roan by my side, and what we had to assume was constant surveillance on me, it was incredibly difficult.

Making my way back to Roan, I carry a few books in my arms. A few stories for me, but also some things I thought he might enjoy. He smiles as I approach.

"I found some books," I say, holding one up.

"I see that." He laughs and shakes his head. "You really do like to read, huh?"

"Yep, but some of these are for you." I dig out one from the pile and hold it up. "I thought you might enjoy this."

"Impressive. A historical account of…what is that?" He looks closer before erupting in laughter. "Barbershops!"

"I thought you'd find it amusing," I giggle. "I insist you check it out."

"Very well, Wife," he says, turning me toward the counter.

As we descend the second story staircase, I catch sight of Sophie ducking out the door. I slow my pace, giving her enough time to escape without being seen. It amazes me how much she looks like my mother did in my last few photos of her.

Roan helps me carry the books as we walk down the street.

"Last stop on your list," he says. "What do you have planned?"

I'm very aware I can't take him to my home, even though we just spent half the afternoon with his parents. I've already gone for the emotional with the cemetery and church, and I hit the Jade-has-people-that-care-for-her spot when I took him to the bakery. Which meant, I needed somewhere that made him laugh. Somewhere fun. Something that would be a good, happy memory.

I only had one place I could possibly take him: the pond.

CHAPTER 11
JADE

he pond is usually a fairly busy place. Today, however, it's rather quiet and I'm thankful. Only a few people mill about, splashing in the water or walking along the bank.

"This was always one of my favorite places to be," I say as we walk to the water's edge.

I back up and set my books on a tree stump that's been turned over to use as a bench. Roan follows suit and sets his pile of books next to mine.

I slip my shoes off and set them by the books. Roan watches for a moment and then kicks his off, rolling up his pant legs.

The moment my toes touch the water I regret it. An icy burst of pain travels up my leg and through my spine. I expected it to be warmer.

"Don't worry, Jade," a young man calls, splashing in the water. "You can get used to it."

"Who's your friend?" Roan whispers, a little harsher than I think he meant to.

"A guy I went to school with," I answer. "Why? You're not jealous, are you?"

"As long as he knows you're married to me and off limits, nope," he responds, raising his hand to wave to the guy.

His reaction stresses me out a little. I don't like to think what would happen if the Commander thought someone might be interfering with his precious plan of revenge.

"Well then, I guess you have nothing to worry about." I kick at the water a little, spraying tiny droplets across the glassy surface.

"When I was a kid, sometimes on the way home from school, if it was really hot out, we'd jump in with our clothes on and then lay in the sun to dry a bit before walking home." I allowed myself to daydream a little of my childhood.

"With your clothes on?" Roan asks, turning to look at me.

"Yeah," I confirm. "What? You've never been swimming with your clothes on?"

I wait for him to answer, but he hesitates. I jerk toward him like I'm going to push him in and laugh when he flinches.

"That was mean, Jade." He laughs. "But not as mean as

this."

He grabs me and before I can think to breathe I find myself underwater. The coolness stings my skin and my lungs burn as he holds me down.

For a moment, I wonder if this is a practice run for him.

Then we burst out of the water, each of us gasping for air.

"So, tell me, Wife. Is swimming with one's clothes on so great *now?*"

I push my hair out of my face. I came up backwards, leading with the back of my neck, so that my tresses ended up cascading down my face. Dunking back down in the cold water, I right my hair and come back to the surface.

"I'll say this much, Husband." I pause, preparing myself for the attack. "I'll get you for that!"

Pushing his shoulders under, I dunk him, catching him off guard. He comes up sputtering and I greet him with a face full of water. He joins in the splashing and we have a water war until we're both dizzy and laughing so hard we can't stand.

Floating in the water next to him, I let his eyes trace over my body. He watches my hair floating along, almost mesmerized by its drifting strands. My hand finds his under the water and I entangle our fingers as I float gently beside him.

When I look back up, I realize we've managed to drift away from where we left our shoes and books. I should say something, knowing that we needed to get moving if we were going to finish all of our stops, but I don't.

A kid jumps off a rock too close to us and splashes our drying faces, ruining the moment. I right myself and we start to walk back toward our belongings.

"How long do you think until we dry off?" Roan asks, his voice sounding almost… content? Happy?

"A bit, I guess. Why?" I ask. "Are we going somewhere fancy?"

"No," he responds. "Well, I was going to show you where I work, but we can do that another day."

"I'm sorry," I apologize, feeling bad for ruining his plans, and ruining my chance to get a feel for the layout of the building he works in.

"Don't be. This was fun," he says, giving me a genuine smile.

I think I'm finally starting to learn the difference between his genuine smiles and his fake ones.

"What was the other place?" I ask as I ring out my hair and dress.

"Better let me carry those," Roan says, reaching for my books. "You're far too drippy to be handling them. And I doubt the library will be happy if we return soggy books."

"You're probably right about that," I say, letting him scoop up all the books.

His shirt is sticking to his chest but he doesn't seem to mind. He scoops up his shoes in his free hand and offers me his elbow. I dangle my heels from their strap, letting them fall at my side, and take his arm with the other.

This would actually be perfect…if he wasn't trying to kill me.

"So where to?" I ask again.

CHAPTER 12
ROAN

y plan was to take her to the small, private hospital where I was born. I figured that would be a good way to connect—all women like babies, right? But as we neared the building, I veered off down a different street.

She's been so personal and candid with me today. She's been open and honest and I feel like if I'm going to convince her to trust me, I have to do something more to connect.

She's still wound through my arm and I'm holding her to my side. Her dress is making strange sounds as we walk, sticking to her legs from the pond water. She tries to pull it away from her body, but she's failing miserably.

At the end of a dirt road, far from prying eyes, is a tiny shack of a building. There are two rooms inside, one for work and one for display.

I open the door for her and usher her inside my child-hood safe haven: the only art studio left in our tiny country, hidden so far away hardly anyone knows it exists, including my father.

CHAPTER 13
JADE

e step inside a small room cluttered with sheets draped over what I assume is furniture. The place smells heavily of paint and something else… something strong enough to make my eyes water.

Light pokes into the room through cracked windows, casting strange shadows everywhere. A layer of dust sparkles in the air as it flits in and out of the light. It looks as if it hasn't been touched in months.

Before I can speak, Roan motions me forward and gingerly steps through the building, as if to avoid disturbing the dust.

There's a door on the far side of the room; it looks cleaner than the rest of the place. When the door opens, it reveals a bright, white room. Hanging on the walls are paintings, even more stunning than those in the Diamond house.

Roan walks off to the right and examines a canvas. I

watch him for a minute as he studies it. Deciding to be coy, I step to the left and start on the opposite wall.

Painting after painting graces the room, each with its own unique colors and textures, each by different artists. It isn't until I reach halfway down the wall that I discover why we are here: *R. Diamond* is scribbled in the corner of a collection of paintings.

I feel him move behind me, realizing I have discovered his secret.

Our country no longer values frivolous things like artwork. It is only for the rich, and only as a status symbol. It is never created, nor is time *invested* in creating it. Which is why the first room was kept in such a disheveled state; very few people ever used it.

"This was my escape when I was a kid. Dad doesn't know about it. A few of us come here every so often. Occasionally we see each other. The man that owns the building wanted to restore it at one point, but there were never enough of us to make it worthwhile.

"He lets us come and go as we please. We help pay for the supplies when we can. It's kind of a place of free expression and relief from everyday life."

"It's lovely," I say genuinely. I almost wish I had known about it growing up, though I never would have been allowed at a place where Roan frequented.

"Tell me about these," I say, leaning against him and resting my head on his still damp shoulder.

"*You* tell *me*."

I think for a minute. If he wants me to tell him what I see, I have to make it good.

"I think it's about loneliness," I start.

"The painting, or my time here?" he asks, amused.

"Both," I reply, looking up at him. "I think it's almost a celebration of loneliness. It's not sad. I don't feel sad when I look at it. But I get a sense of... you were lonely, so you needed to create, and when you did you made something beautiful. Am I close?"

"Something like that," he says. "Look at this one."

He points to a picture further down, moving us away from his collection. We chat a bit about each painting, finishing the wall.

"How long have these been here, Roan?"

"Some a few years, others a few months. We take things down and put them up as we finish them."

"Are you working on anything now?" I ask, hoping for an opportunity to get involved in his process.

"No, I haven't been here in ages,"

"Too busy?" I ask ruefully.

"Yeah, too busy."

"It's a shame work keeps you so busy," I say. "Maybe one of these nights after work we could sneak off and you could come paint. I can read a book outside so I don't disturb you. But that way people will think we're together doing whatever couples do on dates and they won't bother you."

He considers my offer, sizing me up as if it's a test.

"That might be nice. Thank you," he says finally.

I return my gaze to the wall, running my finger over a simple wooden frame as I move along.

After a few more minutes of examining the works on the walls, Roan wonders aloud if we should return home.

"Probably," I say reluctantly, wondering if I made any headway today.

Having mostly dried by this point, I carry my books the rest of the way home, despite his insistence on doing it all himself.

By the time we reach our house, it's clearly night time. I close the curtains and Roan kicks his feet up on the couch.

"You're not going to fall asleep there, are you?" I ask, "Because I definitely can't carry you all the way to your bedroom if you do."

He laughs softly.

"If I fall asleep here, just leave me. It's a decent couch and it wouldn't kill me to spend the night here."

"All right then, if you say so." I let him sit there and find my way to the quiet of my own room, needing to process the day.

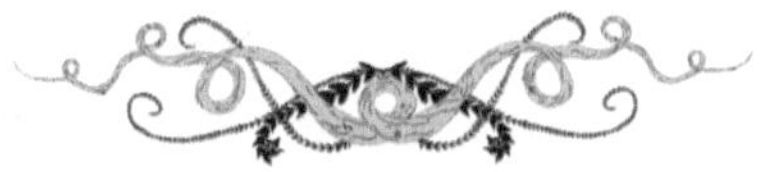

We spend the next day sprawled out around the house, sneaking glances at each other over our books. I don't know if he's caught me watching him, but I've certainly noticed him watching me.

Around one o'clock, he goes outside and sits in the hammock to read. I know he's watching, so I don't even try to make my way around the house. I've explored most of it already anyway.

An hour later he wanders back in and I'm ready for him.

I have to keep our walk yesterday fresh in his mind. The books are a great reminder, but I need more.

"Roan? Is that you?" I call out from the kitchen.

"Yeah," he answers. "Where are you?"

"In the kitchen."

"Are you working on something?" he asks and I hear him walking toward me.

"Yeah," I say sweetly, waiting for him to round the corner. When he does, a look of pure terror washes over his face. "Payback."

The kitchen sink hose is in my hands and I immediately pelt him with water, revenge for the pond the previous day.

His shock wears off immediately and he lunges forward, trying to wrestle the hose from my grasp. Attempting to turn it toward me, I manage to deflect it and mostly hide behind him so he ends up with another face full of water.

Unfortunately, the water has made the floor slippery and my feet kick out from under me. I'm still holding on to him and we both fall, crashing hard against the ground.

"Are you okay?" I gasp, climbing around him to check on him.

He grins as he loops his arm around me and flips me over to the floor. Roan towers over me as he reaches for the silent hose. He poises it over me, ready to soak me. I can see his heavy breathing as his shoulders sway up and down with his chest rise and fall.

I close my eyes, tipping my head to the ground, hoping to avoid a direct hit. One hand slips up, my feeble attempt to block the spray that I know is coming.

And then suddenly he's standing, replacing the hose to its home on the sink. He walks away, leaving me on the ground in a puddle of water. I have no idea what just happened.

CHAPTER 14
ROAN

 should help her clean up the mess in the kitchen but I can't be near her right now.

I'm beginning to wonder if I can do this.

When I had her pinned down, ready to attack, I couldn't bring myself to do it and that was just water from the sink.

A month from now, after she's been seen with us at all of Dad's parties, I have to start messing with her. Not too long after that, I have to kill her.

I don't know if I can.

But I really don't have a choice.

Dad hasn't decided how she's going to die yet. Whatever it is, it has to be personal for her father. We've practiced a multitude of different ways, but I can't imagine using a single one of them on that girl in the kitchen.

I just have to find a way to be cold toward her, at least

for myself. I have to gain her trust, get close to her, but I have to keep her away too.

Maybe if I lie more…

But then, I must keep all those lies straight. No, it's better not to get caught in a lie. But that means I need to let her in. And *then* kill her.

Nothing about this plan is as easy as Dad said it would be.

CHAPTER 15

JADE

he week passes by and I'm glad it's almost the weekend…until I realize I have the office party.

"Roan?" I yell down the hall. "What do I wear to the office party?"

"A dress," he yells back, walking toward my room. His voice softens as he approaches the open door and chuckles. "Haven't you learned that by now?"

"I'm aware of that, thank you," I say in a cool voice. If he wants to be icy like he has been the past few days, I could be icy too. "But how fancy is this party? Sun dress or something more formal?"

"A bit more formal, but not extravagant."

"No worries, I left my ball gowns at home." I swallow, realizing I referred to my father's house as my home. He shifts, but doesn't say anything.

"So, maybe something like this?" I ask, pulling out a soft pink dress.

"Yeah, that's good," he replies before leaving.

I frown, worrying that my plan is failing. Roan had been more distant than usual the last few days. Maybe he was actually angry that I soaked him in the kitchen.

I spend a little extra time looking in the mirror. Pulling my hair down from the knot on the top of my head, I let it fall around my waist in soft waves. My favorite pair of heels finishes off my outfit and I walk out to the kitchen.

"Is this okay for the party, Roan? I've never been to an office party before," I ask, waiting for him to look up so I can twirl.

"Yeah, it's great," he says, barely glancing at me.

When I saw his head start to turn toward me, I began my twirl, but he doesn't stop to watch me move. *Maybe he is angry with me?*

But then I see his eyes grow rounder as he stares at the kitchen counter, reading whatever paperwork is in his hands, as he processes what he saw in that glimpse of my outfit. His face begins to turn to me again, but he snaps it back.

Why is he refusing to look at me?

"Are you ready to go?" I ask tentatively, trying not to upset him.

"Almost," he says, scooting off the chair.

He gathers the papers he was working on and puts them in his briefcase. Few can afford such a luxurious carrier, but as the Commander's son, I suppose he must put on a show. It's like this house—we don't need all this space, but we have it simply because of who he is.

My own father has nothing this fancy. Our house is simple. His briefcase is old and worn, but still useable. But then again, my father never made a show about his position.

I adjust the halter strap on my dress as Roan pulls himself together. One of my favorite things about this dress is that I get to have bare shoulders. I love the way my hair brushes across my skin in the breeze. While many girls prefer showing off other areas, my favorite things to reveal are my shoulders. They may be wide, wider than most, but to me, it's the most attractive thing I can show off.

I push my hair behind me; painfully aware having it in front of me to show off isn't gaining me any points right now. I start toward the pie I made for the party but Roan waves me off.

"That was very kind of you, but best to leave that at home, Jade. The party is catered and no one brings anything with them," he says gently.

"Oh," I say, disheartened. "Okay. Well, at least I tried."

"You did. You're very thoughtful, Jade," he tries to encourage me.

If I had been a normal, doting wife, trying to win the approval of my husband's parents, I might have been disappointed. As a girl fighting to get a man to think enough of me not to kill me while simultaneously making the Commander's friends and family love me to the point where they simply *can't* go on with their plan of revenge, well, that is another story. Not to mention a setback.

As we walk toward the door, he asks, "What kind is it?"

"Raspberry. I picked them yesterday."

"Is that what you were doing outside all morning?" he asks playfully.

"Yeah." I mimic his tone, suddenly terrified at the abrupt switch in demeanor.

"Sounds great. Maybe we could have some tonight," Roan suggests.

"Sure. So you're a fan of my pies then, huh?"

"Seems that way." He bumps into me with his elbow like we're old friends. I return the gesture.

I need to move my timetable up. As much as I don't want him touching me, I need to get him to kiss me. We hold hands in public, put on a good show, but there's no true affection between us. It's a silent pact we somehow made over the last week that we would put up a good front for the world to see. But when we're alone, we're nothing like that.

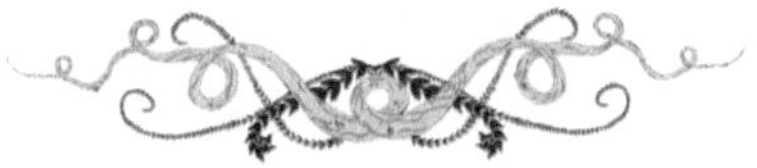

The Commander's house is alive with people, a few of whom I recognize from appearances with the Commander. They all rush to greet me, offering their sincerest congratulations and asking me when Roan and I will have children.

He's just as shocked as I am, but we recover gracefully, saying that we're settling into married life nicely. Most laugh and shake our hands, and leave us on our way.

It takes us fifteen minutes just to get in the door and into the living room.

"Roan!" the Commander's voice booms and I wonder if he had the house specially designed so that his voice would resonate in it. I wouldn't put it past him.

"And here we go…" Roan whispers to me as we walk over to his father.

I get the feeling Roan isn't always as enthusiastic about his father's overbearing loudness as his father would like him to be.

The Commander pulls Roan away from me and starts to talk to his friends for a moment before turning back to me. My father-in-law wraps his arm around my waist and pulls me to his side. I'm so horrified, it's all I can do to not lose my balance; my facial expression doesn't even register as a concern, though it should.

Once I'm against the Commander's side, I plaster a smile on and nod to the other people in the circle.

"Have you met my lovely daughter-in-law, Jade?" he asks jovially, as if he's actually pleased that I'm a part of his family.

I meet the new people in the group, chatting pleasantly, and trying to identify which of them I need to get on my side. Everyone at the party appears to be within a ten-year age gap of the Commander, except for the children running around. I assume when Roan was young, he had more people his own age in attendance, but as of today, we were the only two near our age.

Eventually Roan makes his exit and I follow behind him, claiming I couldn't bear to be away from my husband for more than a few minutes. The ladies of the group all look wistfully at me as I run away to find him. Apparently, everyone loves a good romance. Too bad none of it is true.

I find Roan by the punch, having been cornered by a gentleman old enough to be his grandfather. Clearly, he is the exception to the age rule. I watch for a moment as Roan tries to shy away. The man steps closer, forcing him to engage in the conversation.

I wait just long enough for it to become excruciatingly

painful to continue watching, ensuring Roan's gratitude when I save him.

I sashay my way over to him, intentionally trying to get the attention of the men in the room. The more eyes on me, and the more people inquiring about me in the future, the safer I will be.

"Roan, darling. May I borrow you for a moment?" I take his arm and give a gentle tug.

When it looks like the older man may object, I lean into him and whisper in his ear.

"Act like I just told you something important needs your attention."

I intentionally linger, making sure the tip of my nose brushes against his ear before I pull back and step away from them.

He must have done as I said, because the old man excuses him and we rush toward the kitchen.

"Thanks," he breathes a sigh of relief once we make it to the hallway and out of sight.

"You looked like you could use a hand."

"All he ever wants to talk about is…" he starts, but he doesn't get a chance to finish.

"Roan." The Commander's voice comes as a warning. "Where are you sneaking off to?"

"Just the kitchen, Dad. We wanted to make sure Mom didn't need any help."

"Fine," he says, stepping toward another room, his

voice still warning us, "but make sure you make an appearance with everyone. They all want to see you tonight. You have responsibilities."

Curious. Roan must be one to slip away and hide during these parties. I can't say I blame him.

"Of course, Father."

He waits until his father disappears into the room before grabbing my wrist and pulling me down the hall. He pops his head into the kitchen, backtracks and drags me up the stairs.

"Where are we going? I thought your mother… "

"She wasn't there and she never needs my help," he says, dragging me faster.

"Then where…?"

"We're hiding, Jade, now be quiet before you get us caught," he hisses, though he's not angry with my lack of awareness in our escape.

He glances furtively down the upstairs hallway toward the stairs once before taking me down a second hallway. Opening a door on the right, we step into a chocolate brown room. *His* room.

"So, this is where the great Roan Diamond lives," I say, almost in awe.

"*Lived*," he corrects, "I live with *you* now, remember?"

"You know what I meant." I roll my eyes playfully. "I bet a whole bunch of girls tried to talk their way up here, huh?"

"There were a few," he responds.

I can feel my face go slack, as if he slapped me.

I had been committed to him since I was five. I had never dared to let any other boys into my life for fear of what might happen to them. I'd never dated, never been asked out, never been kissed. I had never even held a boy's hand before the day I married Roan Diamond.

To think that he hadn't lived under the same captive rules…that just infuriated me. Or perhaps it made me jealous. He might not have had a choice, but unquestionably he had options.

He turns to see my face. His eyes grow wide, realizing what he had said.

"I never took them up on it, Jade. I would never do that to you," he tries to convince me.

Sure, he wouldn't.

I didn't even know what to say. I'm so shocked by his confession. He reads me as being flustered which is fine with me.

I'm sure the only reason he didn't have any other girls was for fear of ruining his father's plan. Besides, there will be plenty of time to replace me after I am dead.

"Come on, Jade. Come sit down." He pulls out his desk chair for me and I sit.

He takes a seat on the edge of his bed, facing me.

"Jade, I know we were committed to each other a long time ago, but I won't fault you if you had other men in your life before me. We didn't even know each other until last week.

"And you should know, that while I might have flirted a little growing up, I never touched another girl. For me there was never anyone but you. I knew that from the time we were paired together. Please believe me when I say, I am committed to making this work with you. However long it takes, that's okay. But there has never been, nor will there ever be, any other woman in my life."

He knew all the right words, but then, so did I.

"You've never kissed another girl before?" I ask quietly.

"Not ever," he assures me. "Did you...did you ever kiss another guy?" He sounds hopeful, as if willing me to have waited for him.

I nearly want to lie and tell him yes, just to see how he will react.

"No. I didn't even know that was an option."

He smiles. "It really wasn't, I guess."

"So...then, you'll be the first...and only...man I ever kiss." I stare deep into his eyes, willing him to lean into me.

I let my eyes drop to his lips. His breathing slows and I wait.

We jump, separating as quickly as possible when we hear the noise outside the door. It flies open and the Commander walks in.

"I thought I told you to make an appearance," he growls at his son.

"I'm sorry, sir. It's my fault. I got a little overwhelmed with all the people downstairs and Roan thought I needed a little space so I could breathe. I'm truly sorry." I apologize, casting my eyes down as if I were embarrassed.

Roan places his hand on the small of my back, silently thanking me.

"We'll be right down; she just needs a moment," he tells his father.

He lied…*for me*. To back me up.

In that moment, everything becomes real.

Roan is a rebel.

He doesn't want to do what his father tells him to do, but he feels like he must. He follows orders, but when no one is looking, he breaks free. Like the art house. Like walking away from a party after being specifically told to stay. Like lying to back me up.

All I need to do is guide him into taking more small steps to disobey his father. That way he starts drifting further and further away and when the time comes to stand up for me, it won't seem as hard to disobey. The trick is to make him not just rebel, but rebel *for me.*

And just like that I have a new mission for the evening and the next few weeks.

Roan starts toward the door, but I pull his hand in mine.

"Roan?" I ask once he's facing me. "Are you okay?"

"I'm fine," he seems confused.

"Are you sure?" I question, making him question himself. "You just… I don't know. It seems like you like to make your dad happy, but when you stand up for yourself, you seem… unsure if it's the right thing. I just…I know it can be hard, but I think it's good that you stand up for yourself. I'm sorry I lied, but I didn't want you to get in trouble because of me," I say, "Thanks for backing me up with your dad."

"Of course I want to make my father proud, Jade. But I stand up for myself when I need to. As for you, you wouldn't have gotten me in trouble. I did this myself, and it isn't the first time I've ducked out on a party. And anyway, you're my wife now. I'll always back you up." He leans forward and hugs me.

Astonished, I wrap my hands around his neck and hold on to him. He smells amazing. When he pulls back, I leave my arms wrapped around his neck, playing with his hair with one hand. I smile at him for a moment before pulling away. His hand lingers on my hip until I step out of reach.

I try to leave him wanting more time with me.

"We should get back," I say softly and step out of the room.

I find Roan gravitating toward me more and more during the party. It's mostly boring, a lot of work talk. But everyone has lots of questions about what I do for work and if I'll be going back.

Roan takes considerable pride in talking about the kindly older gentleman I have so selflessly donated my time to assist. None of them know Mr. Eroh's shop, so they take Roan at his word when he tells them what an asset I am to the store.

"She could work anywhere she likes, but she chooses to stay with the man who gave Jade her first job, helping him in any way she can," he says, as if actually proud of my selfless and giving nature.

I was a bit surprised to discover I had a "selfless and giving nature" but if that's what Roan wanted to believe, I'd let him think that. There really was no need to tell him the real reason I stuck around was to learn to defend myself against him. He'd find out soon enough anyway.

I let the women fuss over my dress and tell me how lovely my long hair was. I made sure to complement each of the ladies, finding something unique about them to point out. The men all complimented Roan on a job well done, as if he had selected me himself.

"Hello, Jade." I turn as I hear Alice address me in a low, hushed voice.

"Hello, Mrs. Diamond. This is a lovely party."

"Thank you. I must insist you call me Alice, though," she replies. "Can I get you anything?"

So, Alice was finally getting on board with the make-people-think-we-like-Jade plan.

"I'm fine, thank you. It's all quite a bit to take in. I'm afraid I'm not used to parties or crowds quite this large," I say, reinforcing my earlier statement to the Commander, and hoping I can use it as an excuse to get Roan to take me home early.

"Well, I suppose you'll have to get used to it, Jade. As the wife of the future Commander, you'll be expected to attend and host quite a few of these gatherings," she says as she walks away to find her husband who has the captive attention of all of his underlings.

I never took much time to think that through before. I knew Roan was next in line to be Commander, but for me, there was no Commander other than Robert Diamond. I couldn't even picture Roan as a leader.

I find myself wondering what he would be like as a leader. Would he be fair and kind? Or, would his father force any last shred of humanity out of his son before he turned over power?

"Did I overhear you talking to my mother?" Roan says, sidling up next to me.

"Yes, she seems to be warming up to me," I say sarcastically.

"I told her the crowd is a lot to take in. I thought maybe we could slip away early, if we need to." I plant the idea in his head.

He looks at me, pausing, as he is about to hand me a cup of water.

"You know what, that sounds like a great idea," my husband says and turns to set the water on a table nearby.

So, I had read him right. He wanted out of there as badly as I thought he did.

"Then let's escape," I say. "Anyone you need to say goodbye to?"

"Let me just let Mom know we're going," he steps forward and catches his mother's eye. She is attached to her husband's arm.

Roan motions when his father isn't looking. His mother glances up at her husband, and gives a deft nod when she finds him distracted. Even Alice knew her son needed to escape occasionally.

Outside it was dark, lit only by the moon.

When we reach the front door, I impishly remark, "Now tell the truth, Roan Diamond, you just came home early because you were dying to try that pie, didn't you?"

He smirks, his eyes alight with mischief. "That, my

dear Jade, is *precisely* why we left. Now go fetch me some pie, woman."

I giggle and intentionally walk away from the kitchen and to my room to change. When I come back I find Roan sitting at the island, fork in hand, a third of the way through my pie.

My jaw drops.

"You could have joined me," he taunts, holding a piece up on his fork and waving it around. "You just *had* to go and change first. Too bad, you missed out on your slice."

"Hey now," I say, making my way to the silverware drawer. "I *made* it, I should at least get to taste it."

He slaps my fork away with his, teasing me. "You missed your chance, Wife. This is mine."

"Fine, see if I ever cook for you again, Husband," I say, turning my back.

"Wait," he yelps, wondering if I'm serious.

He pushes the dish at me.

"Peace offering?" he asks hopefully.

"Fine, but don't you ever withhold food from me again," I chastise.

"Deal," he says, sharing the pie with me.

Once I take a bite, I can see why he was reluctant to share. Raspberries are amazing.

"How often did you used to duck out of those parties?" I start, eager to find out a little information.

"Seemed like your dad knew right where to find you tonight."

"Pretty much every time. I never cared much for them. Even when I was a kid and there were other kids around, it just wasn't a lot of fun. Hiding in my room seemed like a better alternative than being cornered by an adult who could care less what I was *learning in school that week,*" he mimicked their voices.

"You make a good point," I agree.

"How about you, attend many parties?"

"Nope. My dad was never fond of the idea of me going to those."

"Not even his work parties?" he asks in disbelief.

"Not even those. Dad was very big on keeping work and personal lives separate. Though, from the sounds of it, he did me a favor."

"I guess if you look at it that way, one point for your dad." Roan takes a mouthful and groans. "Gosh, Jade, this is amazing! Where did you learn to do this?"

"I baked a lot for me and Dad growing up. But this… I learned from a book. It's the first time I've made it."

Roan gives me the saddest look I've ever seen. "You've *never* made this before?"

"Nope,"

"Well… I demand it," he says, flabbergasted. "Every week. All of the time. It's as good as learning you never have to go to work again. Seriously, Jade, it's amazing."

I smile at his eagerness.

"Well, then I guess it will have to be our special occasion dessert then," I say, planting another seed in his mind. "You have a birthday coming up soon. Consider that your cake." *His birthday is still two months away.*

"Sounds perfect."

If my cooking is any indication, I'll be around for at least two months then.

"What else do you like, Roan?"

"What do you mean?"

"I like that the pie makes you happy. I want to know what else you like to eat so I can keep surprising you with special treats."

"That's awfully kind of you, Jade. You realize you don't have to try to please me though. I'm not going to kick you out if you don't cook for me all the time."

"I know," I reply. "I'm just trying to be nice. I know we're getting to know each other, but it doesn't mean I can't make the effort to make you comfortable. It's your house, too. You should be at home here."

He seems to be trying to pick apart my words, looking for hidden meaning. When he finds none, he takes another bite.

"Well, I think I'll go to bed now," I say, standing. "Roan, tonight was nice.

"*This,*" I say, sweeping my hand around the kitchen, "was nice."

He stands as I walk away. It looks like he wants to say something, but he doesn't. The door closes behind me and I let out a breath.

Tonight was murder on my nerves.

Being around that man was the most unnerving, dangerous, infuriating, calculated, horrible, terrifying, wonderful, amazing, comfortable, happy thing in the entire world. I have no idea how I'm going to survive this even if I *do* convince him not to kill me.

CHAPTER 16
ROAN

ying in my bed, I play the scene at the party over and over in my mind.

When Jade wasn't looking, Dad pulled me into his office.

"Tell me where you're at," he demanded.

"I'm working on it."

"Not good enough. Does she trust you yet?"

"I don't know," I brushed his hand off my arm.

"You need to make her trust you. Whatever it takes Roan, do whatever it takes."

"I know, Dad, I'm working on it."

"Take this," he says, shoving something in my hand.

I look down to find a small, plastic container.

"What is this?" I ask, looking up at him from my perch on his desk.

"Poison," he says and my blood goes cold. "Start giving her small doses. It will make her a little sick, but if you space it out every few days, she won't catch on. She'll feel tired, a little nauseous, but worst case, she thinks she might be pregnant."

I'm appalled he thinks that she could even *think* she was pregnant. I haven't touched her and I won't touch her. But I guess to the outside world, we are married and that includes all that is implied with the term *married*.

I couldn't do that to her though. I couldn't do it to *me.* To connect with someone like that and then turn around and end her life? I couldn't live with myself if I did that.

I thought about adding a drop or two to the pie tonight, but I kept the vial tucked safely away in my pocket. I hid it after she went to bed, high on a shelf in the kitchen where I knew she couldn't reach it. I didn't want it in my room, where I could be blamed if she found it.

I'd have to be careful from now on. If I were bringing things into the house she could find, I'd have to be on high alert and ready to explain things away if need be. But I shouldn't worry; I have been trained for this. I know exactly what to say or do to make her believe me.

I'm just not sure I can say or do the right things in front of *her.*

My thoughts drift and I start thinking of nice things I could do for Jade. She's been so thoughtful, thinking of everyone, baking pies for my parents, being a helpful wife. She got me out of trouble with my father, saved me from mindless conversations at the party, even asked for requests for treats she could make me.

Is she really this thoughtful or is she playing me?

I shake my head, trying to clear it. If I can't turn my brain off, I'll never get to sleep. The day after tomorrow, I need to be back at work, and I won't be able to function if I keep having these sleepless nights.

Tomorrow I'll find a way to do something for Jade. Maybe a few simple things and one big thing. I need her to know I'm making the effort.

She needs to trust me, and if I can't trust myself to be physical with her, I have to find another way.

If I could just allow myself to hold her, even to kiss her, it would be so much easier to convince her to put her faith in me. But I don't dare put myself in that position where I could be swayed by her, and touching her would certainly do that.

I can barely think straight when she walks with her arm in mine, let alone *actually* communicate with her through a kiss or an embrace.

I'm beginning to see why relationships are so complicated.

Nothing makes sense anymore.

But I have a mission. And I must follow through.

So tomorrow, I will do something kind for her. And the next day, I start testing her.

CHAPTER 17
JADE

orning comes far too early.

"Hello, Sunshine," Roan says from the kitchen as I step into the room.

"Are you cooking?" I ask, sitting down at the island.

"Yep, but don't get too comfortable. We're not staying."

I look at him, confused. The sun is barely up, I haven't even brushed my hair yet, and he wants me to leave the house?

"Where are we going?"

"On a date." He turns to put the food he has just prepared into a basket.

"We're going on a picnic?" I ask cautiously. He was being too friendly… especially after the last few days.

"Yes, we are. Go get ready," he instructs, sending me off to prepare myself to be seen in public.

Tying my hair up in a ponytail, I pull out a purple t-shirt and a pair of denim shorts. It's been a cool summer, much to my disappointment, but it's still warm enough to wear shorts out.

"Are you ready?" he asks, waiting by the door.

I pause to pull on sneakers and then follow him out the front door.

"So just where are we going on this mystery date?"

I slip my arm through the handles on the basket, so that we're not touching, but both sharing the responsibility of carrying the basket…and intentionally keep us close.

"To watch the sunrise," he says, a glimmer in his eyes.

"But the sun is up," I say, puzzled.

"The sun is up *here*," he says, "and *barely* up at that. But over there… it's still dark there. We're going to have to pick up the pace if we want to catch it."

I look to where his finger points to a still overcast area. He's right; if we hurry, we can catch it.

"Then I guess we should run," I reply, taking my hand from the basket handle and sprinting ahead of him.

He easily overtakes me as we run, but slows to keep pace with me and we collapse under a tree at the same time. The grass is soaked with dew, but we find a place to sit on an exposed tree root that sits a few inches off the ground.

"Here, quick, we have to eat," he says, opening the basket and handing me a container of food.

Miraculously, the food is still somewhat warm and we get several bites into it before the sun starts coming up over the buildings of the town. It glimmers off the glass as it rises. Its golden glow makes even the ugliest of towns look magnificent.

"So… do you want to go for another swim today?" he asks after a bit.

"What's gotten into you today?" I ask before I can stop myself.

"What do you mean?" he asks, turning to face me. He sets down his empty container and I do the same.

"I don't know. You just seemed… a bit distant the past few days and now suddenly you want to be buddies again."

"I'm sorry," he takes my hand in his. "I didn't mean to make you feel that way. Sometimes…"

He seems to be searching for the right words to explain all this away.

"I just… need some space. I'm not used to all this, remember? We're still figuring *us* out. It might take a little time, that's all."

"I understand that. I guess I need some space too. It's good that we'll both be going back to work tomorrow. Then we won't be around each other every hour of the day. Maybe things will be…less complicated then," I suggest.

"I'm sure you're right," he replies, letting go of my

hand. "But as for today, we're still stuck with each other, so what would you like to do?"

Run. Run away. That's what I'd like to do.

"Swimming sounds nice." I smile.

"Swimming it is then. Maybe we could avoid the clothes, though, and go for actual swimsuits," he proposes.

"I think that's an excellent idea," I say, laughing.

"I know a place I think you might like," he says and I'm a bit sad I don't get to go back to my home pond.

"Yeah? And where is that?"

"There's an old pool that's still open we could go to. I know it's no pond, but it's close and I'll bet you've never been in an actual pool before."

"As a matter of fact, I have *not* been to an actual pool before." *I might even be interested in seeing one, but I don't tell him that.* "Lead the way."

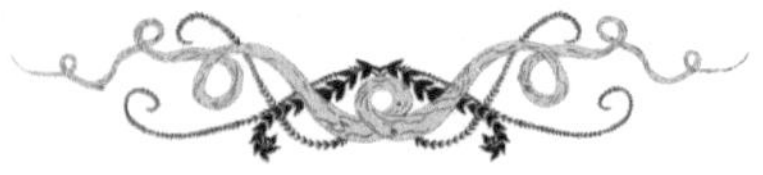

Roan takes us back to our house where we quickly switch our picnic basket for a tote bag his parents left for us in one of the closets. We put our swimsuits and towels in it and start out for this mysterious pool.

It's only a few minutes' walk and no one is there when we arrive. My nerves rush at me, making me incredibly aware that I am alone with a man trying to kill me near a closed-in body of water with no witnesses.

And *then* I realize we're on the backside of his parent's property and that no one will be coming *at all*.

"We're at your parent's house," I say, stepping tentatively into the glass building.

"Yes, but don't worry, they don't ever come out here. They keep it in working condition, but it's more to impress people than anything else."

I set the bag on one of the reclining chairs by the side of the pool, waiting for directions.

"You can get changed in there." He points to a door. "I'll wait."

I take my suit with me and change in the large bathroom. There are rooms with curtains so that several people could change at once, but Roan was kind enough to give me the privacy of the whole room.

He appraises me when I walk out. I intentionally chose a suit that shows me off. It is all black, with mesh details across the stomach. A solid piece of material runs from one hip to under the other arm, allowing only a bit of skin to show through the mesh above and below it. I'm covered, but it alludes to the skin underneath.

His eyes follow me as he walks past me to get changed. Once he's out of sight, I walk over to the steps.

Dipping my toe in, I discover that the water is warm and I don't flinch like I did with the pond. There must be a way to heat it.

I wade into the water, dipping down to my shoulders once I reach waist level. Tipping my head back, I allow the water to soak through my hair and relax me.

The sound of gushing water announces Roan's return. I jerk upright and find him walking away from a nozzle at the far side of the building. He has turned a waterfall on in the rock design at the end of the pool and it cascades down the wall. I must look as shocked as I feel because Roan laughs.

"Everything about your home is surprising, Roan," I say as he enters the water. "I didn't even know things like this existed!"

I can feel the excitement creep into my voice and I run with that emotion. The alternative is to be furious at his family for having such extravagant things they don't even use while the rest of the country is struggling to survive.

"Dad likes to show off. I can't say I mind the waterfall though," he adds. "Go check it out if you like."

I swim over and reach my hand out. The water falls hard against my fingers, knocking it toward the pool water's surface. I reach out again, this time prepared for the gush and it massages my hand.

"Put your shoulders under it," Roan calls out.

I give him a questioning look and he motions for me to spin to face him and back up under the water.

It hits like bricks, but oh, does it feel amazing!

I tip my head back, allowing it to work my hair back into a sleek, straight line down my back. For a moment I close my eyes, enjoying the sensation.

When I open them, I find Roan in front of me, treading water.

"Here, I can scoot over," I say, attempting to make room for him.

He reaches out and grabs my arms, forcing me to stay in place. "No, it's fine. You enjoy it. I used to live here, I've done it before."

I allow him to give me that moment of simplicity.

He treads water, watching me. From time to time, we find ourselves kicking each other as we try to stay afloat. I'm propped against the wall, but it sits at an incline and I keep slipping from it, crashing into his feet. Each time, he reaches for me, to steady me if I need it. I gently place my hand on top of his wrist from time to time, not needing his assistance, but knowing my touch is bonding us together.

"So what do you think of pools then, Jade?" he finally asks, reaching his feet up to the wall on either side of me and kicking off.

He swims backwards, away from me, and I kick off

the wall and follow him, feeling cold now that the water is no longer causing the warm pressure on my back.

"I think pools are fabulous. We should have these everywhere so that all the families can enjoy them," I say dreamily.

"You know, I think that's an interesting idea," he replies, slowing his pace as we reach an area where we can touch the bottom again. "Maybe that's something I could work on for when I have some power."

"I think that would be a great idea. I'm sure everyone would really appreciate your effort to give them something nice like this," I gesture around at the room.

Even if I die, this man will one day be in charge and it won't hurt to give him a few ideas to do something for the people.

He takes off toward the waterfall, looking as if something is weighing heavily on his mind.

"What are you thinking about?" I ask, swimming up behind him.

He turns when I place my hand on his shoulder. I drop my hand and we each brace ourselves off the side of the pool, the water streaming over our forearms.

"Jade, do you think I'll be a good Commander one day?"

So, he's worried about his future responsibilities.

"I know we're just getting to know each other Roan, but from what I can see, you have a lot of potential. I think that in time, if you really focus on doing good, you could be an incredible leader for this country.

"I think you have a good heart. I think you want to help people, to give them the best of this life, like with your art, and I think you want to give the world back the *world*.

"So, yes, I can see you as a good man, a good husband, a good father someday, even a good leader, but Roan... I can see you as a *great* Commander. You just have to stand up for what is right and put the people first. I think you have it in you to be loved by everyone and *trusted* by everyone."

"Do *you* trust me, Jade?" he interrupts, as if the question is so urgent, it can't wait.

"As a leader, yes," I answer after a moment.

He takes his arm off the wall and bobs on the surface. I release my grip and tread water with him.

"Do you trust me as a person, Jade? As your husband?"

Roan wraps his arms around my waist and pulls me close to him. I stop moving and allow him to hold us both up. My hands float to his arms and I take in how strong he really is.

"I..."

He tips his head so we're eye to eye, floating under the waterfall.

"I'm beginning to."

He leans in to me and I get the overwhelming feeling

I've won this battle. His hands rest on my waist, his legs hovering next to mine. Just when I think he's going to incline his lips to mine, the waterfall suddenly vanishes and a deafening silence washes over us.

"I didn't know you were coming over today," the Commander's voice makes both of us duck.

Roan spins me, keeping my back to the Commander so I can't see him.

"Since you're here, Roan. I'd like to see you in the house, please," he says tersely. He walks away, shoes clicking against the hard floor.

"Playtime's over. Sorry, Jade," Roan says scornfully.

I was so close.

"You want to dry off and get changed first?" he asks.

He holds my hand as he leads me out of the pool. I hesitate when he walks into the bathroom, still dragging me behind him.

"I'm not staying, I'm just showing you how to work this."

He opens a narrow door I had ignored before. It was a dark box.

"What is it?" I say, trying to hide my terror.

"It's a dryer," he says, waving me in. "It dries you off so you don't have to wait around like we did the other day."

"It's so small." I'm not worried about its size. I'm worried about being locked in it.

"Do you trust me, Jade?"

No.

"Yes…" I answer instead.

I take his outstretched hand and allow him to help me step inside. The doorway is narrow, but the box itself is fairly spacious.

"Press this button to start it," he points to a green button. "This one to stop. These two control the speed, and these two control the temperature."

He takes a step backward.

"Let me know when you're finished. I'll be waiting outside."

Once he's gone, I shut the door. An overhead light comes on, allowing a soft glow to fill the box. I turn it on and am instantly hit with a stream of air that sends a chill through my body.

After a moment, I get used to it and I lift my hair, allowing the air to dry my back. Running my fingers through my hair, I attempt to get the dampness out of it, but it works quicker than I expect.

I strip my suit off and finish drying, holding it up so it can dry as well. Once it seems mostly dry in my hands, I turn the machine off and carefully open the door. When I'm sure no one is there, I step out and change back into my clothes. I pull my hair back into the ponytail I had it in before our swim and set out to find Roan.

He's waiting right outside the door for me. It doesn't take him long to dry off, and we're quickly on our way to the house. He takes hold of my hand as we walk and I feel like he's becoming more comfortable with me again.

"Do you want to wait out here?" Roan asks as we approach the back of the house.

"No, I'll come in with you." I can clearly tell he wants me by his side.

"All right," he says, still holding my hand.

I wonder what it is about his father that has him so anxious. Other than the fact that they're plotting to kill me, that is.

"He's in the study, darling," Maybelle says with a smile as we enter.

I start to follow Roan, but Maybelle adds, "He just wants you, honey."

Roan looks to me apologetically. I release his hand, giving him an encouraging smile.

"So, Maybelle, how are you today?" I ask, forcing Roan to go.

"I'm fine, darling. Did you have a nice swim? I didn't know you were coming over today or I would have made something for you."

"Oh, that's quite all right, Maybelle, we didn't know we were coming ourselves until right before we came over," I drop my voice to a conspiratorial whisper. "I think we were trying not to be seen, although I can't be quite sure."

Maybelle giggles and continues to fold the laundry. As she picks up a sheet, I move over to help her.

"I see. It must be so nice to be young and newly married. It doesn't hurt that Roan is a fine looking young man," she adds, giving me a knowing look.

I feel myself blush.

"Now tell me," she says, dropping her voice to a whisper. "Did you have a nice swim?"

I laugh, louder than I mean to, "Yes, it was a very *nice* swim," I say, biting my lip and daring a glance at her. I shouldn't have. Her look makes me blush again.

"The Commander always did have the worst timing," she mutters, much to my horror. The Commander had seen us.

Something loud crashes down the hall and I turn quickly, dropping the sheet Maybelle just handed me.

"No, honey," she says softly as I take a step toward the noise.

And then I realize the sound is the Commander, throwing something in his office. I hear yelling, but can't make out what they are saying. I'm positive it's about me.

Turning back to Maybelle, I flinch every time I hear a garbled yell. She doesn't react and I'm left to assume this is nothing new in this house.

"Good heavens, what are you doing?" Alice yelps, walking into the room.

When I look up, I find her staring directly at me and I realize the question had not been directed at her maid.

"Folding sheets?" I say, posing a statement as a question.

When she glares, I add, "I'm waiting for Roan. We came over for a swim and his father asked to speak to him." I point over my shoulder toward the hallway.

Alice marches away, the noise quelling as she enters the room. A few minutes later, they all emerge, wearing forced smiles.

"Mom and Dad are going to come for dinner tonight, is that all right, Jade?" Roan announces.

I freeze, eyes locked on his, searching for what response he wants. He's clearly not happy about their intrusion, but he can't prevent them from coming.

"Of course," I say. "It will be so lovely to have you over. I've been hoping we could host you soon; you haven't been over since we moved in."

A list of things to do races through my mind. I've only got a few hours to pull everything together before they come over.

"Wonderful." The Commander smiles and it's like a punch to the gut. "We'll see you tonight."

CHAPTER 18
JADE

he moment we're out of sight, I start running, catching Roan by surprise. When he catches up to me, he grabs my arm and spins me around to face him, halting me in my tracks. He is wild-eyed and confused as he asks me what I'm doing.

"Roan!" I shout, "Your parents are coming over in *seven hours*. I don't have time for walking, now *move!*"

"Are you *really* that nervous about my parents coming over?" he laughs, amused at my dismay.

"It's the first time they'll be at our house, Roan. They're judging us on this. Everything has to be perfect. I have to cook an amazing meal, clean everything, make sure the garden is in perfect order, pick an outfit, *actually get ready*, make sure dessert works out, and...*oh gosh...Roan*, the guest room. Do they know you're in the guest room?"

His amusement fades, eyes growing wide again.

"Let's go," he says, turning to run with me.

Once inside the house, I task him with cleaning up the living room and dining room areas while I race through the kitchen deciding what to make. Between the two of us, we come up with a game plan for the meal and settle on another pie for dessert.

When he's finished picking up the living room and dining room, I send him out to pick up more raspberries for me. I hurriedly make my way through the bathrooms, hallways, closets, and porches, cleaning everything in sight.

Roan returns with the ingredients for the pie and while I start to bake, he starts transferring his belonging into the master bedroom.

Two hours before his parents are set to arrive, we start cooking and finish the cleaning. We make our way out to the garden, Roan focusing on the yard, and I focus on the flowers. Once I'm pleased with the way everything looks, we settle into the island barstool chairs and take a deep breath.

"The place looks spectacular. They can't hold anything against you," Roan says encouragingly.

What he doesn't realize is he said "you" instead of "us." One more nail in my coffin, clearly stating that his family will hold things against me, but never against him.

"Yes," I smile. "We did a good job today. Though I

guess it's a good thing we got to relax a bit this morning, on our very last day of freedom from work."

"Yeah, sorry about that," he grins ruefully. "We'll find more time to relax."

"We have to get better at sneaking into the pool though," I say, making him smirk.

"Hey, Jade, did you really mean that earlier? About thinking I could do good for this country?"

"Of course," I say, surprised he would bring it up again. "You're a good man, Roan. *I* can see it and I haven't even known you for two weeks."

It struck me how little time had passed since I married him. It was hard to imagine only a matter of days had passed since I angrily dyed my wedding dress in protest. Hardly any time at all had gone by since I last saw my father. And only a few days had passed since I was in my town and my people saw me and passed along information to my father.

What was he thinking now? What was he doing?

"What do you think of my father?" he asks abruptly.

"Your father?"

He nods and waits for me to reply. I know he's asking what I think of him as a Commander. Do I side with my father? Do I hate him? But instead, I choose to answer differently.

"I think your father loves you, Roan, I think it's just a little hard for him to show it the way you want him to sometimes. I know he can be a bit hard on you and he can be demanding, but I think, beneath everything, he is a man who just wants what is best for his son."

He seems shocked by my answer. I've given him more to think about.

I sniff the air loudly and stand up from my perch. "Smells like it's almost ready." I go check on my meal. "Do you want to taste test it?"

I need to shift his focus, and food is an easy way to do that.

A moment later, there is a knock on the door and we both freeze.

"We'll be okay," Roan says, as much trepidation in his voice as is running through my head.

"We can do this," I agree.

He requires a push before he starts walking toward the door. I turn my back on him and take a deep breath. This is one test that I must pass.

The Commander walks in with his usual, boisterous greeting. He claps Roan on the back and makes a big show of telling us how nice our house is. The house *he* picked out for us. And furnished. And controls.

Alice tips her nose as she surveys the house. I put on my best hostess smile and walk over to greet them. We exchange greetings and Roan moves to my side.

"Would you like to take your parents out to see the

garden, Roan? I could bring drinks. How does lemonade sound?" I turn my attention to his parents.

I can see the Commander sniffing the air, clearly pleased with the smell of the food. He may hate me, but he has no problem eating my food, apparently.

"I'll help you," Alice says, suddenly very eager to assist.

"Thank you," I say, a bit flabbergasted.

She must think I'm going to poison them.

Technically if I were going to, now would be the best time. They're all here and I have access to their food and drinks. Too bad I can't do anything like that.

Alice's gaze sweeps around the kitchen, which I have made sure is still spotless. When she sees nothing to criticize, she reaches for the cabinet to retrieve the glasses. On my first full day in the house, when Roan and I rearranged everything, I also purposely moved everything in the kitchen. She grumbles, searching for the right cabinet.

I step next to her, opening the door, and hand them to her, offering her the kindest smile I can.

"Roan wanted to put our own spin on the house, I hope you don't mind we rearranged things a little."

"Yes," she says in a flat voice, "I did notice that."

"Roan has been wonderful about making sure this feels like a home for us," I comment, pouring the drinks into the glasses.

"I see," Alice replies, picking up two of the glasses.

She walks away without another word. I scoop up the remaining two glasses and follow her through the house.

It's hard for me not to smile too brightly. I like aggravating Alice. Grinning, I hand Roan a glass and he gives me a questioning look. I latch on to his arm and sink against him. Resting my cheek firmly on his shoulder, I cuddle into him, making sure Alice has a very clear view of her son.

She scowls, but the Commander seems pleased. He probably thinks he's winning and that I'm falling for their little trap.

Roan seems a bit lost as to what to do, so he allows me to be affectionate toward him.

"Father was just saying how lovely you've kept the garden, Jade," Roan says, trying to start a conversation.

"Yes, Jade. You've done a magnificent job. Not a weed in sight," the Commander says, "You must spend a lot of time ripping the weeds out, removing their very existence from the beautiful flowers."

"Not at all sir," I say, "I suppose the weeds know enough not to try to choke out my garden, as I haven't seen a single one this whole time. Or perhaps it's the heartiness of the garden itself, when all the flowers band together, they can overtake any weed that tries to hurt them."

I shouldn't be challenging him, but I can't resist.

"Flowers must be tended to, dear. If they aren't looked after, they die," he replies.

"Or flourish." I smile.

"Well, dinner should be ready," Roan says, purposely interrupting. "Let's go inside."

He tugs at me before anyone can protest, and I nearly trip up the stairs as he tows me up the steps.

Inside, we have set out the best dishes, even folding the napkins in a fancy manner. This is my first dinner party and I need to set the bar high. If I am expected to be the wife of the Commander someday, people must know I will be a good one. The people in this room all know I'm not supposed to live long enough to host my own parties, but the outside world must hear of my abilities to entertain at a dinner party—even if it *is* only for my murderers. They all wait for me to take the first bite, probably still wary of the idea that I might poison them. I decide to have a little fun with them. I take my time preparing my plate. Just when I look like I'm about to eat, something conveniently distracts me, and both the Commander and his wife lower their forks.

Roan is oblivious to this, and digs right in, much to his parents' horror. Finally, I take a bite, encouraging them to eat. Suddenly I make a face, gasping slightly as if something is wrong. Panic washes over Alice's face and I nearly laugh.

"You need refills," I say, biting back my laughter. I race to the kitchen and return with the pitcher of lemonade.

Alice is glaring at the Commander, who has clearly said something to Roan.

"Is everything all right?" I ask as innocently as possible.

"Everything is fine, Jade," Roan says, "everything tastes wonderful, doesn't it?" He turns to his family.

They murmur their responses. I listen as the three of them chat.

Toward the end of the meal a thought occurs to me. I need to get Roan's attention back to me. I need to start pulling the attention away from the Commander.

Gliding my foot forward, I skim it over Roan's foot. He pulls back, giving me more space, but I do it again, making him look at me. I smile and run my foot up his ankle.

His eyes widen and he glances away. Pulling my foot back, I wait a few seconds and do it again, nearly causing him to jump out of his skin. He swallows hard pushes his chair back.

"I think it's time for dessert," he says moving toward the kitchen.

"Oh here, let me help," I follow him, placing my napkin gracefully on the table. I can't help but grin when none of them can see me.

"What are you doing?" he turns on me when his parents can't see.

"Helping you get dessert," I say right on cue.

"No, in there," he whispers as he points.

"Oh. I just thought you could use a friend in there. I wanted you to know I was there to support you if you needed me. It seemed like your father was pushing you a bit, that's all." I brush past him and pick up the pie. "Can you grab the plates?"

I turn and Roan is towering over me. He's not particularly taller than me, but when he stands at his full height, I need to tip my head up to make eye contact with him. With the pie between us, he looms over me and suddenly I feel very small... vulnerable. He watches me for a moment.

He wants to say something, I can feel it. But then he scoots around me and picks up the plates. He slips a smile back on his face and we return to the dining room.

"Fresh, homemade, raspberry pie," he announces, "I had some the other day and it was like heaven. Jade is magnificent with pies."

"Yes, it does seem to be a staple with her," Alice mutters, casting me a sarcastic smile as I hand her a plate.

Once we've finished, Roan helps me in the kitchen with the dishes. The Commander practically demands we take care of them now instead of waiting to clean up later. He and his wife make their way to the garden to wait for us.

The water from the sink is loud as Roan washes dishes, but I manage to hear some activity over the spray of water hitting glass. I want to find out what is going on: clearly someone is in the house, but I don't dare leave Roan's side. With the way his father switches moods so easily, Roan may be the only thing keeping me alive this night.

He pretends not to hear, though I can tell he notices. I force us to go faster, finishing as quickly as possible. The sounds get louder and I turn to investigate.

"Jade!" Roan says, spinning around from the sink and catching me around the waist. "Thank you, for having my back in there. I appreciate having someone on my side."

"You're welcome," I say, trying to get away. "Did you hear that?"

"Hear what?" he asks.

"That noise in the living room."

"Oh, that's probably Mom and Dad out in the garden. You know how Dad's voice carries."

He follows me as I push my way out into the living room, but there's nothing there to see. Whoever it was must have heard the water turn off and went back outside.

The Commander and his wife stay just long enough to give us the details for the party they are throwing us the next weekend. After a few very specific instructions on when to arrive and what to wear, they leave.

The sun has very clearly set and in just a few short hours, Roan and I are expected to be back at work. We decide to call it a night and make our way to our rooms. That is, until we realize Roan's entire room is now in my room.

An hour later, in complete silence, we have moved him back into his own space. He says goodnight and I collapse on my bed. Tomorrow I would see Mr. Eroh again and this all would seem more bearable.

As I try to fall asleep, I make plans to go to the bakery for lunch tomorrow, where I can tell anyone who will listen all about the fabulous dinner party I threw for the Commander and his wife. I need to get word out about the effort I put into the evening. People like to talk about the Commander, especially in his inner circles. If word could reach them, I would be in good standing with them, and that is exactly what I need.

CHAPTER 19
ROAN

e was careless tonight. He nearly got himself caught when he was traipsing through the house while we were doing the dishes. I don't know what he was up to, but I covered for him. I'll have to ask him what he was doing tomorrow.

Jade, however, was flawless tonight. She did everything so perfectly, people wouldn't believe it if they didn't see it. She was polite, efficient, hospitable…everything a Commander's wife should be.

She even made sure I knew I could count on her when my father got harsh. Is it possible this is really all an act with her?

Once, when I was about ten, I saw Jade for a few minutes. I was with my father on one of his trips into one of the towns, which I presume was her town. It was a market day, a rare and special event in the towns, and the entire town seemed to be out to buy and trade.

I saw my father stiffen and heard him say something about James Jareau. I knew the man was the cause of the rebellion and I knew my job was to help make sure he never did it again.

When I looked for him in the crowd, I was enraged that he would continue to show himself in public. He should have run away like the coward that he was.

But then, from behind him, a little girl ran out, smiling. She took his hand and walked along side of him for a moment. Then she saw a younger kid get pushed down. She darted forward and picked them up. The kids had stolen something from the little boy, but had run off when Jade approached. She held the little boy's hand until his mother turned back and saw he had fallen. Jade disappeared before the mother could even thank her.

Jade made her way over to her father and begged him for something. He finally gave in and handed her what turned out to be money. She raced to a nearby shop and picked up something, paid for it, and ran. I assumed whatever it was had been meant for her, but she wove her way through the crowd and found the mother and boy. Jade gave it to the child and his face lit up. Throwing his arms around her, he hugged her tightly. When he looked back to show his mother, Jade disappeared again.

I thought it had all been an act; something she did for the attention. But maybe not. Maybe it's just who Jade is.

Tomorrow I have to start testing her. Which means I have to stop thinking about her like this...like a *person*.

She can be nothing more than a target to me.

CHAPTER 20
JADE

"Y ou're welcome. Have a lovely day," I say, handing the wrapped box to Mrs. Thompson.

She smiles and takes her package, escorting her son outside.

"You seem glad to be back, Jade," Mr. Eroh comments as he walks past the counter.

"I am. It was nice to have a few days off, but I'm glad to have something to do again."

"That nice young man of yours didn't keep you busy baking all week?"

"Well, maybe a little," I admit. I told him a bit about the impromptu dinner I hosted the night before, hoping he'd catch on to the things I intentionally did not say.

"I see, and just how did you find yourself in a position of having to host a last-minute party?"

"Roan and I decided to take a swim in his family's pool and when we *went inside*," I say, hoping he'll understand the Commander forced us inside, "Roan and his parents made plans for dinner. It all worked out quite nicely."

"Yes, it sounds like it there were some very nice plans being made yesterday," he commented, a clear warning to me that it sounded to him as though the Commander was plotting against me.

"Indeed," I say, confirming his thoughts.

"How does your husband like that little gem of a wind-up toy I gave him? Did he put it somewhere nice?"

So, it was his intention for it to look like a gem to remind Roan of me.

"I'm actually not sure what he did with it. I'm sure he's got it in his room somewhere." I realize I just admitted to being in different rooms after saying it out loud.

Mr. Eroh glances around. No one was near but he was always incredibly careful of listening ears. I could see the relief on his face when he discovered we weren't sharing a room, a sentiment my father would share as well when word got to him.

"Well, I'm sure you'll see it again sooner or later. Come help me with these boxes, won't you?"

We spend the next hour reorganizing the back room of the store. Eventually he sends me off to get lunch, knowing my plan for spreading word of the dinner party.

By the end of the day I am exhausted. The walk home gives me a few minutes to relax before entering my home and worrying if it will be the last time.

Just as I'm about to cross over into Roan's side of town, I see a figure dart into a store.

Aunt Sophie.

I look in the direction she came from and find a small candle shop. I pause for a moment, and decide to go in.

Looking around, I examine each piece as if I'm selecting one for a very important reason. In truth, I know my aunt had recently been there.

"Hello, dear, looking for anything in particular?" the shopkeeper asks.

"No, just looking for something nice to take home to my husband. We are newlyweds and I thought maybe I'd light a few candles for dinner tonight," I say sweetly.

"Ahh, well, now that is an important choice," the woman says, walking over to me. "I have some nice ones over there, perhaps you should take a look."

She watches as I walk to the shelf she pointed at.

Green labels. Jade green.

Of course my aunt would use my name as signal and of course the shopkeeper would be on my side. Most of my side of town knew what had to be going on. They were all trying to help in whatever small way they could.

The note was tucked inside of the label hanging off the top of the candle jar.

"Rumors. Targeted. Planning."

So even the town was hearing rumors of what the Commander planned to do. I don't know how he thought he could keep this quiet.

I kept looking around the store, finally settling on a few unscented candles that might look nice around the house.

"These please," I say, walking to the counter.

"Anything else, sweetheart?" the woman asks.

"No, just these, thank you," I smile politely.

She rings me up and hands me two receipts.

"Sign here, please." She taps both papers.

Usually the second one would be for me, but she's giving me an opportunity to respond to my aunt without raising suspicion.

Unsafe. Stay away. Love.

I write as little as I can, hoping she understands that they can't save me.

The woman frowns slightly as she takes the papers back from me.

"Take care, dear. Hope to see you soon. If you order two more candles next time you come back, you get one for free."

"Thank you, I'll be back then," I say, confirming if I need to get a message out, I'll return. But I know I never will. It's too dangerous to involve other people in this.

I beat Roan home, so I settle into the kitchen to start dinner. Once it's cooking, I wander through the house, looking for places to put my new candles.

I don't sit on the couch often—usually Roan occupies that space—but since he isn't home, I flop down onto its soft cushions. Stretching my hands over my head, I wiggle down into the fabric. I let my hand trail along the back of the couch, dropping it to my side, pinning it between my thigh and the couch back.

That's when I feel something strange against the back of my hand. Pushing it deep in between the cushions, I grasp something cold and hard. I pull it out, sitting up. A vial.

I haven't made any headway with Roan and this vial confirms that...because this vial is meant for my destruction.

I shove it back into its hiding place as I hear the front

door open. Jumping away from the couch, I pretend to set down the last candle.

"I bought some new candles on the way home from work," I say, holding it up, thankful I had picked up unscented versions. "Do you like them?"

I point out the other two and he nods.

"How was work?" he asks.

"Good. It was nice to have something to do again," I say, making my way back to the kitchen. "How was your day?"

"Long," he replies. "Can I help with dinner?"

"You can get dishes out," I say, nodding to the cabinet.

Once he sets them out, I inform him we still have a few minutes until it's ready and that he can go relax if he wants.

Right now, I can't stand to be around him. I knew he was trying to kill me, but to see the proof of it was so unnatural that I wasn't sure how to cope.

CHAPTER 21
ROAN

ade seems a little flustered as I arrive home. When she practically kicks me out of the room as she's making dinner, I feel like all the momentum we've gained has just been iced over.

I wander into the living room and sit down on the couch. Staring at her new candles, I wonder what could have happened to make her switch so fast like that.

But when my hand finds the vial tucked in the couch cushion, it's *my* blood that runs cold.

Jade is planning on fighting back.

I swallow, eyes darting around the room. What else has she brought into this house that I don't know about? Suddenly I have to start being extra careful, because it's not just me with revenge on my mind, but the woman I am living with as well.

My father said this might happen. After all, she *is* James Jareau's daughter. He had no problem hurting people to get what he wanted and his daughter clearly turned out just like him.

When she enters the room, I hide the vial, leaving it where she left it. I smile and join her in the kitchen. We eat in relative silence. I make an effort to ask a few questions about her day and she responds with questions of her own, but it's obvious neither of us wants to talk.

We both hurry off to our own rooms as soon as we're done eating and cleaning up. I'm relieved when I don't have to be near her any longer.

I get up early and leave the house before Jade comes out of her room the next morning. Usually I enjoy listening to the birds on my walk to work, but today I glare icily at them. Silence is my friend today, and the animals aren't helping.

During the night, I resolved myself to do what I had to in order to stay alive. Never once growing up did I think I'd be defending myself as I was preparing to kill my wife. The concept has shaken me enough that I need to rethink my plans for making this happen.

I had to at least get through the Command party in a

few weeks so that everyone would know my family accepted Jade and wished her no ill will. We had to make them believe that she was one of us. Then we could stage an accident of some kind without casting suspicion on ourselves.

I sit at my desk all morning, trying to focus on my paperwork. Dad has always thought that I needed to spend time on paperwork to truly understand how to run the country. He's given me more responsibilities over time, but he still insists that I spend several mornings a week going over his paperwork. Really, I think it's an excuse to get out of doing it himself.

"Roan!" a voice calls sharply from the main office.

"What is it, Daniella?" I ask politely.

"Come quickly!" Her tone is panicked and I jump to my feet.

I rush into the main office lobby Dad and I share.

"Something happened, Roan," our secretary says, motioning me over.

Outside I can see a commotion in front of the building. People are rushing around. Suddenly a path clears on the walkway.

My mother pounds up the pavement and into the lobby.

"He's okay," she starts, setting me on edge.

"What happened?" I ask, grabbing her shoulders as much to steady her as to steady myself.

"There was an explosion. No one died, but a few people were injured, including your father."

I can feel the blood drain from my face.

"How? What…?"

"We don't know yet. You need to come home with me; they're taking your father there now."

"Did he go to the hospital? Was he checked out?"

"Yes, he was at the hospital. No, I don't know how bad his injuries are, but they wouldn't move him if he weren't stable. Now come on," she says forcefully.

I wasn't used to my mother being so strong. Usually, with my father around, Mom relied on him and let him take the lead. She simply followed along. She never stood up against him. He was always in charge. To see her so assertive was strange.

I let her tug me along, taking me all the way back to the house. We arrive as the paramedics are leaving.

"He's inside, ma'am. He told us you'd be home and to leave," the first man informs us.

"We tried to stay, but he ordered us out, ma'am," the woman explains, clearly trying to avoid my mother's wrath for leaving my father alone.

"Thank you," she murmurs as she rushes past them.

I don't even bother trying to talk to them.

Inside, my father sits on the couch, arm in a sling and a bandage over his eye.

"What happened?" my mother says, surprisingly calm

considering the nail marks she put in my arm on the trip home.

"I'm all right, Alice," he brushes her off.

"Dad, what happened?" I reiterate my mother's question, keeping my voice low and calm.

"There was a small bombing, really, everyone is all right. We lost a building, but nothing that can't be repaired in time," he says flippantly.

"A bombing?" I question incredulously.

"Son," he tries to calm me, "it was James Jareau. He was trying to make a point but we stopped him and we got everyone out without any major injuries. We'll get him to stop. Don't fret over it."

James Jareau nearly killed my father today to make a point. And Jade had plans of her own. Clearly, they were working together to start a new rebellion by disposing of my father and me. Well, I won't let them. I'll protect my father and this country from the rebels, no matter what.

"I'll make them stop," I say through gritted teeth. "Jade and James won't get away with this?"

"Jade?" he questions.

"I found a vial last night, one I didn't hide in the house," I admit.

"She's trying to poison you?" my mother gasps. "No! No, I simply won't have it. I want him out of there right now, Robert. I won't have you risking our son's life for this stupid campaign against a rebel leader..."

"No," I interject. "I'm staying, Mother. This has to be taken care of. Dad could have died today. The Jareaus need to be stopped. I can do this. Now I know what she's up to and I can be careful. I can strike first.

"We have to get through the Command party," my dad interrupts. "We can stage an accident on the way home from the party. It's not too far away. You can make it."

"I…" my mother starts, but we silence her.

"This is happening, one way or another," I tell her. Turning to my father, I add, "You just stay safe until we can take them down."

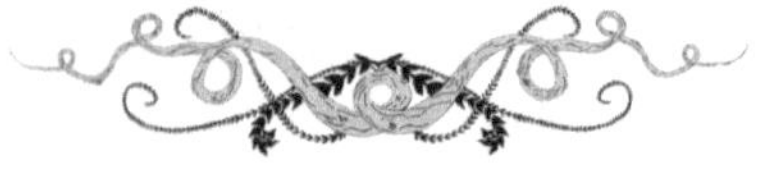

I spend the rest of the day with my parents, trying to decide what to say to Jade when I return home. I can't let on that I know about the vial or about her father's plan.

We decide not to tell the public it was James Jareau who

set off the explosion, but rather say it was being investigated. The less I had to tell Jade, the better.

My father finally forces me out the door as the moon starts rising in the sky. Reluctantly, I walk back to my house. Jade is at the door as I start walking up the steps.

"Are you okay? Where were you?" she asks, as if truly concerned.

"There was an explosion today, Jade," I say, not bothering to hide the tiredness in my voice, "my father was hurt, but he's all right."

She looks stunned. She's an incredible actress.

"Where? Were you there? Are you hurt?" she asks, but I can't bear to listen to her.

"I wasn't there. I'm fine," I brush her off as I walk by.

"Do you want to talk about it?" she asks, following me through the house.

"No, Jade. I really don't. I think I'd just like to go to bed."

Tomorrow I would apologize and play the part of a good husband, but tonight I am exhausted and need to regroup.

"All right then," she says, almost dejectedly. "I'm here if you change your mind. Can I get anything for you? Are you hungry?"

"No, thank you," I add as she continues to trail me through the house.

I turn around to face her. "Jade, I'm fine. Really. Why don't you go get some rest too and we'll talk about it tomorrow?"

"If you're sure," she says, though she looks uneasy.

I start toward my room when I hear her one more time.

"Roan? Is your mother okay?"

Is she really concerned about my mother? This girl is incredible!

"She'll be fine, Jade," I drag my hand down my face.

"Okay," she backs up. "Good night,"

I close the door behind me. Tomorrow my newly redirected mission starts to unfold.

CHAPTER 22
JADE

'm shocked when I hear the news… and a little disappointed that the explosion didn't take the Commander out. For a moment, I found myself actually being worried about Roan's well-being. I can't believe I cared for even a second after I found that vial yesterday.

I have to find out what happened tomorrow. I didn't hear anything about it today in town. From the sounds of it, it happened early in the day, if Roan was at his parents' all day. I can't believe word of it didn't make it around town.

As I'm pondering how in the world the explosion could have happened when the Command is so careful about regulating everything, I hear Roan moving around the house.

I open my door as silently as I can, trying to see what

he's up to. He stumbles back with a glass of water and I close the door. From this moment on I will always be terrified when I hear that man in this house.

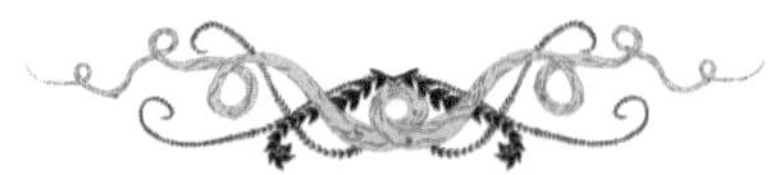

I barely sleep. I wait to hear his door open in the morning and time it so we bump into each other.

"Oh. I'm sorry. Are you okay?" I ask, running my hand through the hair on my head to brush it out of my eyes, an attempt at flirting without being obvious.

"I'm fine, are you okay?"

"Yes. Are you going to see your parents today? I could come with you, I'm sure Mr. Eroh will understand. He must know about the explosion by now."

"No, he won't know. The Command is keeping it as quiet as possible for now. Only a few people know. It wasn't just an explosion, Jade; it was a bombing. We don't want the people panicking until we know what's going on," he says.

A bombing?

"Oh. Well, we should still go see your parents…"

"No. You need to go to work, Jade. You have a job to

do and so do I. While my father is recovering, I'll be taking on some of his responsibilities. I'll check in on him sometime today, but he wants for both of us to keep up business as usual."

As it turns out, Roan is right and Mr. Eroh knows nothing about the bombing. During lunch, he sets out to find some details through his contacts.

That afternoon an elderly woman walks into the store.

"I'd like to trade this," she says to us, unfolding her hand to reveal a hair comb. It's jeweled with dark green, purple and clear jewels.

"Of course, what would you like ma'am?" Mr. Eroh asks.

I find it strange because he usually has a process he goes through to determine value and see what the client wants in return.

"I'm looking for an old clock, dear," she tells him.

Mr. Eroh points out a few and she finally settles on one. Mr. Eroh inspects it and I notice him specifically move the hands on the clock while he's checking the back with his other hand in a grand flourishing movement.

It's a signal.

The woman thanks him and leaves with her clock.

"Well now, what am I going to do with this?" Mr. Eroh asks, inspecting the hair comb.

"I was wondering the same thing," I say, curiously.

I take it from him as he holds it out to me. I inspect it and finally hold it up to my hair, showing it off for Mr. Eroh.

"It's lovely. Jade, why don't you keep it? I have no use for it."

I'm about to ask why he traded for it, but then I remember the clock hand signal.

"Jade, your father is worried about you." He tips his head and whispers.

And then I understand. It's a two-way message. My father sent the hair comb to me.

"The tip, dear."

I take it back out of my hair and pull on the end. It slides out revealing a sharp edge, almost like a tin sword. It's covered in a liquid and I quickly put it back in place. Poison. My self-defense carefully hidden in the jeweled object, waiting should the need arise.

Amazing how something so small and so beautiful could be so deadly.

I tuck it in my hair before I walk home, knowing I'll

have to explain it to Roan once I get there. He notices it as we sit down for dinner.

"What's that?" he asks as his eyes narrow.

"It's a hair comb. One of Mr. Eroh's good clients came in with it to trade today. Mr. Eroh likes her, so he traded even though he had no use for the comb. I happen to hold it up to my hair and he decided it looked good, so he gave it me."

"That was kind of him," Roan says, taking a bite of food. "It looks nice."

"Thank you. How is your father?" I dare to ask.

"He's doing better," he says, still looking at his plate.

"I'm glad to hear that. Can we take him anything? Maybe cook something for your mom so she doesn't have to?"

"Maybelle is cooking, but thanks,"

Of course. Sometimes I forget they are privileged enough to have a maid.

"Would you like to take a walk after dinner?" he asks suddenly.

"Oh. Umm...okay. Yeah, that would be nice," I stumble.

"I thought maybe we could go to the art house," he says casually, as if we often frequent the place.

"Sure, if that's what you'd like."

I couldn't imagine why we'd be going, but if he

wanted to do something, I'd better play along. I needed to get back in his good graces.

We finish eating and set out for the art house. The sky is still light as we walk, and I'm grateful, thinking I might end up waiting outside. Roan walks right up to the building when we arrive.

"I can wait out here," I suggest, hoping he won't ask for space.

"No, come in with me. Maybe you could work on something too."

"If you're sure," I say hesitantly.

"I am."

Once inside he wanders around the workroom a bit. The sheets cover furniture, as I had guessed. He picks out a chair for himself, dragging it to the middle of the room. He finds an easel tucked behind a couch and sets it up for himself.

"There are supplies over there, go see what you want," he instructs.

I wander over and find a massive number of pads of paper, brushes, paints, pencils, and inks. I know I can't use the paints; it would be a disaster, especially if Roan is watching. I edge toward the pad of paper and a pencil, but in the end, I go for the ink.

When I turn around, I hold up my choices for Roan to see, asking his approval. He nods and motions me over. He flings the sheet off an old couch, catapulting dust into the air. He bats at it momentarily, but leaves me to sit.

I lean against the arm, nestled into a pillow. Reclining back, I settle in to create. Only I have no idea what to do. I see Roan settle in out of the corner of my eye, but I refuse to look up. We both need our space, but at least we're having our space together.

My hand flicks over the paper, mimicking actions of drawing, though I never touch the paper. Back and forth it travels, my hand hovering just over the sheet.

When pen and paper finally connect, it's magical. Lines flow out of me as if I have no control. I don't know how long we're lost in creating but when I finally look up, it's dark.

It's as if we're taking a collective breath at the same time. Roan and I both look up and suddenly there is life in the room again. He stands, and moves toward me.

"Can I see?" he asks.

I turn the pad of paper and reveal the drawing I was working on. My pond has come to life on my page. I didn't realize at first what I was working on, but as the water and the trees and rocks started to take shape, I quickly recognized the scene.

It was my safe place, my happiness; a reminder of my childhood…of my father and my life *before*.

"The pond," he muses. "You do nice work."

"Thanks… I've never actually done this before."

"You've never tried drawing before? Not even as a kid?"

"I had other things to learn as a kid," I say. "What did you make?"

We walk over to his workspace and I find a portrait of myself looking back at me. He captured the way my hair swayed as I sat, the intensity in my eyes as I drew, even the way my lips pouted as I was lost in thought. It was eerily similar to what I saw in the mirror.

"You painted me?"

He shrugged as if it were nothing. "You inspired me. I didn't realize it was you at first, but it turned into you about halfway through. I went with it."

"It's beautiful," I say, wanting to reach out and touch the still wet paint.

I couldn't decide if I loved it for being so good or hated it because this deranged man had captured me so beautifully. I wanted to cradle it in my arms while simultaneously gouge it to pieces.

"It has to stay here," he warns, reminding me that this place is secret and what we do here, must remain here.

"Of course," I hand him my pad of paper and he tears the sheet out.

Walking into the gallery, he tacks it to the wall.

"Here, sign it," he says, handing me a pen.

I scribble an unreadable version of my name on the paper, never wanting to be connected to it.

"Ready to go home?" I ask, returning the pen to him.

"Yeah, I'm ready." We close the door behind us.

"Thanks for coming with me tonight," he says, taking my hand as we walk.

"Of course. It was very therapeutic," I reply, and it *had* been.

"Why did you draw the pond?" he asks thoughtfully.

"Why did you draw me?" I respond, giving him a smile. He smiles in return.

"Things have been weird between us," I say as we near our house. "Can we talk about it?"

"I'm sorry; it's my fault," he says, accepting the blame. "I've been under a lot of stress lately and I'm bringing it home with me. I shouldn't; I'm sorry. I know this is a stressful situation to begin with, we've only been together for a few weeks, and I shouldn't be complicating things."

"It's not all you; I haven't been the most helpful either. We just seem to be going from being on each other's side, to being *not* on each other's side. I'm not sure what we're doing here."

"I think we're figuring each other out. We're discovering who the other person truly is. Now that we've had some time and we're getting over the initial be-really-good-so-the-other-person-likes-me phase, we're figuring out how to exist together."

"Sometimes I wonder," I sigh softly, "if I'm not what you're looking for."

"Jade, you're actually exactly what I'm looking for in a mate. You have no idea *how much* you are *exactly* what I'm looking for." I sense a deeper meaning behind his words. "I'm going to try harder. I promise."

And somehow, I think that promise holds an entirely different meaning than what he's trying to suggest.

CHAPTER 23
ROAN

've spent my day sitting in my office, trying to work out a new plan. I need to force Jade out into the open, revealing her connection to her father's rebels.

"How was your day?" she asks me as she sets the table.

I turn my back to the food I'm cooking to look at her.

"It was fine. How was the shop?" I ask, leading into my plan.

"I helped fix a broken sewing machine today. It was practically ancient; I don't know how Mr. Eroh got it working at all, much less working properly," she comments.

"Sound interesting," I respond, turning back to the food.

"How's your father? Did you go see him today?" she asks the question I've been waiting for her to ask.

"No, I was too busy today. The Command is close to

making arrests for the rebels responsible for the bombings."

I turn to see her reaction. I expect her to flinch or look worried. Amazingly, she doesn't seem worried by the news.

Of course, I made the arrests up. My plan is to follow her tomorrow as she goes to warn the rebels that the Command is closing in. Once I find out how she is communicating with her father, I can catch her and put an end to both of them.

When she goes about setting the table, completely unfazed by my words, I begin to wonder if she has any knowledge of the attack at all. But she *must*. There's no way her father could have done this without her knowing.

"That's good," she murmurs as she finishes and slides into her chair to watch me. "He's doing better, though?"

"Yes, he's doing better," I say, frowning. When she catches me, I add, "I just wish he hadn't been hurt in the first place."

"Will he be better in time for the Command party?" she asks, bringing me back to the task at hand.

"I'm sure," I say. "Have you decided what to wear yet? We'll have to coordinate outfits."

"Oh." She seems surprised. "I'll wear whatever goes with your outfit, just let me know."

"No, you pick your dress first. It's easier for me to match to you."

"All right, if you're sure. I'll have an answer for you by tomorrow, if that works."

"That's fine," I say, trying not to sound too forced. I'm supposed to be wooing the girl, after all.

"Are you going to wear that hair comb all of the time now?" I ask, noticing she's wearing it again.

Her hand floats up to where it sits in her hair. She fingers it gently and then brings it back down.

"I like it. You don't?" she pauses, seeming unsure of herself. "It holds my hair back when I'm working, which is helpful."

Her hand waves to her off center part and the mass of hair that falls to one side, currently being held back by the comb.

"It's very nice, you just seem to wear it a lot, that's all."

"It's the only one I have and it's functional. I'll have to buy a few more so I have a few to choose from," she suggests. "I think I might work out in the garden a bit after we finish eating. Do you want to come outside with me?"

"Sure," I respond, not knowing a graceful way out of it.

Outside, the sun is starting to set, giving the entire yard an orangey golden glow. I've always loved the golden hour; the time of day where the light is so perfect, it takes your breath away.

Jade tends to the flowers and I make my way over to the wall surrounding the yard to pull some weeds that have started sneaking through. She focuses on watering the flowers as if her life depends on it. Maybe she thinks it does.

"Oh look, Roan! A butterfly," she calls.

I walk over to stand beside her. We watch as the orange thing flits around from flower to flower. Butterflies aren't very common anymore, so it's a rarity to actually see one in our yard.

It bobs through the blades of grass, hopping like a frog. Its vibrant colors stand out against the green. Jade tips her head as she watches it. It almost looks like she wants to reach out and touch its delicate wings.

She's entranced by the winged creature, which is why her shriek is so terrifying. Jade jumps backward, clinging to my arm. A bird had swooped down, snatching the butterfly in its beak before either of us could react. We had both wanted to save it, but neither could move fast enough. Jade looks like she wants to wring the bird's neck and I can't say I blame her.

When I look back at Jade, her eyes are filled with tears. She tries blinking them back, but it doesn't do much good.

"Hey," I say softly to the visibly shaken girl, "it's okay,"

"No. It's not," the tears in her voice are almost enough to undo any man. "It was cruel and awful."

"The birds need to eat too, Jade," I try to convince her, though I'm not happy about what just happened either. "It was just trying to survive."

"Survive by killing someone else? Somehow that doesn't seem fair," she points out. "Is survival worth it, when someone has to be killed for it?"

She makes her point.

"It was just a butterfly," she presses, "It wasn't doing anything by flying around. And that vicious bird, it just swooped in, no warning, and snapped it in two. It just took off. It didn't care. How could anything be so careless?"

Now the tears are really flowing. I try patting her arm, but it doesn't seem to help.

"*We* didn't even see it coming. The poor little butterfly didn't even have time to *try* to escape. It was alive and happy one minute and dead the next."

She folds herself into my arms and leans against my chest. I let her cry against me, holding her in my arms. It amazes me how she could care so deeply about a little butterfly but not care about all the people she and her father are hurting.

"I'm sorry," she says as she pulls back. "I guess I just have a lot on my mind."

Pulling away, she starts back inside. I mean to say something kind, something husbandly, but I can't find the words, so I simply follow along.

Inside, she looks around, seeming a bit lost.

"I think I'm going to read for a while. I need a distraction," she announces. Without waiting for an answer, she leaves.

Once she's gone, I check the vial in the couch. It's still where she left it. At least I know I can keep tabs on it there.

I think about the vial my father gave me, safely tucked away in a secret compartment he added in the kitchen before we moved in. If I start using it now, she might get suspicious. Then again, maybe a little terror would help the situation.

Only a few more days until everyone would see us at the Command party. I just needed to get through that and I would be free of having to make these decisions.

I leave for work before Jade does. Except, I'm not going to work, I'm following Jade.

She slips out of the house not long after I do. She takes her normal route to Mr. Eroh's store, not stopping once. I hide down the street and manage to stay out of view of the other people walking around.

She doesn't leave until work is over for the day, not even to go out for her lunch break. She said she usually just stays in the store all day, but I know sometimes she takes a trip to the bakery midday.

On her way home, she avoids all the stores. She doesn't talk to anyone. Jade doesn't even do anything remotely suspicious. No signals, no communication, nothing. No one even came into the store all day. And unless that old man she works for is passing messages for her, she hasn't told anyone about the Command gaining in on them. Mr. Eroh seems to like her enough, but I doubt he could even figure out *how* to pass a message. Besides, she has to know the store is being watched.

Frustrated, I make my way back home. I circle the block, and come back from the direction I should be returning in from work so she doesn't get suspicious.

I need a new plan.

CHAPTER 24
JADE

oan has been trying everything in his power to keep me away from his family since the explosion; the explosion that no one in my town seems to know anything about. Which means I need to find out what is going on.

He barely spoke to me last night after we both got home from work. If he won't talk to me, I'll have to find out for myself.

Mr. Eroh gave me a basket before I left work. On my way home, I stop by a few shops and pick up some things. I order a few cookies from the bakery. While I'm there, I send one of the younger girls to get a relaxing candle from the shop on the edge of town. I don't want to go in myself and get the owner in trouble. I pick up a few teabags from the bakery as well.

During my walk home, I pick a few wildflowers and add them to the vase Mr. Eroh gave me. With my care package in hand, I veer off from the road to our house, and continue on toward the Commander's house.

I start to second guess myself as I approach the front gate, but once the guards have seen me, there is no turning back.

"I'm here to see the Commander and Mrs. Diamond, please."

They allow me inside and I walk to the front door. Maybelle answers when I knock.

"Well, look who's here. I haven't seen you in a few days, dear. Where have you been?"

"Hello, Maybelle," I greet her. "Roan told me about the explosion. I wanted to come sooner, but Roan said the Commander needed his rest. I finally couldn't take it anymore. Roan's been over here almost every day, but I've been dying to bring a care package over myself."

Holding up the basket, she looks impressed.

"I don't have to see him if he's too tired, but maybe I could check in on Mrs. Diamond?"

"Oh, don't be silly. The Commander is doing just fine. I'm sure he'd love to see you. You can give this lovely basket to him yourself. You put so much effort into it." She smiles. "And are those cookies I see? I'll let you in on a little secret. The Commander has a bit of a sweet tooth."

"It seems he passed that trait on to his son as well," I lean in conspiratorially and wink.

She laughs and motions me forward.

"Commander, look who dropped by to see you," Maybelle announces as we walk into the living room where I find the Commander sitting on the couch, papers sprawled all over the coffee table.

He looks up, an easy smile on his face until he sees me. It falters and even Maybelle notices. He quickly arranges it back in place and stands to greet me, one arm in a sling.

"Thank you, Maybelle," he says, dismissing her. "What do we have here?" he peeks into the basket.

Once Maybelle is gone, the Commander drops his façade. Grabbing my arm with his free hand, he jerks my arm back, nearly causing me to drop the basket.

"What are you doing here?" he growls.

I'm so taken aback by his brutality that I don't know what to say. I had thought he would at least keep up the act until it was time to kill me. Maybe he doesn't care if I know he's after me. Maybe it was only Roan holding him together long enough to complete the plan. Without Roan here, there is no one to rein him in.

"I… I brought you a care package. Roan said you were hurt in an explosion." I wrench myself away. "He said you needed some space, but I thought it wouldn't hurt to bring over some cookies and flowers for you. I even picked up a candle to help you relax." I offer him the basket, keeping as far from him as possible.

"You shouldn't be here," he growls again. "You're interfering with my plans."

"What plans?" I ask innocently.

"Don't be coy, Jade. You know what's going on here. You're a smart girl and your father must have prepared you for this."

"For what?" I gasp, as if it is all new information to me.

"Let me be clear, young lady. You will play your part in all of this, mark my words, or else. Your father started the rebellion and I know you've been working with him all this time. I know he's not done yet, but when I'm finished, he will be. No one will revolt against me."

"The rebellion?" I ask.

He slaps me so hard across the face that I fall back into a chair. Never have I been so grateful for a chair in all my life.

My hand flies to my face and I can feel the pain radiate through my entire body.

"You will be a good girl, Jade, and do everything I tell you to do. Because if you don't, someone else will pay."

"You wouldn't hurt your own son," I say, assuming he means to threaten my husband.

"It's not Roan that will pay. It's Sophie."

I feel myself falter. He knows about Sophie. We'd been so careful all these years to keep away from Sophie, to keep her safe, but also to keep her a secret in case we needed her help. Now it didn't matter; he would target her.

"Someone has to pay for what your father did, Jade. It can't be him—it's too public. It can't be Sophie, because it's not personal enough. But she *is* personal enough for *you*. So, if you don't do as I say, she'll pay the price. And if that's not good enough for you, then I swear to you, I'll find a way to make your father pay. Do you understand?"

I nod, still clutching my face.

"You will go to the Command party and you will be the perfect bride, the perfect daughter-in-law. You will show the world you love us and are one of us. You will conclude your work in your hometown. You will have no further contact with those people."

"If I quit, they'll know something is wrong."

"Then phase it out. Give notice. I'll give you a week or two. And Jade," he says eerily. "If you tell Roan of this little chat, you'll regret it."

I glare at him.

"Oh, and one more thing. Roan isn't to be touched. You hurt him, and I'll rain horrors on you that you never knew. I can destroy your town and blame it all on you if I like," he grins. "So don't push me."

He starts toward me, ready to throw me out. I leap to my feet and scurry to the door, unwilling to be touched by that monster.

Maybelle sees me flee, but I don't stop.

I make it to my street before I stop running.

The Commander isn't hiding anymore.

When I wake up the next morning, I feel ill. Roan promises he'll send word to the shop for me that I can't come in. Mr. Eroh will know something is wrong, at least.

I might have forced my way through the pain, but I have another plan. If the Commander wants me to fall in line, I will. But subtle defiance has never been my preference. I prefer overtly covert defiance.

I set to work, preparing for the party. I need to look just right.

There is a dress code and that is: *fancy*. I told Roan what colors I would be wearing the night before, but now I had to make the dress actually happen.

The nuance might slip past the rest of the crowd, but I'm positive the Commander will get my message.

Roan shows me his outfit that night. I approve, saying it will match mine perfectly. He has no idea what I have planned.

I leave work early the next day, having filled Mr. Eroh in on everything. I spend the afternoon getting ready. When Roan comes home, I call out from my room, telling him to go get ready so we aren't late to the party.

In fact, we will be late; I'll see to that. We need to make an entrance.

I made sure he was delayed coming home from work, so we were already running a little behind. I hid his cummerbund behind his dresser as if it had fallen down. His socks were conveniently "*accidentally*" mismatched. I rather enjoyed hearing him grumble.

Before he arrived home, I selected a few flowers from the garden and cut them, laying them in Roan's room. He has no idea he's part of my plan for showing up the Commander.

When he finally steps out of his room, I'm standing in the living room, perched on the back of the couch. My dress drapes over my legs so that I'm showing them off at precisely the right angle.

He freezes when he sees me, taking me in.

"You look stunning, Jade," he says.

He hasn't realized what I'm wearing yet.

"Thank you. You look very handsome yourself," I flirt.

Walking over to him, I adjust the flower in his lapel.

"This is the one I would have picked too," I smile up at him through my lashes.

I actually feel his heart stutter under my touch. Running my hand down his chest, I straighten his lapel.

"Are you ready to go?" I ask.

He makes a grunting noise; an indication that we should leave.

As I walk, the fringe of my dress bounces around my ankles. The detail work on the bodice was always my favorite part of the dress, even if I despised it as a whole. It once bound me to the Diamond family, but now, in its shredded, styled form, it will free me of them.

I can't wait to see the look on the Commanders face when he sees I repurposed my tea-stained wedding dress. I was rebellious about it the first time I wore it, changing its color, but now I'm positively shouting my defiance against him.

I admit, shredding it to pieces and recreating it was one of my favorite moments ever. It looks so much better this way, anyway.

I even added my own personal butterflies to the waistline and chest from the extra fabric I took out of the underside of the dress.

I try to hide my smile as we walked, arm in arm, to the party. I would see my father tonight. It had been so long.

I know people have kept him informed, but I need to find a way to see him tonight. The Diamonds can't keep me away from him in such a public place. They can keep me from being alone with him, or really talking to him, but they can't keep me from his presence and that's really all I need.

There is a special building kept by the Command that is used only for formal events. Most times it sits—quiet and unused—an absolute waste of space that could be used for something to help the country. Tonight, it is brimming with people.

The Command always makes a show of the party, or so I have been told. The lights are bright and the music is loud, even from out on the street.

I lift my skirt up as we walk up the stairs to the building.

I revel in the way it crashes around my feet. It is my confrontational heart song, and every time it connects, I feel rooted deeper and deeper to my new cause. I may have to give up my life, but I will do it boldly and with no regrets.

Inside, people are everywhere. I search for my father. Several of his friends catch my eye and nod to me in greeting. Roan is approached by his father's colleagues and I'm forced to make polite small talk.

Finally, I see him across the room. I let out a breath. He can't hold back his smile when he sees me. I want to rush to his side and cling to him. We're both trapped in mindless conversation, and neither of us can move. He notices my dress and a smirk spreads across his face. How I've missed him. He nods in approval, raising his glass a bit as if to toast me.

I see my father's grin fall and he straightens a bit, shifting his gaze to the side of me. I turn to find the Commander walking over to us.

"Hello Roan, hello Ja—" He falters, discovering what I did to his precious wedding dress. I lean into Roan, resting my head on his shoulder.

"Hello, Commander. It's so nice to see you this evening. The party is so lovely."

I can tell he is livid, but we're in public, so he slips on his mask of deception and plays along.

"Thank you, Jade, it's lovely to have you," he turns to a

man next to him. "Have you met my daughter-in-law, Jade? Roan is so lucky to have a girl like her."

I notice Alice with her back mostly to us, listening over her shoulder, trying to cover her eye roll at her husband's words. I keep my eyes fixed on the Commander as he speaks, not wanting to give anyone any reason to doubt me.

"There she is, my beautiful daughter," I hear my father's voice as he sidles up next to me. His hand slips around my waist.

I feel myself deflate. For a moment, even just for that moment, I am not in this alone and the realization of it washes over me.

I want to melt into him, but I can't let go of Roan. My hatred for him grows.

"Hello, Roan." My father moves to shake his hand with his free one. "Taking good care of my girl?" he asks jovially, as if they talked all of the time.

"Of course, sir."

I expect Roan to look uncomfortable, but he exudes confidence. I can see how he'd make a good Commander someday.

My father chats with the men in the group, purposefully avoiding the Commander, which is just as well because the Commander avoids him. Eventually the Commander gets pulled away, leaving Roan to watch over me.

"So tell me, my girl," my father leans in to me and says just loud enough that Roan can hear too, "how has married life been? Do you like your new house?"

"I've missed you," I say, not able to adequately say just how much I've really missed him.

He looks at me, his eyes demanding to know if Roan has mistreated me.

"The house is nice," I add.

"Your dress looks lovely," he smiles. "It was the perfect choice for tonight."

"Thank you. I think so too."

It's almost amusing that Roan is the only one unaware of the joke.

Alice walks over to the group, clearly not having noticed my father standing next to me. She probably didn't even see *me* at all.

"Roan, why aren't you with your father?" she asks, taking his free arm.

Roan looks to me and Alice's gaze follows along.

"Oh. Hello, Jade." She does a double take. "Good heavens! Is that your wedding dress?" she yelps.

I look down at my dress virtuously. "Oh, yes, it is. It was such a lovely dress, I thought I should wear it more than once, so I repurposed it," I smiled as if destroying and redesigning the dress was the most natural thing in the world.

She flounders and my father squeezes my hip, enjoying the hilarity of the moment.

"She looks lovely tonight, doesn't she Alice?" he asks, prompting her to publicly respond.

"Yes, it was a lovely choice," she replies and turns to find anywhere else to be.

"That's your wedding dress?" Roan whispers, a bit amazed.

"Yes. Where did you think I got it from?" I frown, trying to upset him publicly.

"I… I have no idea. I just… it's really your wedding dress?" he asks again, inspecting it.

"You saw me wear it once, Roan, you *should* recognize it," I reply, making sure it sounds like a disheartened joke. The crowd around us looks amused.

If the Commander wanted me to look accepted by his family, I was going to make it hard for them. I wanted the world to know there was trouble in the paradise the Commander told them of.

My husband clearly doesn't pay attention to me, despite my best efforts to please him. I was satisfied that I was disturbing the Commander's plans.

"I'm sorry, I guess I just assumed it was new," he tries to recover.

I look away, downcast.

The bystanders try to tell me what a lovely job I did

with the dress and I thank them kindly, coming back to life like a wilted flower given water.

They see the change in my demeanor and hover around my father and me, complimenting him on what a lovely daughter he raised and how proud of me he should be. Eventually they force Roan out of the circle and he wanders back out of view.

As if the room was suddenly given air again, I feel as though I can breathe. I may be in the presence of the Diamond family, but I'm separated from them. I'm near my father. For a moment, I can pretend life is normal again.

Had I not fallen into the trap of the Commander's revenge, it was very likely that I'd be here anyway, in this same location now. I may be married. I'd have a job I enjoyed. I'd probably be working with my father to make our country a better place. And I would certainly be on my father's arm here tonight at this very party talking to these exact people. One thing is for sure; I *wouldn't* be looking over my shoulder, waiting for my executioner to make his move.

The music switches and the dancing starts. I watch a few dances as we continue to talk. Just as my father is about to take me out to dance, Roan interrupts.

"I'd like a dance with my wife, sir, if you don't mind," he addresses my father a bit formally.

"Of course," my father nods his head to Roan and releases me.

"You seem to be spending a lot of time with your father tonight. I've hardly seen you."

"You see your father all the time, Roan," I spit, "I haven't seen mine since the wedding, and I barely saw him then."

"That's *your* choice," he replies and I want to hit him.

"Yes, because I have so much free will in this," I mutter under my breath.

"What was that?" he asks.

"I said that you're a very good dancer, dear."

He spins me around the room, and surprisingly, he *is* a very good dancer. After a while, we forget we are fighting and find ourselves genuinely enjoying dancing together. I catch sight of my father once and he gives me a surprised look when he sees me genuinely smiling.

I'll have to watch myself. Sometimes I find myself forgetting I'm dancing with the enemy.

The Commander makes sure to send plenty of people over to my father to keep him occupied the rest of the night. I don't even get to dance with him.

As the music fades, Roan announces it's time to go. Reluctantly, I follow him to the door.

"Leaving so soon? I've barely had time to see you, my sweet girl," my father says, causing my heart to ache.

"It was wonderful seeing you," I say.

He embraces me gently; though his muscles are so tight I can tell he doesn't want to release me. Kissing the top of my head, he tells me he loves me.

"We'll see each other soon," he comforts me.

"Yeah, there's always the Command party *next year*," I say wistfully, and he gives me a look.

Can he tell I'm giving up?

He looks sharply at Roan.

"You take care of her," he commands.

"I will," Roan responds. My father stares him down for a long time before Roan rips his gaze away.

One final squeeze of the hand and my father lets me go. I can see the pain in his eyes.

Roan tugs on me and waits for me to turn around. I loop my arm through his and follow behind him.

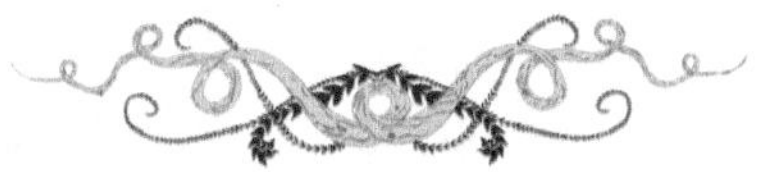

The streets are fairly empty despite the people leaving the party early. The cool night air feels good on my face. I hadn't realized how warm the room had become from all the dancing and talking.

I lift my hair off the back of my neck, letting the air soak up the sweat.

"Did you have fun?" Roan asks.

"Yes, it was a nice party," I reply.

"It looked like you had a nice visit with your father," he comments.

"Yes, it was so good to see him again. You should get to know him sometime, Roan. I think you'd have a lot to talk about." Though getting those two alone would probably result in a very injured Roan.

"Don't move," a voice behind us says. Their tone is so volatile that we both instantly freeze.

"Turn around," he says. We oblige.

A man stands in front of us, face obscured. He holds a knife in his hand. He takes a step toward us and I realize what is about to happen. I have only a second to decide how to respond.

This man has been sent by the Commander; I am his target. It's to look like Roan and I were mugged on the way home from the party. By the time the sun rises Roan will be mourning the loss of his bride to a tragic accident.

I can fight. If Roan fears at all that he will be seen, he must defend me. If he's good, he can make it look like in the process of saving me, he lost me.

I can use the poison tucked in the comb in my hair, but that will give it away. I'll never be able to use it again and Roan will question everything from now on.

I could run, but I'll be caught.

Before I can decide on the best option, I hear people walking closer. Witnesses. The man must move quickly.

Roan starts shouting to the man, trying to scare him off in front of the people. Just as I'm about to take my chances attacking the man, a cart comes flying out of nowhere. It plows into the man, sending him careening into the street. In the process, the knife cuts Roan's arm.

Everyone scatters and Roan pulls me away, knowing the plan is over. I silently thank whoever pushed that cart.

We run all the way home. Roan tries to explain it away, rationalizing it as an unusual occurrence and assuring me he'd find out who tried to attack us.

I sit with him, cleaning his wound and sewing it up, another talent I learned at the feet of Mr. Eroh. Roan doesn't question where I learned to sew a person up.

The attack is all anyone can talk about the next day. Unlike the news of the explosion, this traveled quickly. Everyone stops me to see if I'm okay. It takes twice as long to get to work. The bakery is packed at lunchtime and I'm overwhelmed by questions. The entire town is silently furious at the idea of me being hurt. I'm thankful for the people who care for me.

Strangely, Mr. Eroh doesn't even mention it when I walk into the shop. Not one word. I know he must have heard about it. Usually he's so concerned, but it doesn't seem to faze him.

When he still hasn't said anything in the afternoon, I'm worried that he thinks we're being monitored. I give him the signal, asking if we were being watched.

"Not that I know of," he says out loud.

"Then why haven't you asked about last night?" I ask.

"Because I don't need to ask, Jade, I know you're fine." He smiles at me knowingly.

Because it was Mr. Eroh that pushed the cart that foiled the Commander's plan. He saved me.

I smile back, thanking him.

"Now come on, we have work to do," he says.

CHAPTER 25
ROAN

he plan failed. The mugger never got the chance to attack Jade. I am almost relieved; I didn't know if I could stomach what promised to be a brutal attack.

I knew Dad was going to try something, I just didn't know what. When the man showed up, I played along. I knew it was an option; we'd been over the finer points of how I should react and how I needed to move to make it look real without getting myself hurt.

But the plan failed.

I had thought after last night, I'd be free of this nightmare. It *should* be over. But it's not.

Jade is a hard woman to kill.

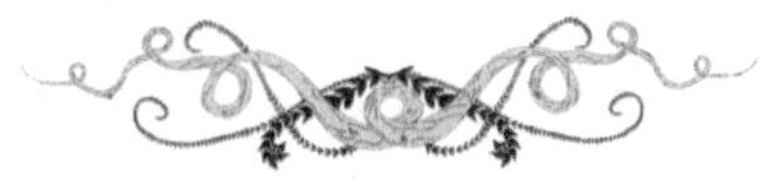

"Roan, we need to talk." Jade's voice is icy as I enter the house.

I find her sitting on the armrest of the couch. She has one leg folded over the other, foot dangling in the air. One arm is crossed over her body as she leans forward on her knee. The other is tucked in at the elbow, holding something in her hand toward me. She bounces her foot in the air, making her whole body sway with the motion.

"What is this?" she demands.

I look closer and see she is holding the vial in her hand.

"You tell me," I lower my voice, crossing my arms across my chest.

"I found this in the couch," she growls angrily. "Why was it there?"

"Because you put it there," I challenge her.

"*You* put it there, Roan. *You* were trying to poison me," she says spitefully, anger flashing from her eyes.

She's right, but *that* is not my vial.

"Don't lie to me, Jade, it's beneath you." I step toward her, trying to intimidate her. She doesn't back down.

Leaping to her feet, she stretches as tall as she can.

"I know what you and your father are doing, and it won't work. I'll fight you until my last breath, Roan Diamond. I will not bow down to you or *that man.*"

"I won't let you or your father hurt this country, or *my father*, again, *Jade*. We know it was your father's rebels who set off that explosion that nearly killed my father." I lost my temper.

"My father did no such thing!" she yells at me. "He would never hurt people, even people he opposed. He *never* has!"

"That explosion didn't just make itself happen, Jade!"

"You mean the explosion that no one but *your father* has ever heard of? *That* explosion, Roan? *That* one?" she screams, throwing the vial on the ground.

"Stop lying, Jade. We know everything."

"You know *nothing*! You're a murderer, just like your father. You have no soul! You'll follow in your father's footsteps and destroy this country, just like he is doing now!" she starts to storm away, but I grab her arm and spin her to me.

She claws at me and I release her.

"I am not a murderer and neither is my father," I start but she cuts me off.

"You're trying to *kill* me!" she shouts in my face, making her point. "And you know what? You're going to. Because I'd rather die than let you selfish, horrible people touch my father or my aunt or any of the people of this country. If my death is what it takes to end this insanity, so be it! Here! *Here*!" she shoves her wrists at me as if waiting for me to slice them open. "Kill me, Roan. Do it! Get it over with!"

I push her hands away, and step back.

"No."

"Come on, you coward. Do it!" she shouts again. "Or isn't it part of the plan? It's not time yet, so you can't? Does your father control every last bit of you that you can't even think for yourself? I'm letting you do it—I'm giving you the opportunity and you can't even decide for yourself to take it."

She huffs as she breathes, not getting enough air.

"You're *weak*, Roan," she says sadly, quietly.

"*Go to bed*, Jade," I say through gritted teeth, willing her away before I do something I regret.

"So you can kill me in my sleep? Yeah, *great idea*," she says bitterly.

"*You* were going to poison me, Jade," I point out to her, motioning to the vial on the floor.

"*Drop it*, Roan. Your act doesn't fool me. I know it's yours and I know you're trying to kill me. Stop acting like you're not." She starts to walk away, but turns back. "But I swear, you'd better kill me *soon, or else*."

She made it sound as if the vial wasn't hers. But if it wasn't brought here by her then how did it get here?

And how does she not know about the explosion?

Maybe her father didn't tell her about his plans. My father keeps secrets from me and does things without consulting me. Like dinner the other night.

Dinner.

When someone was in the house.

And then suddenly the vial appeared.

It's not Jade's.

I'm so quickly aware of everything that's happened that I become light headed. Sitting on the couch where Jade was balanced only moments before, I try breathing to calm myself down.

My father pitted me against Jade. He set it up so that we would both find it, blaming the other.

Does that also mean the explosion was fake? How could he have pulled that off? But if no one else but the people directly involved after the explosion know about it, is it possible it was a set up as well?

CHAPTER 26
JADE

ow we know.

It's out in the open. He knows that I know. He didn't deny that he was trying to kill me. Now it just becomes a matter of time.

My ceiling isn't getting more interesting as I stare at it. It's cloudy out, dimming the moon's usual glow in the room.

I know he can't do anything tonight; it would be too obvious. But I can't take the waiting for much longer. I just need this to be over, no matter what that means for me.

We avoid each other the next day, intentionally occupying the common spaces in the house at different times. The following day is the same, the house as silent as the cemetery we had once visited together.

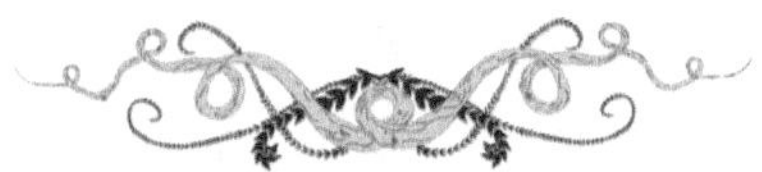

"Jade, get up." Roan knocks on my door late that afternoon.

"What do you want?" I ask through the door.

"We have to go out. People need to see we're all right after the mugging the other day," he replies, his voice slightly muffled through the door.

"You mean the murder attempt?" I scoff.

"Just come out, Jade."

"Fine, one more public appearance won't kill me," I say opening the door. "Or will it?"

"Don't be like that, Jade."

"You know what, I'm going to make you a deal. You're going to tell me when it's going to happen, and I'm going to try not to stop you," I say, shocking even myself.

He looks at me in horror. I brush past him leaving him standing in the doorway.

"Excuse me?" he finally says.

"You heard me. I want to know. Otherwise I'm going to fight you. If you want this to be easy, you could at least do me the courtesy of telling me before you hurt me."

"I doubt I'll know, Jade. I didn't exactly do what I was supposed to do," he finally responds.

"Well figure it out, *Husband.*"

He cringes at the word.

"Was any of it true?" I ask. "Any of that kindness you showed me at the beginning? Or was it all an act?"

"I'm not a bad person, Jade," he tries to convince me.

"I find that hard to believe."

"Jade, I don't *want* to have to hurt you," he insists.

"But you're going to do it anyway. So your words are invalid," I turn toward the door. "It's too bad, because that guy I saw pieces of... *He* could have been a decent guy."

I stomp out the door and down the front steps. He catches up with me and I weave my arm through his and plaster a fake smile on.

"Where are we going?" I ask tightly.

"What do you want to do?" he asks.

"What is this, my last wish? Suddenly I'm dying and I get to do all of the things I've always wanted to do?" My voice rises in mockery.

"Might as well. I can at least give you that." He almost sounded remorseful.

"Fine, we're going to the bakery. I want to see my friends again."

"All right, but don't get any ideas," he warns.

"What ideas, Roan?" I whisper, "Do something stupid and *your* dad turns on *my* dad. No. I've accepted this."

We make small talk whenever we pass by people. I put on a spectacular show.

Inside the bakery, I slide down into my seat and close my eyes as the cool air washes over me. One last time I take in the scents of the bakery, the sounds of the people I love. I know I'll never see them again.

I do my best to ignore Roan, focusing on the people around me. They swarm me as usual, silently begging the man with me to spare my life.

Being as flirtatious as possible, I reach over and take the last half of Roan's scone. I'm not actually hungry, but I want to take something from him. He takes my life; I take his scone. Seems fair.

He allows me to, knowing I need my say. For being so adamant about ending my life, he certainly is giving me a lot of leniency.

It disgusts me as he waves goodbye to the kids in the bakery. I feel sick that one day, this man will be leading them and making decisions for them.

He doesn't try to talk to me on the way home. He lets me drift into my thoughts and memories.

Eventually, he pulls on my arm, breaking the cherished silence.

"Come on," he says.

"Get off me," I hiss, pulling away from him. "What do you want?"

He looks at me, frustration written on his face.

"We're going to the pond," he says.

"Why?" I ask spitefully, not wanting to see the pond that was now polluted with memories of Roan.

"Because we can. Now, come on."

I let him pull me toward my childhood watery playground. We walk along the edge and he lets go of me, allowing me to walk ahead of him. I close my eyes and breath deep, letting my hands trail behind me in the air. I tried memorizing every bit of the scene—me and the water—alive and desperate for more.

I step out onto the dock. It creaks as I move. Swaying in the water, I balance myself, accustomed to the way it shudders against the water. I can tell Roan follows me, but he gives me space. Leaning against the pole, I close my eyes and lean far out over the water. Minutes pass, and I'm far away in my thoughts.

The crashing sound of the water's surface breaking jerks me out of my daydream. The water ripples, and I know someone has fallen in. It's late in the day and no one else is around.

Looking around, I discover Roan is gone.

He must have fallen. He doesn't know enough not to step on the board over there on the end.

When he doesn't surface, I start to worry. As kids, we were always told not to jump off the dock. There are nets and dangerous things under the dock. Only adults are supposed to go near it.

Bubbles make their way to the surface.

I know I can't leave him there to drown, as beneficial to me as it might be. Kicking my shoes off, I dive wide. The abnormally cool water takes my breath away. Enough light filters through the water that I can see Roan just in front of the dock.

Entangled in netting and old fishing cage rigging, he's struggling to free himself. I swim toward him. When I reach him, I pull myself down his leg and into the ropes and metal entrapping him. Glancing up, I can see the panic in his eyes. I pull on the ropes, motioning for him to stop struggling. As I fight to free him, I can see him slipping away.

After what seems like an eternity, I release him. When he can't make it to the surface on his own, I wrap his arms around my waist and kick. I surface first and the air is glorious. A moment later Roan comes to the top, gulping in air. I tug him over to the shore, leaving him at the water's edge as I climb out.

I did my job; I saved the man. But that didn't mean I had to stay.

He struggles after me, but I keep up my brisk pace, walking away with my arms wrapped around me. I hear him coughing and choking behind me. I think about going back to help. A few more steps and I realize I can't just walk away.

Turning back, I wedge myself under his arm and help support him on the walk back home. He rests heavily on me as we walk. We're nearly dry by the time we make it home. I leave him at the door.

"Jade," his voice is still weak from coughing so much. "Why?"

I raise an angry eyebrow at him, shaking my head once to let him know I don't know what he wants.

"Why?" he repeats.

He wants to know why I jumped in after him.

"The rest of us are smart enough not to go out on the end," I reply, turning my back again.

Before he can continue, I make my way to my room, closing the door between us, leaving only one thought echoing in my mind.

I'm not like him. I could never be the cause of someone's death.

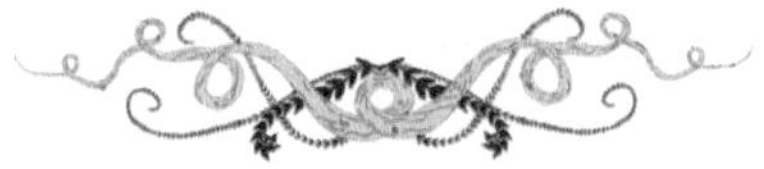

My decision is confirmed the next day when Mr. Eroh looks at me proudly. It's the same look my father would have given me.

"Life is important, Jade. *All* life," my father once said.

"You're a brave girl, Jade. Your father raised you right," Mr. Eroh tells me.

"Thank you, Mr. Eroh. Not just for saying that, but for everything. You've taught me so much."

"No. None of that, girl," he stops me. "I'll not have you saying your goodbyes yet."

I sigh deeply. He always *could* read me.

"I don't have much time," I say so softly that no one but my boss could hear, even if there were other people in the shop.

"We'll see about that," he says.

"Please don't interfere anymore," I plead with him. "You know this has to happen. And I need you to promise me something. Once it's over, don't let people use it as an excuse. I realize that people know, and I don't want them to rebel again because of it. My life will have been for nothing."

"Your life will never have been for nothing, Jade. Look at all you've done. What you mean to say is that your *death* will be for nothing, and *that,* Jade, I can assure, *is* the case. Because no matter what happens to you, ending your life will have accomplished absolutely nothing. Not even for the Commander."

Those words makes me rethink things. He has a point.

"It doesn't change anything."

"Maybe not, girl, but your life will always have meaning. Live it the *right* way through till the end," he says.

I need to stand tall and make the right choices, all the way up until my death. Like saving Roan, despite knowing he's going to hurt me.

"You're right. I will," I agree.

"You have more integrity than this entire country put together, Jade," he smiles sadly at me. "You would have done remarkable things had you been given time, more than you've already done."

I sit next to him and put my head on his shoulder, tears burning my eyes. If I couldn't have my father, Mr. Eroh was a good alternative.

"You know I can't come back," I say softly. "He's even taken this away from me."

He pats my hand and we sit together for the rest of the day.

"I told Mr. Eroh this will be my last week working at the shop," I confess after work.

"Why?" Roan looks confused.

"Because your father said so," I say glumly.

"He told you to quit?" he asks, realizing the answer before I have to speak. "Oh."

"Did you find out when it's going to happen yet?" I inquire.

He looks up at me suddenly.

"No. Do you honestly want to know, Jade?"

"Yes, I do. I told you, with every fiber of my being, I'm going to fight to stay alive. If you want me dead, I need to know so I can force those instincts down. It's for your benefit, really."

"I'll see if I can find out," he says with resignation. "Why did you help me yesterday, Jade?"

"Because no one should have to drown, Roan. It's an awful way to go," I pause. "Hey, do me a favor and don't drown me, okay?"

He almost smiles. "Okay."

"I'm going out," I announce. "Don't follow me."

He nods and I retrieve my shoes.

I walk to the art house. Breaking in is easy; I watched Roan do it last time. I find the place empty, as I was sure I would.

My original intent was to find paper to write a note on. But once inside, I find myself drawn to the show

Your Jade.

I hadn't realized until that moment that I myself had forgiven Roan. He was only trying to protect his father, just as I was protecting mine. I would die for my father; Roan would kill for his.

Just as I was tucking the folded paper into the waistband of my pants under my shirt, I noticed the painting of me hanging on the wall. Walking over, I take my pen to the paper. Under Roan's name I write, "I forgive you." Maybe one day he'll see it and he'll know I understand why he had to do it.

I go the candle shop. Catching the woman's eye, I watch her as she watches me move around the room. I drop the papers behind one of the stands, making sure she sees me.

I purchase a small candle and thank her.

"My father would love these," I hold it up to her.

"I'm sure he would, dear," she nods, promising me to get the message to him.

CHAPTER 27
ROAN

 skip work the next day, instead opting to go to the art house. I've given Jade all the space I can give her, but now I need to think, and art will help with that.

I spend the morning creating, though what it is, I can't tell. Ink and paint on a page. Frustration poured out onto paper.

When my stomach rumbles, I realize it must be past lunchtime. But I can't bring myself to leave yet.

I wander through the show room, eyes raking over works I've seen a hundred times before. I fixate on one for what seems to be an eternity, though I gain no insight on it. Finally, I shake my head and move on.

Finding myself in front of my own works, I look for some deeper truth in them. I find nothing... until I see her.

"I forgive you," I read aloud.

She was here.

That's when I notice her drawing is gone.

She forgives me.

She understands.

I can't.

I can't kill her. She's innocent in this.

Everything about this is wrong.

She saved me when she could have let me die. She'd rather give her life up than have the people she loves suffer. She knew nothing about the bombing or the poison. She's been kind to every person she's met, including my parents when she *knew* my father's plan.

I have to try to end this.

I run all the way to the shop. Flinging the door open, I see that I've clearly surprised Jade and Mr. Eroh.

"I have to talk to you," I say. When she doesn't move, I run through the store and around the counter.

Mr. Eroh looks as though he's ready to take me on when I reach for her. She holds up a hand, waving him off. Tears start to flow down her face as I pull her away, but I can't stop, I need to get her out of there.

"Goodbye," she chokes out, and I know she must believe I'm leading her to her death.

She's sobbing by the time I get her out of town. She stumbles behind me as I run, but I can't slow down, and she doesn't try to pull away.

Finally outside of the town, I mean to stop, but I don't. I keep pulling her all the way to our house. She can't breathe by the time we arrive. Pulling her inside, I slam the door behind me.

"Jade," I say as I pin her against the wall as I feel her survival instincts kick in under my hands.

She flinches so hard I nearly pull back.

"Jade, look at me. I'm not going to hurt you." I fight for her attention through her waterfall of tears. "Look at me, Jade. I'm not going to hurt you."

I plead with her again and again until she looks up. When her eyes connect with mine, I feel like the worst person alive.

"I won't hurt you...ever. I promise." I'm breathing heavily as I try to convince her of my sincerity, struggling to hold her together. "I'm so sorry, Jade, I won't hurt you. I won't let them hurt you."

"You're a liar, Roan," she finally says, a knife to my heart. "And I don't believe you." She ducks under my arm, but I catch her.

"I get it now, Jade. I do. You don't deserve this, and I don't care what my father says, I won't let him kill you over this."

"Leave me alone, Roan," she insists.

"No. I *won't*. I'm going to protect you."

"Why would you do that?"

I lean closely to her, looking deep into her eyes, hoping to convince her. "Jade," I whisper, brushing away her tears carefully.

My hands have somehow found their way into her hair and I'm brushing it over and over again. My arms are bracing me against the wall, preventing her escape and holding me inches away from her. I want to lean in and tell her.

When she hesitates and turns away from my question of a kiss, I pull back a little.

"I won't let him hurt you, Jade. You said you forgave me." Her head whips back to me so fast we almost collide. "Now *trust* me."

"You went to the art house," she whispers.

"This morning," I confirm.

"You weren't supposed to see that until after."

"Why after? Why not tell me now? You think it wouldn't have changed my mind?" I ask.

"Let me go, Roan," she says after hesitating.

"I'm on your side now, Jade," I say, releasing her from the wall. "You were right… about everything. My father planted that poison in the couch. Neither of us knew. I think you're even right about the explosion. I think he's been manipulating me this whole time. I see it now, Jade, and I'm so sorry… about everything,"

She can tell how defeated I am. I see her shoulders drop as she understands how fallen I feel.

"I'm sorry," I say again. I slide down the wall behind us and sit on the ground.

Jade walks over to me cautiously. I *hate* that I've made her into this scared creature I see before me.

She kneels down beside me and ducks her head to be on eye level with me. She stares for what seems like the longest time. Jade nods only once and utters the word, "Okay."

"Okay?"

"I believe you," she says, absolving me of every act I've ever committed against her.

CHAPTER 28
JADE

I sit down next to him and wait for him to calm down. I believe him when he says he's going to try to protect me. I don't believe he can actually do it, but, miraculously, he saved his own soul in time.

Maybe one day he *can* be a great leader.

"I believe you, Roan, just breathe."

When he regains his composure, he turns to me.

"I'm sorry, Jade."

"I know, you said that."

"I want you to understand how much I truly regret everything."

"I get it, Roan, it's fine."

He puts his head on my shoulder, and I give in, resting mine on his. "So now what?"

"I don't know," he says honestly. "Now we figure it out."

"Okay. We figure it out."

"First," he says, formulating a plan, "we need to start treating each other like allies."

"Like friends?" I laugh. "Didn't we try that once?"

"Yes," he mocks back. "I believe it ended in us trying to kill each other."

I can't help it. I laugh at the absurdity of it all.

"We're really messed up, you know that?" I ask.

"Yeah, we really are."

"Okay," I say, spinning toward him. "If we're going to do this, we have to be completely honest with each other."

I think about testing him, but I look into his eyes. I have to believe him. And even if he fooled me, I need to believe the best in people no matter what. I need to live with integrity and honesty until the day I die.

"I promise. Honesty," he says, holding his hand up as if making a pledge to me.

"I promise, too," I say solemnly, mimicking his pose. My grin gives me away.

"Okay, what do we know so far?" he asks.

"I'm supposed to die," I say.

"Really? That's the first thing you're gonna go with?" he mocks again.

"Well, what do you want me to say?" I ask.

"Let's start at the beginning," he says. "Now don't get mad, I really need to know this. I need to know your side of the rebellion. The first one... when we were kids."

He set me on edge a little, but I can see why he would need to know.

"When we were kids, there was a rebellion," I start, "My father led that rebellion. It wasn't to gain power or control anyone. It was to free the people. My father wanted a democracy, not a dictatorship like we have now.

"I know," I say holding my hand up, "the politicians get to vote, but we both know those votes don't actually count. They are for show. My father wanted a government where the people get a say in the way things are run, the way it used to be before the war.

"My father never killed or hurt anyone," I assured him.

"Why did he let you come here, Jade?" he asks me.

"He didn't have a choice. He tried for years to get your father to take it out on him. But Dad's a public figure. If anything happened to him...*ever*...the people would know. I, however, have always been fair game. I think forcing my father to live with that knowledge all these years was part of the torture." I see him flinch at the last word.

"Did you ever have a normal life?" he asks me, reaching for my hand.

"No." I smile. "It was pretty much keep-Jade-away-from-Roan, try-not-to-let-her-get-killed."

"So I was always the enemy, huh?" he asks scornfully.

"Since the day it was proclaimed," I confirm. "I was always the target?"

"Since *before* it was proclaimed, I'm sure," he says, waving his hand dramatically.

"Okay, no targets, no enemies. So where do we go from here? How do we find peace in all of this?"

"We have to stop the plan," he says. "Do you think your dad is planning anything?"

"No, he's honoring my wishes. I think the others are as well."

"Others?"

"Roan, that entire *town* has a pretty good idea of what is going on," I give him a be-realistic look.

"Point taken," he holds up his hands in mock surrender. "They kind of love you over there."

"I like to think so," I say quietly.

"No, Jade, I've seen it. They adore you and nothing about that was faked for my benefit. I thought Mr. Eroh was going to kill me today…"

"Mr. Eroh!" I yelp, realizing the state I left him in. "Roan, we have to go back, tell him I'm okay. We have to tell him before he tells my dad."

We're on our feet instantly.

"Wait!" he says, stopping me before I can run. "We're a

wreck, we can't go out like this. Go splash some water on your face."

I rush to my bathroom and he heads for the kitchen. Having put ourselves back together, we run for the door.

"Slow," he says taking my hand. "We can't let on that we're in a hurry."

I nod and wind my arm through his. We walk as quickly as we can through the streets. A lifetime later, we reach my town. Together, we start for the shop.

"We can't get to your dad, can we?" he asks, knowing there are eyes everywhere.

"Doubtful."

Just then I catch a flash out of the corner of my eye. It ducks into the bakery.

I have no idea how Sophie keeps finding me at the exact right moments, but she does.

"Let's get a scone," I suggest.

He looks at me confused, but I tug on his arm and he follows.

We take a seat and food is set before us without even ordering. I've always loved that this place knew me well enough that I never needed to order.

"Roan, go get me some sugar for my tea," I say quietly, nodding to a bar of drink accessories on the side of the room. "Three packets please."

He questions me again, but does as I ask. I watch him

count out the packets. He unknowingly sent a sign to my aunt: Roan is one of us.

I empty one into my drink, even though I rarely use sugar. Setting the other two against the side of my saucer, leaning at an angle, I finish the message: I trust him.

Sophie looks affronted, but barely looks at me. She chats animatedly with one of her friends.

"Should we get you back to the shop, Jade?" Roan asks after a few minutes, wondering why I'm suddenly so relaxed.

"Sure, let's make our way over."

Walking to the shop, I take his hand in mine, trying to communicate that I got my message across. He squeezes back, and I'm afraid my message failed him.

Mr. Eroh looks so relieved when I walk back in, I fear he'll have a stroke. He still looks ready to destroy Roan, so I step between them.

"You remember Roan, don't you?" I shake my head up and down until he catches on.

"He's changed?" his whisper is harsh and accusing.

"I'm looking out for Jade," Roan confirms.

"Why?" Distrust.

"Because she doesn't deserve this."

"And you would turn on your father?" he questions. "Just like that?"

"No, not just like that," he says honestly, "It's taken me

a very long time to come to this conclusion. But I made it, and I won't let him hurt her."

Mr. Eroh watches him intently for a long time. "There might be hope for you yet, boy."

I shuffle around the room for a minute, as if I had forgotten to do something earlier. I call to Roan and have him help me move a big box; that would be our cover story if anyone asked why we came back.

"We can't stay," I interrupt the light conversation, knowing someone is watching.

"Go," Mr. Eroh shoos us toward the door. He adds quietly to me, "As long as you're safe."

"I trust him," I whisper back.

"We have to act normal," Roan says, walking back. "My parents want us to come over in a few days. Are you going to be okay with that?"

"I trust you." I have no other choice.

"Good. I'll do my best to keep you away from them. I have an idea, actually. If we take our swimsuits, we can slip away to the pool. At this point, he still doesn't know I figured all this out, or that *I* know that *you* know. He thinks I'm still trying to win you over, so we can play up that angle."

"That's a smart idea."

I hate the idea of going back to that house, but at least he's trying to help me escape.

"We need to be public again. We've been hiding out the last few days. People need to see us together, more specifically, see *you*."

"In that case, what do we do?"

"You've been acting like a happy wife and I've been acting like a happy husband. We were just in *your* side of town, so now we need to be out in public on *our* side of town. So tomorrow, you're coming to work with me."

I do a double take. I'd never been to Roan's work before, and I'm fairly certain that I don't ever *want* to go.

"I think it's better if we stay close," he explains. "Besides, I told you before I was going to show you where I work. And if they're supposed to think you might be leaving the shop, you'll need something else to do, so it's only logical we'd get you a job with us."

"Will your father be there?" I ask, knowing they share an office.

"Probably," he answers slowly. "Now that everything is out in the open with you, he's got to make sure he is really on top of things. But I won't leave you, Jade. You'll be with me all day."

"If we have to," I finally say. I'd much rather be in the

safety of Mr. Eroh's shop, but I need Roan to stay on my side, which means going along with his plan.

"Good. Now, as for tonight, let's take a walk around town. Just once around the block, but it will be enough to be seen by some people."

We wave to some of our neighbors as we walk down the street. They seem a bit nosy, but that's probably because Roan and I have stayed close to our house and stuck to the main roads in town. Everyone waves back, commenting on how nice it is to have us in the neighborhood.

"Hey," I say as we turn the corner. "Do you want some fresh fruit or vegetables? I saw someone set up a stand this morning on my way to work."

"That might be nice," Roan says, perking up a bit.

It takes a few extra streets we hadn't planned on walking, but we manage to catch the vendor before they tear down for the day. Roan and I walk away with a basket full of fresh strawberries, blueberries, green beans, carrots, and raspberries. I tease him all the way home about his addiction to my raspberry pie.

Inside, we turn on the lights and start to put our food away. I find it amazing how quickly we switched from being enemies to being friends once we found we had a common foe. It was nice seeing the real Roan after all this time.

"Jade, look at this," Roan says.

I walk over to discover a tiny green caterpillar crawling on one of the berries.

"You called me over to show me a worm?" I ask skeptically.

"Yes. We should name him. He can be our first pet."

I laugh at his suggestion.

"Get rid of it, Roan."

He frowns at me and lets it crawl on his finger. I bat at his hand when he holds it out to me.

"I'm serious, Roan. Get rid of it."

"Fine, I'll take the little guy outside," he gives up.

I watch him walk away to set the creature free. Much like he did with me.

CHAPTER 29
JADE

I dress up a bit to go to work with Roan. I need to look like I could fit into their office, even though I've never been one for business attire.

"That looks perfect," Roan says when I step out. "Good choice."

"You ready?" I ask.

"Almost. I figured we could take lunch with us today; that way we don't have to leave the office unless we really need to."

"I like that idea," I mumble, following him to the kitchen.

It only takes us a minute to put together some sand-wiches. Roan and I have become so accustomed to working with each other over the last few weeks that we fly through the motions of kitchen work. It's almost as if we've been working together our whole lives. Never once do we get in each other's way. We know exactly what the other needs before they need it and have it ready to hand off to them. We move at the same time, working in fluid motions. It's almost as if we choreographed a dance, and we've been keeping time these last few weeks despite our spats.

"Now we can go," Roan announces as he picks up the container carrying our lunch.

I tap my hair comb back into place. I no longer need it for Roan; I'm not scared of him anymore. But I keep it just for the sake of security against the Commander should the need for it arise. I wonder how Roan would react if I used it against his father.

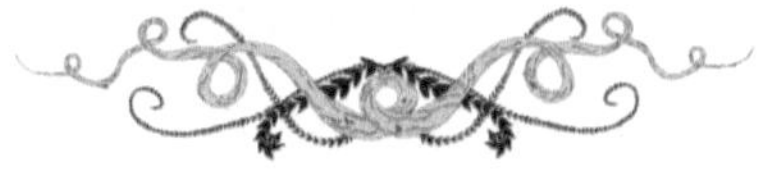

The Command Building isn't nearly as big as the building they use for events, but it is impressive nonetheless. The floors are made of the most marvelous marble. Paintings of the past Commanders hang on the wall, much larger than life.

Aloysius Diamond, the first Commander, poses proudly in his picture. Next to it hangs an image of his family, including a small, equally as evil, Robert Diamond as a child. Robert's picture is next. He's unable to hide his sneer even in this. Next to that, hangs a picture of the Commander, Alice, and Roan as a child.

Roan looks small; I'm guessing the picture was created before the rebellion. He sits on his mother's lap. It's strange to see Alice smiling. I've never seen anything but disgust from her.

"Jade?" Roan asks, and I realize I've stopped to stare at the picture.

"You were little," I say softly, slipping my arm around his back in case anyone was watching.

"Roan?" a female voice interrupts us.

Turning, I find a short, blond-haired woman staring at us.

"Daniella, you've met my wife, Jade. She'll be spending the day with me today," Roan addresses her. "Jade, you remember Daniella from the Command party."

"Of course, so nice to see you again, Daniella. How have you been?" I was grateful Roan placed her for me.

She looks at me skeptically, but reaches out to take my extended hand. "I'm fine, thank you, Jade. It's nice to have you with us today. If you need anything, please let me know."

"I will, thank you."

"Come on, honey, we should go to my office," Roan says, tugging on me. "You'll really like it, it's a great space."

His voice trails off as we leave the secretary behind.

He steps up to a door and pulls out a set of keys. The door swings open and reveals a fairly large room, bigger than what I'd expect an office to be. The walls are dark brown and bare except for the windows on two of the walls. A large couch sits off to the side, facing a small coffee table and two chairs.

Roan takes a seat at his desk. I notice the stacks of neatly organized papers taking over practically every inch of the space. There are bookcases lining the wall without windows and I wander over to look at the books and binders resting on the shelves. I wonder if any of these books could have possibly been selected by Roan, or if it was all his father's choosing.

"You can read them, if you like." Roan's voice cuts through my thoughts. "But the one you brought might be more interesting."

"Can I help with anything?" I ask, looking back at him. "Organize papers or anything?"

"Yeah, because they'd be thrilled *you* touched the paperwork here," he smirks.

"Ha. Ha," I reply curtly, swaying my way back to the couch before dropping into its slightly uncomfortable cushions. "How do you rest on this thing?"

"When you're exhausted, it's comfier than you think," he replies, not bothering to look up from his paperwork.

"Sleep on it a lot then?" I question.

"More than you'd think," he mutters.

I couldn't imagine actually resting on that couch, but then, I also couldn't imagine being able to handle this less-than-personalized office either.

I settle in and start my book, finishing long before lunch. Not wanting to disturb Roan, I sit quietly on the couch, staring off at nothing. For a while, I watch him work, hunched over his desk, writing and making notes, reading and sighing.

The knock on the door startles us both. Clutching my hand to my chest, I will my heart to slow down.

"Sir, your father would like to see you," Daniella says as she opens the door.

"Can it wait, Daniella? I'm in the middle of…"

"No, I don't think it can." She gives him a look, trying to indicate that the Commander knows I'm in the building by tipping her head slightly toward me.

"All right, I'll be right there," he says, dismissing her.

"What do you want to do?" he asks me, coming to kneel by the couch. "Do you want to come with me or do you want to stay here?"

I weigh my options. On one hand, I shouldn't leave Roan's side. On the other hand, the last thing I want to do is see the Commander. I might even consider whipping out my poisoned hair comb and ending it all now.

"You go," I finally answer. He gives me a hard-to-read expression and stands to go. I nod when he looks back, assuring him I want to stay.

Daniella appears in the doorway, clearly meant to watch me. Heaven forbid I should be in the office alone. Who knows what kind of damage I could do? Then again, Daniella isn't supposed to know about the Commander's plan, so why is it that she dislikes me so much?

"I haven't been able to help Roan very much today," I say in a sad voice. "Is there anything I can help *you* with? I've very good with organizing, or even delivering coffee."

She sighs at me, recognizing that I'm trying to be helpful, but still not wanting my assistance.

"No, Jade, thank you though. You just enjoy some time off."

"Well, if you change your mind, please let me know. I finished my book earlier than I thought and I've just been sitting here this last little bit." Then I add, "I'm afraid this couch isn't the most comfortable thing in the world."

She shakes her head and gives me a half smile. "The Commander keeps telling Roan to get a new one, but he hasn't taken the time to pick one out yet. Maybe you could convince him to update his office a little more."

I smile back at her. "Well, I can certainly try. It does seem a little devoid of any personal touches."

"Roan's a very straightforward man. He's not one to make a lot of fuss. This is the office that was given to him, and he hasn't changed a thing. Most of this is from when room. On the wall sits my drawing of the pond I once loved so much.

Taking it down, I fold it as small as I can. I scribble a note to my father on the blank sheet.

Dear Dad,

I'm so sorry I didn't get to say goodbye. Please know I love you and I only want what is best for you. Look after Aunt Sophie; they know.

You should know that Roan regrets what he must do. I can tell he doesn't want to hurt me, but he feels he must protect his father. I believe the Commander has lied to him the way he has lied to the country. I don't think Roan has all the facts. I know he's going to regret this for the rest of his life. Try to forgive him.

I'm including a picture I drew for you to remember me by. Don't forget all of our wonderful times at that pond; it's one of my favorite childhood places.

Tell everyone I loved them very much and that I thought of them until my last breath. Don't let them lose sight of why I did this when they hear about me. Remind them that my life is to be the last. Hold them accountable and don't let them use me to do something they shouldn't.

I love you, I love you, I love you.
Goodbye, Daddy.
Love,

it was the Commander's office. He, of course, took his personal things with him to his new office."

"And Roan just hasn't taken the time to do anything with the space yet," I finish her thought. "That makes sense. Daniella, you know how this office works better than anyone. If you could spruce this room up a bit, what would you do?"

This seems to win her over and she launches into a litany of changes and updates she would make for Roan. Some of them seem perfect for the man I am getting to know, while others seem to lean more toward the Commander's tastes, but I catalogue each suggestion in my mind as she drones on. If I'm around long enough, I plan on implementing a few of her ideas. *That* should at least win me some points with her.

Roan looks frustrated as he walks back into the office. Daniella cuts off her sentence immediately when she notices him and back out of the room. I call a thank you out after her as she closes the door.

"What happened?" I ask, unwinding myself and climbing off the couch.

"He's angry, but I convinced him you were thinking about getting a job here at my request after you told me you were leaving the shop. He bought it, for now at least. I also told him I found more poison in the house and think it's you."

"Bet he is overjoyed," I mock.

"The good news is, he made it seem like it's going to be a bit before he goes after you again. He wants us at a few more events over the next few weeks."

"Great, more events," I say with a fake smile.

"Great, more *life*," Roan chastises me.

I roll my eyes and go back to the couch. "Are we really going to sit here all day?"

"No, that's the other thing. We're going out this afternoon. I'm really sorry."

He doesn't have to say why. I already know it's because his father will be with us.

"Lunch first though," he says, motioning for me to scoot over to the table.

He retrieves our food and sets it on the coffee table. I start to reach for my sandwich, but deciding I can't bear another moment on that couch, I slide to the floor, trapping myself between the table and the couch. Roan gives me a curious look, but then pulls the table toward him to give me a little more room.

Pushing the chair he is sitting in back, he slides to the floor and joins me. I smile as he does, approving of his choice to join me.

"So," Roan says, "Tell me what your dad is really like."

I look up at him, horrified he's asking at his father's request and that this is all a set up. But the honesty in his eyes tells me otherwise. He really *is* making an effort to be friends with me.

"He's really kind. He always looks out for people. He takes care of them the best he can, even when it means taking on some of the problems or suffering himself."

"Sounds familiar," he comments.

"Even when I was little, Dad would always teach me about helping people. *We* always came second. For a long time, I felt like I was inconvenienced all the time, just so Dad could help someone else. When I grew up and realized what was happening, I saw just how much of a price we really paid for Dad being so helpful to others. Now that we're here, I understand, but it wasn't always easy to know that as a kid."

"There's a lot we have to go through based on our parent's actions," he says. "You've told me a bit about your mom. I know you were little when she died. What happened?"

Taking a deep breath, I steady myself.

"Another time. It's hard to get through that one without crying a bit and if we have to go out, I probably shouldn't be all teary-eyed."

"All right, another time."

"Tell me about *your* mom. I know she loves you and hates me, but I don't think I've seen anything but her distaste for me. What's she really like?" I ask.

"She's...unique," he starts, trying to find an accurate way to describe her. "She loves me. She doted on me growing up. I was her only kid, after all. She hated that my father committed you and me to each other. She was terrified of your father and what he might do to retaliate. She always hated the training my father put me through…"

"Training?" I interrupt.

"Oh," he frowns and sets down his food. "Well…"

He's clearly upset over the turn the conversation has taken. He takes a deep breath and starts again.

"You were trained to survive, right?" he asks and I nod. "I was trained to make sure you didn't."

"I suppose I should have seen that one coming," I grumble. It bothers me the lengths the Commander has gone to in order see me die. "So you learned to kill."

"Mostly it was about manipulation and getting you to trust me. If I could get you to trust me, the killing part was supposed to be easy. Although, I had a hard-enough time betraying your trust… I don't think I could have brought myself to actually go through with killing you. That's why Dad took it into his own hands with the mugger."

"Well, at least we both know we're manipulative."

He laughs before growing serious again. "Jade, was any of it real? In the beginning…about wanting to be friends or even wanting to take it slow?"

Now it's my turn to set down my food. Ever since becoming friends, we seem to be having a lot of these deep conversations.

"In the beginning, I was convinced you were going to kill me. I barely slept, I tried never to turn my back on you. I didn't trust you at all. So those first few days—that was all me trying to survive.

"After that, I thought maybe, *maybe,* you weren't a part of the plan. And if you weren't a part of it, maybe I could get you on my side. So, yes, I was trying to manipulate you into befriending me for real, and part of that was to actually become friends with you."

"So it wasn't real."

"It was survival, Roan. And you did the same thing."

"But we've started over now."

"Yes, we have," I agree.

"You trust me now, don't you, Jade? You trust I'm going to try to save you."

I notice he said "try."

"I trust you Roan, or I wouldn't be here."

I pick up the remnants of my sandwich and finish it off.

"We're friends, Roan," I reassure him.

"It's almost time to go; we should finish up," he says, glancing at the clock on the wall.

"Where are we going, exactly?" I ask.

"I don't know yet. Dad has some meetings and I have to go along. We usually go to two or three different places while we're out. It will probably take the rest of the afternoon. We might actually be able to go home from the last place, so we'll take everything with us."

"That sounds like a good idea," I say, packing up our things.

"Time to go," the Commander's voice calls from the other side of the closed door. He pounds on it to get our attention.

"He's not used to not being able to walk in whenever he likes." Roan frowns.

"Yes, I sensed a lack of privacy—and personal space—with him," I joke.

"Oh, you noticed that too?" he says playfully.

"Come on, let's go get this over with."

I am largely ignored until we reach a public area. I walk several feet behind the Commander and his son as they discuss their first appointment. The swarm of people surrounding them keeps me far enough away that I can't hear what they are saying. Roan frequently turns to make sure I'm okay.

Once he's had enough, he deliberately slows his pace,

reaching his hand back for me. Clearly, he is taking his new role as protector very seriously.

Reaching forward, I wrap my fingers in his, but I keep a safe distance away from them as they continue to talk.

"You're Jade, right?" a voice says next to me.

I turn to find a man a few years older than Roan and I walking next to me.

"I'm Lucas. We haven't officially met yet." He holds his hand out to me. I reach out with my free hand in a strange effort to connect.

"Nice to meet you, Lucas," I reply.

"I heard you're thinking about getting a job at your husband's office," he says casually, though I suspect his real motive is to keep me from listening in to the Commander's conversation. In the background, I can hear him lecturing Roan about something.

"Yes, my old job is so far from home; it makes more sense to work around here, and Roan thought it would be nice for me to work in the office. I've always been good at organizing, so I think it might work out nicely."

"So you want to be a secretary, then?" He scoffs.

"Is there something wrong with that?" I say, suddenly offended that this man is judging me.

"You don't look like the type to sit behind a desk all day and be happy with pushing around paperwork."

"Neither do you," I retort, knowing that if he's working under the Commander, it involves paperwork.

"Touché." He holds up his hands in surrender. "That's not all we do though, you know. I'm sure your husband has told you of all the other things we politicians manage to fit into our day."

"Mmm…social engagements?" I ask snarkily.

"Your father was a politician, wasn't he?" he says a bit coolly.

"Still is," I say shortly.

"Of course, I know who your father is, Jade. I spoke with him just last week. I just meant that, growing up, he was a politician, so you should know what kind of things we do."

"I'm very aware of what a demanding job it is," I say, wanting to get away from the infuriating man. "Aren't you a little *young* to be a politician?"

"Looks like we're here. Maybe we can chat later." He winks at me and splits off.

I stop short, pulling Roan to a stop. When he looks back at me, I quickly shake my head and motion for him to go on. "Sorry."

As we walk up to the school Roan once showed me, I see a line of small children standing outside. They look curiously at the group as we approach.

"Boys and girls, what do we say?" a woman, who I assume is their teacher, asks.

"Welcome, Commander Diamond. We are honored to have you today," they carefully repeat the lines they have obviously been practicing.

"Very good," she nods to them. "Commander Diamond, politicians, we are so grateful to have you visit us today. Please, have a seat."

There is an arrangement of chairs sitting on the lawn and several of the men take seats. Lucas offers me a seat, somehow finding his way next to me again.

The Commander is ushered toward the group of children as they find seats in the grass. He stretches out in a chair and looks down at the young kids.

I decline the chair, wishing instead to stand at the back of the group. Lucas sits in the chair he had pulled over for me, which was still positioned next to me.

We're far enough away from the class that we can barely hear what the children are asking the Commander. After a few minutes, he straightens in the chair, gaze sweeping around his entourage. He waves Roan over, and his son reluctantly leaves my side. Standing with arms crossed, I watch as he takes a seat next to his father.

Roan sits politely as the children remained focused on his father. The Commander is clearly enjoying showing off his son.

"You must be so proud." Lucas smirks beside me.

"I'm sure you realize that *he's* up there, and *you're* back here," I point out.

"You don't like me," he grins next to me.

"Well you're certainly not making it easy," I say.

Switching to baby talk, I add, "And anyway, aren't you about their age? Do you want to go sit with the kids?"

I'm not sure where this hostility is coming from.

"You think I'm too young for this job? Well just remember this, Jade: I'm older than that husband of yours, and he's preparing to lead the country. You and I aren't that different, Jade. I'm surprised you haven't realized that."

What is he getting at?

"Somehow I doubt that."

I turn from him and focus instead on Roan. The children have started to engage with him and he's animatedly waving his arms around, answering questions. I smile; it's nice to see how he would have been if the Commander hadn't forced him into his plan.

I hear a gasp from the group. A few of the kids look horrified. One little girl is almost in tears. Then Roan stands up and waves to me. For a moment, I'm frozen, realizing I'm being called into the spotlight.

"Look who's in the spotlight *now*. Ready to play politician's wife, Princess?" Lucas whispers next to me.

I throw my shoulders back and step forward toward the crowd. Someone scurries to get me a chair, but I wave them off. Kneeling in the grass next to Roan, I get down on the children's level.

"Hello. I'm Jade," I say softly. "It's so nice to meet all of you. I was over there watching, and you all look like a very well-behaved class. It's so nice of you to be so kind to my husband. He's a really good guy, isn't he?"

They all nod and say yes.

The Commander tries to break in, but I talk over him when I see a little girl's hand shoot up. I call on her to ask her question.

"You're really married?" Her voice is so tiny it makes me grin.

"Yes. I'm really married."

"Why did you marry him?" another little girl calls out.

"I actually picked Jade out as my son's wife a long, long time ago," the Commander commandeers the conversation.

"Why?" a little boy asks.

The Commander seems puzzled at first, not having expected this line of questioning.

"Because Jade was a lovely girl. She was raised to be my wife, just as I was raised to be her husband," Roan interrupts. "Do you know what my wife likes to do? She likes to read. Do any of you like to read?"

We discuss books for a few minutes before the Commander takes back over. At the end, the class sings the praises of the Commander...literally. They *literally* sing about him. He beams as they wave goodbye.

Placing his hand on my back, the Commander leads me away. Roan rushes to keep up, standing by my side. The Commander ushers me away, proclaiming me as belonging to his family for all to see. Gritting my teeth, I try not to tense up. I struggle to find a way to get away from him, but can't without being too obvious.

Roan wraps his arm around my waist and pulls himself in to my hip. His father's hand still rests on my back. With each step, I can feel his muscles tensing around me. Every step reveals more of his hatred for me, but we're in public, so he can't say anything to me.

Once we're out of sight of the school, Roan pushes his way between his father and me. He starts a conversation, asking him where we're going next.

Lucas sidles up next to me, hovering just far enough behind me that I block him from Roan's peripheral vision.

"Well that was fun," he says, smiling.

"Something like that," I reply.

"How does it feel to be paraded around as the Commander's daughter-in-law?"

"Much like the rest of my life since I got married."

"Seems you're coping well," he says quietly.

"I didn't realize this was something to *cope* with," I say, hoping he wasn't sent to test me.

"I think your father might see that differently," he replies and then slips away.

I don't know what to make of that man, but for security's sake, I'm going to go with *not* liking him.

The second stop is much duller. We tour the site of a

project the Commander will be working on. He's claiming it is for community advancement, though I sincerely doubt it will help anyone but him and his official people. Roan takes special interest in the area. I can tell he has his own ideas for the space, though he'd never question his father's use of the land.

Our third stop is a bit out of the way. We walk to the town's edge and cross over into my town. Worry washes over me and I know this can't be good. The Commander keeps looking over his shoulder to check on me.

"Hey, Roan, how's it going?" a voice asks. *Lucas.* "We haven't had a second to catch up today."

"Hey, Lucas," Roan turns to greet him with a smile. "It's been a busy day. How's it going?"

"Pretty good. I met your lovely wife earlier," he nods to me.

"Jade, Lucas and I have been friends for ages. I'm actually surprised this is the first time you've met him."

He turns back to Lucas. "We'll have to have you over for dinner sometime."

"That would be lovely. It would be great to get to know your wife some more. I'm free tomorrow, if that works for you."

I'm shocked at how easily he invited himself over.

"Yeah, that would be great, right, Jade?" Roan asks me.

"Uh…sure. Tomorrow is fine," I stammer.

"Great, I'll come over after work." Lucas grins like he won something.

"Here we are," the Commander says gleefully.

I look up to find myself standing in front of the library. *My* library.

"Roan?" I whisper, but he seems just as uneasy as I am.

"Well, come on then." The Commander grins, unable to hide his delight.

He makes his way to the front steps of the building. Turning in front of the door, he addresses his crowd.

"This, gentlemen," he focuses on me, "is the site of our new office building for this part of the country. Work begins next week. We'll be tearing down the inside and putting up new walls to form offices for all of our politicians who live over here."

His eyes venture from mine and land on Lucas.

"Lucas, Timothy… I'm sure you'll both find your new offices very suitable. Be sure to let the others in this area know we're providing them with these stunning new offices."

He babbles on for another minute, preaching the benefits of the new office building and the lack of need for the current library. Anger wells up inside of me, but Roan holds me down. I can see Lucas take a slight step toward me, but he holds back.

"It will be okay," Roan whispers over and over to me.

I'm shaking by the time the speech is wrapped up. The

Commander turns, and in a display of show, he attaches a sign to the door, saying the library will be closed at the end of the week.

I see the librarians and patrons watching out the windows. Clearly, they hadn't been given advanced warning. The Commander sends in someone to explain what will be happening in the coming weeks to the workers.

They can see I'm clearly distraught, but their eyes plead with me to do something. There's nothing I *can* do.

The Commander looks at me victoriously.

He's trying to take everything from me.

The moment we're released, Roan guides me away from the group. We take the long way home, though the only thing I want is to bury myself in my pillow and cry. The direct route would have required walking with the rest of the people and Roan knew I couldn't handle that.

He lets me cry quietly on the walk home. He apologizes over and over, wishing there was something he could do, but there is nothing. The Commander wants to take the library away from me and he will; there's nothing that can change that.

CHAPTER 30
JADE

I discover the next day that, in fact, the library staff had been told of their dismissals and only had the rest of the week to wrap up any library business. Books were being given away at the end of the week; any not claimed would be destroyed. Mr. Eroh said that one of the librarians was holding a few of my favorites for me.

Roan promises he'll go with me at the end of the week to the book distribution…assuming I survive that long.

We hustle about the kitchen preparing for our guest. I don't like the idea of Lucas being in our house, especially when I'm concerned he's working for the Commander.

Roan assures me that Lucas would never betray him like that, but I'm not so sure.

Lucas arrives right on time, and Roan answers the door. I can hear them chatting as they walk toward the living room. I walk around the corner and greet him.

"Hello, Lucas. Can I get you guys something to drink?"

"A water would be nice," he says. When Roan turns to address me, Lucas smirks at me.

"I'll take a water too, thanks, Jade," Roan says appreciatively. When he turns back, Lucas drops his grin.

Everything about this dinner is weird.

I return with two glasses and the three of us walk out to the garden. I find myself spending entirely too much time there for being allergic to the flowers. I suppose it's something I put up with so that I can be out in the fresh air.

"It's a shame that your father is closing down the library," Lucas starts, "that was always a big draw for the town."

"Yeah, I agree," Roan says.

"New office will be nice, though," he continues even though he knows I'm upset over the topic. "Maybe your father and I will have neighboring offices, Jade."

"Maybe," I say curtly.

"How is your father? I haven't seen him since last week."

"I don't know; I haven't seen him either."

"Did you hear about the bakery adding outside seating?" he asks casually.

"No, I didn't know that. Though, I haven't been over there in a few days."

"Ahh, well it's all anyone can talk about. They're thrilled to have more places to sit. You know it can get quite crowded in there at times."

"That is true. I'm sure they're thrilled to get more customers," I say, relaxing a bit. "I should go check on the food."

I start toward the house, but Lucas stops me.

"Let Roan check on it; we're busy catching up on hometown news." He waves Roan off. Roan reluctantly goes inside at my nod.

"Yes, I didn't realize we were from the same place." I turn back to Lucas.

"I tend to keep a low profile," he says.

The moment Roan is inside, Lucas lashes out at me and grabs my arm.

"Listen to me, Jade, I'm working with your father; you have to trust me."

"Get off me," I hiss, wrenching my arm away. I stare at him, wide-eyed. I won't trust this man, not when he's so closely connected to the Commander.

"The hair comb, Jade. I'm the one that gave it to him to give to you. Our fathers were friends. I'm Asher Montgomery's son. You remember him; he worked with your father. When he died, I picked up where he left off. I've always looked out for you, Jade, I just kept far enough away that you didn't know." He cuts off his rushed words as Roan rejoins us.

My head is spinning. Wouldn't my father have told me about Lucas if they were really working together? Then again, I don't know most of my father's contacts.

I seem to remember Asher Montgomery spending a good deal of time with my father off books. I vaguely remember some of the secret meetings my father took part in before the rebellion was discovered, and I remember Asher being a part of them. In the years that followed, my father kept his distance from everyone associated with the overthrow for their safety.

Could Lucas really be on my side?

But if he was, he certainly wouldn't be friends with Roan, the man charged with killing me.

And wouldn't he know Roan was now on my side?

"Looks like it's ready; come on inside and we'll eat," Roan announces.

Lucas offers me his hand to help me up the steps. Unable to decline his offer, I take his hand. Roan gives me a smile and turns to go inside. He trusts Lucas. Maybe he shouldn't.

Lucas watches me, forcing me to look at him. He's willing me to believe him. But I can't; not yet.

Inside, I serve the food, and we sit down to chat. I let Roan guide the conversation, only jumping in when needed. I'm so busy trying to figure Lucas out that I nearly miss when they speak to me.

"I'm sorry, what?" I ask, blushing.

"Are we boring you?" Lucas asks playfully. "Roan, my friend, we'll have to find a more interesting topic than work. Come, Jade, tell us, what would you like to talk about?"

"You weren't boring me. I just thought of something and slipped out of the conversation for a moment, that's all. Please, go on."

"Well, let's switch topics and talk more about our hometown and we can leave Roan out of the conversation for a bit, shall we?" His eyes sparkle as he speaks.

"Sounds fair enough," Roan chuckles.

"I'd rather talk about how you two became friends," I say, plastering a smile on my face.

"Oh, well that's easy," Roan says. "We met a few years ago, back before Lucas started working with Dad. His father was a politician and Lucas stepped into his position after his father passed away."

"This was back before either of us were politicians," Lucas adds, "We were some of the few people our age at one of the Command parties. We all banded together and hung out. The rest is history."

"What happened to the other people your age?" I ask.

"Lucas and I were the only ones that hung out after that. Eventually, Lucas started his job and I saw him more frequently through work. We hang out when we can, even now."

"It's been awhile though," Lucas says.

"And why aren't you married, Lucas? Most people our age are at this point," I search for information.

"Let's just say I've been busy with other things. I'll get around to finding the right girl one of these days…if I ever manage to slow down a bit. Looks like some of my work load might be wrapping up soon though."

He nods to me. If he's telling the truth about working with my father, his lightened workload means my death. Lovely.

"Maybe Jade has some friends she could set you up with, buddy," Roan says jokingly. Roan knows I don't have any friends.

"Yeah? There was this girl from when we were young; Jade, maybe you know her. I've been wanting to talk to her for years. When we were kids, she was out walking one day and this runaway bicyclist came flying toward her. I pulled her out of the way, but I never got to talk to her. Her aunt came flying around the corner to check on her. Any idea who she was? Lovely girl. I'd love to get the chance to see her again. I told her I'd always be looking out for her, but I never got to speak to her again."

He is, of course, talking about me. I was the girl who was almost trampled by the bicyclist and Sophie was the aunt who ran to check on me despite the fact that she was staying away from us at that point. And Lucas had apparently been the boy that saved me. He had whispered in my ear that he'd be looking out for me, and then he'd vanished. When I didn't see him again, I assumed he figured out who I was and kept away. Clearly not the case.

So maybe he has been on my side all along. If his father made him a part of my protection, then he really is on my side. But why is he in politics and why is he friends with Roan?

Lucas smiles at me, waiting for me to give him some signal that I understand.

I look back and forth between the two men before me. Roan is starting to grow suspicious of my silence.

"What's going on here?" he finally asks.

"Do you really work with my father?" I challenge Lucas openly.

His eyes grow wide in fear. He doesn't know about Roan yet.

"He says he's working with my father," I address Roan, whose head whips around to face his friend.

"Why are you here, Lucas?" he confronts his friend in a low, dangerous voice.

Lucas looks cornered for a moment, but then comes out swinging.

"I'm here to protect her from *you*," he growls, rising out of his seat.

He looks ready to sweep me behind his back and single handedly take Roan out to protect me.

"I won't let you hurt her. She's innocent in this."

Roan rises from his seat and moves toward me.

"Don't you touch her!" Roan demands.

"Stop," I demand, moving closer to Roan. "Roan is protecting me."

Lucas looks doubtful.

"You can't honestly believe that, Jade. He's been trained for most of his life to kill you. This wasn't supposed to happen like this, but I can't leave you here with him. Come on, I'm going to get you out of here." He steps toward me.

"I'm not going anywhere, Lucas. Roan really is protecting me," I insist.

Roan's eyes dart to mine as if I'm insane for telling him.

"I believe him when he says he's working with my father. That story, about the girl—that was me. He rescued me. His father was friends with my father. I think we're in this together, boys."

I see Roan ease, but Lucas remains ready for a battle. I edge away from Roan toward Lucas. Placing my hand on his arm seems to relax him, and he lowers himself back to his normal standing height.

"Why are you here, Lucas?" I ask, returning to my seat.

"When we were kids, my dad told me to look out for you, but never to approach you unless I couldn't help it. That's why that day I pulled you out of the way, I didn't stick around." My thoughts flash back to the bakery—the first time I took Roan. It had been Lucas who looked away that day. "You weren't supposed to know me, and people weren't supposed to associate us as friends. When I saw Sophie, I knew you'd be okay, so I left."

"You know Sophie?" I question.

"I know a lot about you and your family, Jade. My father was right there with your father in the…" he trails off, eyes darting to Roan again.

"He's with us, I promise," I assure him.

He sighs, resigning himself. "Fine. It could have as easily been me and my dad as it was you and your dad who got caught."

"So, your dad told you to protect me?" I ask.

"Yes, pretty much. I was told to watch out for you— and I did, from a distance. When Dad died, I slipped into his role and have been playing the game ever since. I figured I might be able to do some good, but I also knew one day, I'd be in a position to help you. You may not know it, but I consider us friends, Jade."

"So…all this time… you, *what*? *Targeted* me to help Jade?" Roan asks, realizing he had been played.

"Sorry, buddy," he shrugs unsympathetically, "I went after you as a means of protecting her. Nothing more. I mean, you seem nice enough, but knowing you planned on hurting Jade one day, it was pretty much all I could do not to strangle you a few years ago just to prevent all this."

"Wow. Thanks," Roan grimaces.

I'm starting to like this guy.

"So, did my dad send you?"

"No. He doesn't even know I've made contact with you. I just saw you yesterday and knew it was my only shot. I haven't talked with your dad since last week. In fact, once I started taking over for my dad, we made sure to stay as far away as possible. Most of my communication is through Sophie, and even that is extremely limited. We couldn't risk the connection.

"Actually, your dad doesn't even know how involved I am. He knew my dad had me looking out for you, but that's about it. Sophie hasn't really kept him in the loop about me."

"Good grief, is Sophie running *everything*?" I say, exasperated.

Lucas chuckles, "Maybe." He shrugs playfully. "Now, I need to know what you two know."

"Such as?" Roan asks confrontationally.

"What the plan is. I suppose *you'd* know more than *she* would. So, let's have it, Roan. What's dear old dad got planned for Jade's demise?"

"We're not sure," I answer before Roan has a chance to speak.

"You don't know?" he asks incredulously and shoots Roan a look.

"I've always known I couldn't *actually* hurt Jade, and

it shows in some of my actions. My dad isn't trusting me with all the details, especially after his last plan failed."

"The cart?" Lucas scoffs. "Thank goodness for Amos Eroh."

Roan looks at me in surprise. I nod, indicating I knew of Mr. Eroh's involvement, though it's strange hearing anyone refer to Mr. Eroh by his first name.

"So, then what's your plan for combating the Commander?" Lucas presses.

"Well, right now, I'm not letting Jade out of my sight."

"Yes, because that's such a fool proof plan," Lucas retorts spitefully.

"Take it easy, Lucas. We're working on it."

"It's hard to *'take it easy'* when I've spent my entire life trying to protect you, only to have it taken over by the *enemy-turned-good-guy-without-an-actual-plan.*"

"You either have to work *with* us, Lucas, or you can get out now." Roan faces him down.

"Or, I can get Jade out now before your father finds out," he counters.

"I can't just leave, Lucas. They'll go after my dad and Sophie."

"Why I am *just* hearing about Sophie?" Roan interrupts.

"You knew she existed," I say, waving him off. "'I'll explain the rest later."

"You *can* leave, Jade. We'll figure out a way to get you *all* out," Lucas interrupts.

"Out *where*? There's nowhere *to* go." I point out, annoyed.

"We'll hide you. We'll find a way, but you can't stay here, Jade. If you do, you *will* die," Lucas insists. "The people will hide you; they love you."

"Oh sure, and drag them into the line of fire too?" I say quickly.

Lucas shakes his head at me in dismay.

"I have half a mind to gag you and drag you out of here right now."

"*You'll do no such thing*," Roan says protectively.

I drag my hands across my eyes in frustration.

"I'm not going anywhere. This is the way it has to be. I appreciate you both for wanting to help me, but there's no way around this. Let's just get it over with."

I cast a pleading look to Roan, begging him to turn me over to his father so I can be done with this mess.

"No," they both shout at once.

Throwing my hands in the air, I lean back against my chair.

Talking to them is pointless.

"And don't you go getting any ideas about turning yourself over to the Commander either, Jade," Lucas adds, clearly having read my mind.

"Don't you dare, Jade," Roan sits up, concern ringing in his voice.

"It's going to happen one way or another, so why not just deal with it now? It saves us all a lot of trouble."

"Because this will kill your father and you know it," Lucas warns me.

"He has to deal with it sometime, Lucas. Someone has to pay at some point."

Lucas turns on Roan, pointing his finger at my husband's chest. "I swear, if you let her out of this house, out of your sight, I will find you and—"

"I'm *not* going to let her out of my sight, *Lucas*. Before you came along, we were doing just fine."

"If '*fine*' means getting her killed, maybe."

Both men are on their feet, facing off around the table.

"Enough!" I shout, quelling their argument. "My life, my choice. Now *sit down!* Both of you!"

Lucas sends Roan a threatening glare. I watch them both uncurl their fists and realize just how close I came to having to separate their impending brawl.

I have no idea how we would have explained away both of them having black eyes and split lips the next day.

"Does Sophie know about Roan?" Lucas finally tears his gaze away and faces me.

"Yes," Roan flinches again as he learns I have more secrets. "I signaled her at the bakery the other day. Mr.

Eroh knows too and I'm pretty sure the candle lady knows as well."

"Erica's been a lifesaver." Lucas attempts to smile. "Okay, let's talk about what we need to handle immediately. What's the plan for the next few days?"

"Well, we have to go to the Commander's house tomorrow," I say, glancing at Roan.

Lucas glances at him too, then back at me. "Stay by his side, don't ever walk away from him. No matter what."

"We had planned on that. We also came up with a way to avoid them while we're there," I say.

"We're going to spend some time in the pool. We went swimming there once before, so it makes sense we'd want to go again. They don't know I've figured all this out and plan on helping Jade, so we're still operating under the cover of me trying to win her trust."

"Unfortunately, the Commander knows that I know."

"Meaning?" Lucas inquires tentatively.

"Meaning he flat out told me I was going to die and I had to play along or Sophie would pay the price."

"Well that's helpful," Lucas says sarcastically, sitting back in his chair. He rakes his fingers through his dark brown hair as he thinks.

I marvel at the fact that Lucas could keep himself hidden for so long. Even as a politician, I barely knew of him. Granted, my father kept me far from that world after the rebellion faltered. The fact that a man that looked as put together as Lucas Montgomery did could keep from being the talk of all the girls in town was astounding.

"Lucas, how did you keep such a low profile? I'd barely heard about you until yesterday."

"Well, now, that's not going to help *you* much. You're already high profile, my dear," he joked.

I roll my eyes at him. I kind of wish we *had* been friends for all those years.

"Listen, now that we all know that we all know, let's just take tonight and think things through and we can come up with a better plan later," I suggest. We won't be getting anywhere if the conversation keeps up like this.

They both reluctantly nod in agreement, grumbling about how absurd this all is. I can't say I disagree.

We make plans to meet again the day after tomorrow. The arrangement is to casually meet in town, faking a run in, and spending some time together. It seems like the safest plan we've come up with so far.

"I don't like him." Roan turns to me once he's gone.

"You don't *know* him," I counter.

"Neither do you."

"Well, if *that's* the standard we're going with, Roan, I don't exactly know *you* either."

"That's different," he objects.

"Apparently, I've known him longer than I've know

you, Roan, and *he* works with my *father*," I stare at him, waiting for an answer, to which I only receive a sigh.

"I'll trust him if you do, Jade, but can we drop this for now?"

"Sure," I give in. "Let's clean up and go to bed. I think we need to relax before tomorrow."

"I think that's a good theory," he moves toward the sink and I follow.

CHAPTER 31
ROAN

"**R**eady?" I whisper as we step up to the gate.

"Mhmm," Jade murmurs back.

"Just stay with me and we'll be okay," I coach her as we step through and walk to the front door.

"I was so happy to hear you two were coming over today," Maybelle says, taking the bag with our swimsuits in it from me. She gives me a big hug now that she no longer needs to be as formal around Jade and moves over to her. I refuse to relinquish her hand and I'm caught in the embrace.

"What's all this?" Maybelle asks, eyeing the bag in her hand.

"We were thinking about taking a swim. It's a shame the pool doesn't get used more often and Jade really likes it," I answer.

"What a lovely idea. I'll take your bag over there now, if that's okay with you."

"That would be very helpful, thank you, Maybelle," I smile.

I lead Jade into the living room and find it empty. We take seats on the couch, and although she keeps a safe distance from me, I feel like she wants to be as close as possible.

She stays remarkably calm when my father walks in. He sneers at her and it makes me sick.

"Hello, Jade. Welcome back."

"Commander," she addresses him with a curt nod.

"Where's Mom?" I ask, redirecting his attention to me.

"I'm here." She breezes into the room, seeming lighter than I've seen her since this whole process started.

"Hi, Mom. You look good," I say, standing to hug her. Jade stands too, and my mother reluctantly hugs her as well.

"You're early; we weren't expecting you for a bit."

"We thought we might take a swim," I say. "Maybelle was kind enough to take our bag over. Do you mind?"

She pauses for a moment to consider me. I can tell she wants to say no, but she really doesn't have much choice. "Of course not, you kids go right ahead. I'll call you when lunch is ready."

"Thanks, Mom," I give her the biggest smile I can and draw Jade away from the living room.

"No, you let those kids be, Mr. Diamond. They need some alone time." I hear Maybelle flag down my father. She has no idea how grateful I am for her assistance. I know she'll keep an eye on him and keep him away. She's still convinced we're a happy couple who want time to be alone.

"Thank goodness for Maybelle," Jade whispers when we're out of earshot.

"She's been a lifesaver for years," I agree.

The pool house is warm. I close the door behind us, sealing us in against the war raging between us and my father.

"Here, you can get changed first, I'll wait out here," I say, scooping up the bag and handing it to my wife.

"Maybe you should come in, too—there are separate areas in there."

"Don't want to be out here alone while I'm changing, huh?" I give her a knowing look.

"Precisely," she replies and opens the door to the changing area.

She ducks behind a curtain, leaving the bag in the middle. I slip behind one of the hanging pieces of fabric and emerge a minute later. Jade steps out after me, that same black mesh suit from before gracing her curves.

She follows me out to the pool and jumps in before I can get to the steps. I laugh as I'm pelted with drops of water. Stopping in my tracks, I wait for her to surface.

Once she's emerged, I jump in next to her, soaking her in the process.

"Really? That was nice, thanks." She grins, clearly happy to be away from the house.

She swims to the far end. Maybelle was kind enough to turn the waterfall on for us, so I didn't have to get out and turn it on myself. Jade swims to it and turns her back so that the deluge cascades down her back and shoulders. I watch as she tips her head backwards, forcing her hair into a line down her back.

We swim for a while, this time uninterrupted by my father. For the briefest of moments, it seems like Jade nearly forgets everything we're involved in. She splashes me, throwing water at my face, and laughs, tossing her head back like she doesn't have a care in the world. This is the real Jade; the one who lives and loves and cherishes every moment of her existence. This is the Jade that would have taken over the world with her smile if she hadn't spent every moment running for her life. This is the Jade that her father, her friends, her people, will remember. This is the Jade *I'll* remember.

I pull her close, *in case anyone is watching*, and she allows me to hold her. We bob in the water together, rocking on the waves we've created.

I'm surprised by the amount of time we've spent in the water for having such limited access to it. The pond that first time we were introducing each other to our lives, the time we were in the pool and Jade experienced the waterfall, the time she saved me, and now this moment.

She reaches up to brush a piece of hair out of her face and my breath catches. She's lovely. When we first found ourselves in this mess, I knew she was pretty. I had to guard myself against it, but as I got to know her, every-thing—every wonderful thing—came out of her and made her so much more stunning.

She's breathtaking in the water. In this moment, I've never seen anything quite as... perfect.

"Jade, I'm sorry," I murmur to her, still holding her in my arms.

"I know," she confirms.

"But you don't know," I say sadly. "I *did* hurt you, Jade."

"Yeah, but you were only following orders, and you're making up for it now. Besides, scaring me isn't *that* bad."

"I didn't just scare you Jade," I pull back from her, knowing I have to say what I'm about to say, but hating that I have to say it. "I *actually* hurt you. That poison we both found wasn't mine, but it also wasn't the only poison in the house."

She takes a sharp breath and I regret even more what I'm admitting.

"That day you were sick, Jade, the day you shredded your wedding dress... I did that to you." I can't hold eye contact with her. I can't bear to see the look of betrayal I know must be on her face.

"You poisoned me?" she says after a moment, no hint of accusation in her voice.

"I'm so sorry."

Jade swims to me, closing the distance. Her hand finds its way to my arm and I flinch.

"Roan, you were following orders, I understand," she says, determined to get beyond this. "I forgive you."

"But…"

"No," she interrupts, forcing me to look at her. "It's done. I forgive you. Moving on."

I shake my head in disbelief. How could one girl be so compassionate?

"You're amazing, Jade. Simply amazing."

"Yeah," she tosses her hair and grins. "Well, I try."

Her attempt at levity breaks down my final wall and I pull her into a hug. She embraces me back…and then I drag her under.

We come up gagging and spitting, splashing each other relentlessly until we make it to the stairs. Climbing out, we drag ourselves up the steps and across the room. She throws a towel at me from where it rests on a lounge chair and I catch it one handed. She applauds and dries off her face.

"Maybe we can sit in here for a bit after we dry off?" she requests.

"Anything you want, my dear."

She smiles and we walk into the other room to dry off. I hold the door to the drier open for her and she steps inside. She turns it on, leaving it open just a crack so she can keep an eye on me. I watch her for a minute, trying not to make it too obvious that I'm staring at her.

When I can't take it anymore, I open the door a bit more and slip in. Her back is to me and she didn't see me coming. She's frightened at first when I put my hand on her shoulder to let her know I'm there.

I pull the door closed behind me and we're surrounded only by the muted light of the box. We face each other and let the air dry our skin and hair. I know I'm smiling like a fool, but I can't help it. She grins back, amused at my antics.

Suddenly I find my hands in her hair, her hands wrapped around my wrists. We look at each other, her hair flying around her like we're caught in a windstorm. It's stunning and beautiful and all together alluring. And I can't help myself; I kiss her.

With her hair dancing and whipping around us and the air tossing our careful thoughts away, she lets me kiss her, bringing my lips to hers again and again. When I pull away her eyes are on fire, sparkling with an iridescent light I can't even describe.

Her hands make their way to my waist and I realize I have no shirt on. Her hands are like fire against my skin, burning me to my soul. She runs her fingers up my chest and I ache for her as she cleanses me of all my sins against her.

My hand traces its way down her back. She's soft and warm and intoxicating. I kiss her again and I can barely think. The wind in the box is taking my breath away, or perhaps the lack of oxygen is from being unable to pull my lips from hers.

My hands make their way around her waist and to the mesh on the front of her swimsuit. How I wish that mesh wasn't there so that I could touch her, connect with her skin that I so crave.

I sigh into her, only encouraging her as she brings my face closer to her using the hand wrapped in my hair. I move to her cheek, her jaw, her neck, her shoulder.

"Roan," she murmurs my name, ordering me to snap my head up. I look into her eyes and see my own desire reflected.

"Jade," I reply.

Our foreheads come together for only a moment before I can't stand it and have to kiss her. I moan against her skin and she guides my lips to that place between her shoulder and neck. She cringes into me, begging for me not to stop. Her lips find their way to my neck and I can see why she enjoys it so much.

Her kisses grow soft and gentle and she pulls back from me, hands still curled in my hair. She's breathing heavily, trying to recuperate from the loss of oxygen. I still can't catch my breath.

Jade smiles at me and I lean into her as she rests on the drier wall. At some point, she has managed to turn off the air, but I have no idea when.

"Well that was unexpected," she finally says.

"Really? Because I've known that was coming for weeks," I sigh.

Her eyebrows shoot up in amusement.

"Did you now?" she asks, stroking the back of my neck absentmindedly.

"I'm married to *you*...there's *no way* I could avoid thinking about kissing you," I admit. Somehow this girl has made me drop all my defenses and I have no way of not giving her everything she wants, including answers.

"And now that you have, are you ready to trade me in? After all, I *am* the starter wife," she jokes.

"*Never*," I say with such desperation in my voice I'm sure she'll run for the hills.

Instead she leans forward and kisses me once, so lightly I can barely perceive it on my lips.

"Admit it, woman, you're just trying to make sure I'm hopelessly devoted to you," I tease, pulling back slightly. "And if I wasn't before...*I sure am now.*"

I grin and lean forward to touch her again, but she pulls back, licking her lips, taunting me.

"Are you? Devoted?" She drops her voice.

"Absolutely," I say, nodding.

"Good," she whispers and allows me to kiss her.

I smooth her now-dry hair back and lean against the wall.

"Do we have to leave?" I plead.

"Unless you want your father coming in here, finding us like this, then, yes, I'd say we have to leave."

"I guess we kind of gave up our time to lounge out by the pool," I say as she pulls me out of the box.

"Would you rather have done *that*?" She looks at me in surprise.

"Well…" I weigh my options and she throws a towel at me.

"Shut up, *husband.*"

That's right. I am her husband.

And she is my wife.

And I've finally kissed her.

"Come on, let's get changed," she directs, tossing me my clothes.

CHAPTER 32
JADE

e kissed me. I didn't think he would... I didn't even know if I wanted to, but when he kissed me... I could taste how heartbroken he was over hurting me, how much he longed for me, how much he wanted to protect me.

He kissed me and all I could think of was kissing him back. I wanted him and he wanted me; two enemies who wanted nothing more than to be wanted by the other. In those moments, I knew he could be my husband. I knew he'd be loyal to me. I knew he'd protect me.

I felt safe.

Roan was not at all the man my father had warned me about, but rather the man my mother had prayed for me.

And he was mine.

And it was all thanks to the Commander.

That thought brought me crashing back to reality. If I hadn't made it out of my foggy state of delirium at that point, the Diamonds' back door brought that reality rushing forward.

Inside Maybelle catches my eye and I can't help smiling back at her. Alice walks through the hallway as we enter and her eyes dart back and forth between us. She knows something happened. I glance up just in time to see Roan attempt to hide his smile. I can't help myself; I blush.

"Roan, may I speak to you for a moment?" Alice asks.

"Sure, Mom," he takes a step forward, pulling me with him.

"Alone," she clarifies.

He hesitates, but I touch his hand, pulling it away from mine. He carefully steps toward the end of the hall, keeping me in sight the whole time.

"Are you falling for that girl?" Alice whispers harshly.

They argue for a minute, Roan constantly glancing at me. Alice keeps her voice low but I hear a litany of my faults as she lectures her son. He vows he has no feelings for me and she's wrong, saying I'm just a mission. The words sting, though I know he doesn't mean them.

When I hear the Commander's footsteps coming, my eyes dart frantically up at Roan. He hears it too and ends the discussion with his mother. He strides easily to my side and takes my arm, leading me to the dining room. Roan seats me on his far side, keeping himself between the Commander and me.

Except Alice and the Commander don't join us. After a moment, we hear a commotion in the other room, much as I did that first time when Roan and his father were yelling about me.

"I heard you...that first day here. When you calmed your father down," I admit quietly, turning away from the noise in across the house.

"You heard that?" he asked in disbelief. "Jade..."

"No, I needed to hear it...I wouldn't have been able to protect myself if I hadn't."

He brings my hand to his lips, quickly setting it back under the table. Shows of affection for our fake relationship were required; shows of *actual* affection could be deadly.

The Commander stomps into the room.

"We're having guests. Roan, go outside and greet them," the Commander orders.

Roan looks a bit surprised but he stands.

"She stays," the Commander says as he walks across the room.

"She needs to come with me. Whoever this is, they need to see Jade can handle the obligations of being a good hostess. She is my wife, and will one day be a Commander's wife. This is a valuable time for her to show off her abilities."

The Commander looks his son over, doubt written

across his face, but he dismisses us with a wave of the hand.

Alice stands in the hallway, looking furious.

"There are people on their way," she huffs.

"Yes, we're going out to receive them now," Roan says. "Who are they?"

She glares at me and turns back to the curtain she is holding open by the door. She flings the curtain back into place and marches away after scowling at me one more time.

Looking to Roan, I rush to the window. A group of men walk up the drive. I spot Lucas and my stomach jumps into my throat. I'm positive the Commander knows something. But then I see another man—this time, my heart falls on the floor so hard I'm convinced I can't survive it.

I have the door open, rushing out. I nearly fall as I make my way down the drive toward the men. Roan calls out after me, trying to catch me. But I don't care; I keep running. I push my way through the crowd of men and throw my arms around my father.

"Jade, stand up," he whispers to me, compelling me to remember myself and where I am.

I hold back my tears, pulling back to look at the man I never thought I'd hold again. My father was here. I am overjoyed and horrified all at once.

"Why are you here?" I ask, trying to hold my voice steady.

"The Commander set a meeting for today; this was the only time he could fit it in," Lucas answers for him.

"Gentlemen," my father addresses the crowd, "you all remember my daughter, Jade."

The men greet me politely but give me space to walk with my father. We linger behind the crowd, his arm wrapped around my waist as we walk. We only stop when Roan looms in front of us. He holds his hand out to my father.

"Mr. Jareau," he says politely, though we can all tell the meaning behind it. He's apologizing for his actions and promising him to care for me all in one look. He refuses to move until my father takes his outstretched hand.

Once he nods and returns Roan's greeting, insisting he call him James, we fan out and start back to the house.

The Commander seats my father across the table from me. I am seated between the Commander and Roan, which puts my father on the end of the opposite side of the table, directly next to a fuming Alice.

I conclude the fight must have been over Alice's pure hatred for my father. She must be horrified that she must sit next to him as he politely makes conversation with her and the others at the table.

Roan appropriately joins in on the conversation, but Alice and I sit in general quietness. We are not politicians and we are only involved because they couldn't host this lunch without us. We remark quietly when asked a question, but we offer no opinions.

The Commander directs an obscene amount of questions toward my father. He's clearly the target of today's affair and everyone notices.

Amazingly, Lucas never reacts. He's the picture of perfection several seats away from my father. His ability to stay calm is fascinating. I wish I could study him and learn how he does it.

At the end of their meeting, they go about talking on endless topics that would bore the dullest of us. But soon I find *myself* the topic of conversation.

I was so busy watching my father and Lucas that I somehow missed the transition to discussing me. It wasn't until the Commander slipped his hand under mine and lifted it to the table that I became aware the he was focused on me.

I watch in horror as he begins stroking my hand, like I'm a pet kitten or some prize he won.

"It's so lovely having Jade in our family. Roan is quite smitten with her. Even Alice is taken with the girl's graces, isn't that right, dear?" he croons to the table.

Roan reaches under the table, grabbing my free hand, clutching at me as though he can will us both away. I stare at my hand in the Commanders and force myself not to pull away.

My father's foot inches forward, I can see him shift in his chair, but he can't reach me. He locks eyes with me, willing me to keep calm.

"Yes, Jade certainly is lovely, isn't she?" the Commander directs his comment to Lucas and one of the other younger politicians at the table. "Roan couldn't have found a more *attractive* girl. I'm sure you think your daughter is lovely, don't you, James? I bet the men couldn't keep their hands off her growing up. I'm sure it was all you could do to keep them away from her, knowing that she was committed to Roan, wasn't it, James?"

"Jade was always a good young woman, Robert. She always honored her commitment to your son," my father remarks without any inflection in his voice.

"Yes, and now she's Roan's. And I'm sure he takes *very* good care of her," he taunts my father.

"Mom, lunch was wonderful, thank you so much," Roan says louder than necessary, attempting to redirect the conversation away from me.

But the Commander stands and walks around behind my chair. He leans against the back of it and begins stroking my hair. His hand glides down the same path Roan's did only two hours before.

My father flinches as he restrains himself from standing up and beating the life out of the Commander. The Commander's hand lingers on my shoulder and down my arm. I focus on a spot on the table and try to control my breathing.

He's talking about me, but I can't hear what he's saying. A shiver runs down my spine.

"Jade *loves* being a part of our family, don't you, Jade?" he leans down to me and hisses in my ear.

I nod, hoping he'll move away.

"What was that, dear?"

"Yes. Yes, of course," I sputter.

Lucas catches my eye and he no longer bothers to hide his horror. Everyone around the table looks ready to object to the Commander's behavior as he continues to pet me. Taking my hand again in his, he places it on my shoulder, near his face.

"You're right, Father," Roan leaps out of his seat. "Jade *is* just too lovely to share," he pulls on me so hard I collide with the Commander's jaw. "If you gentlemen will excuse us, Jade and I need to be going now. We have plans for this afternoon."

The Commander grins wildly from his new place back at the head of the table where he stands behind his chair. "Well gentlemen, looks like I may have grandchildren very soon after all!"

He dares a look at my father who is remarkably still in his seat. The Commander gives him an evil grin, making sure he's aware that I am Roan's wife and he must surely be taking advantage of that fact.

"Come on, babe," Roan tugs on me, eager to get me away from his father.

The Commander takes a few easy strides and blocks our path. He hugs his son as Roan pushes me backwards toward the door. I duck around him and rush to my father to say goodbye.

He holds me in his arms, protecting me from the Commander.

"Let me walk you out," he says loudly as he notices the Commander approaching.

"Goodbye, Jade; we'll see you soon," Robert Diamond says, pulling me out of my father's embrace. He holds me so close to him that I can feel his heart beating furiously in his chest. His hands roam from my back to my arms as he finally releases me. Kissing me on the forehead, he holds me far too long.

Roan pulls me away and my father follows quickly.

"Are you all right?" they ask at the same time once we step outside.

The shaking begins and they both try to catch me.

"I'm so sorry," Roan apologizes.

"You tried to help, there wasn't much you could do without giving yourself away," my father says. "But don't you *ever* leave her alone with him, do you understand me? Or *her* death isn't the only one you'll need to worry about."

"I swear I'll protect her, sir," Roan vows to my father as he once did to my mother.

"He did this for my benefit. He's trying to torture me by humiliating you," my father says to me. "Keep away from him. We're working on a plan to get you out of here, just survive until we can."

"You can't get me out of here, Dad. This has to happen."

For a small moment, I allow myself the relief of imagining freedom from all this. I think about the life I could have with Roan and I realize I could be happy with him. But the hope is strangled by reality. We'll never get away and even if we did, someone else would pay.

"I have to go back in. Stay strong, Jade. We're going to fix this, I promise you." He kisses me and hurries back inside.

"Get her out of here," he instructs Roan over his shoulder.

"I'm so sorry, Jade. He never should have done that."

"He was proving a point to my father. He owns me now and there is nothing my dad can do about it."

"You're not his wife, you're mine. I won't let him touch you like that again."

"I doubt he will. He was doing it purely for my father to see. It makes me sick."

"I wanted to rip you away from him…" Roan starts.

"You couldn't. He would have caught on. We have to stick with the plan, Roan."

"I know," he says reluctantly.

"Roan," I say after we walk a bit. "You know there's no way out of this for me. I *have* to die to end this."

"No, you don't."

"Yes, I do," I say sadly.

Only our footsteps create noise as we walk back home.

"What happened back there, in the pool house..." I start and his face lights up, "Roan, we can't do that again."

He stops in his tracks, pulling me back. His face is awash with concern. "What?"

"We can't do that again," I say, unable to look at him. "It's going to make all this too hard."

"It's going to make *what* too hard?" he prompts.

I hesitate, rocking on my toes. "Letting you go," I finally say.

He closes the space between us. He kisses me lightly and adds, "I'm not letting you go."

I turn away from him, pulling myself out of his arms.

"See, that's the point exactly. I'm going to die, I *have* to die, and if I'm attached to you like this... I don't know if I can go quietly."

"But you're not going quietly...you're not going *at all*. I *want you*, Jade, more than I've wanted anything in my life. If you die, it will kill me. I can't lose you, and if you're going to give up like this, I'm going to have to give you a reason to fight." He closes the distance between us again and his hands work their way through my hair as his lips trail over me.

He walks me backwards, down our street as he kisses me. Guiding me up the stairs and into the house, he closes the door behind him.

"Roan, stop," I beg, finding it hard to think.

"Only if you promise me you'll fight."

"I can't…" my complaint is cut off by his lips. *"Roan, stop,"* I whisper.

"I *can't,*" he says.

He touches every place his father touched, erasing the memory and replacing it with this new one. I lean into him and let my tears fall. I'm going to hate saying goodbye to this…to *him.*

"I'm not losing you," he says finally, pulling back.

My hand finds its way to his as it sits on my cheek. I stroke it softly, letting my eyes drift shut. Again, I see my future with Roan…the future we'll never have. Happiness…a family…love. It's all standing there, just out of my reach.

He brushes away my tears.

"You see it too, huh?"

"See what?" I ask, letting him pull me to the couch.

"Our future." He sweeps my hair over my shoulder.

I nod and he bends his head toward me. We lean against each other, taking in the moment.

"Do you honestly not want that?" he asks in a pained voice.

"I want it, Roan, I want it with *you,* truly. But you've always known my fate."

"Do you wish I hadn't kissed you back there?" he asks. His forehead still rests against mine and he places my hand on his chest under his hand. I feel his every breath.

"I'm glad you did. At least I know," I answer. "Would you take it back, knowing I'm going to die?"

"No. I wouldn't take back one moment of time I spent with you. I care about you, Jade. I know we're new at this, and I know it's not love yet, it can't be yet, but I also know one day it *will* be."

Love. Such a funny word. Love is what got me into this mess. Love for country, love for people, love for my father and family. Now love was making it hard to say goodbye.

I had made my peace with dying for those I love. Now love was holding me back and making me question everything.

"I need some time," I say, tearing myself away from him. I flee to my room and lock myself in.

I hear Roan lean against my door. He slides down it and rests against the floor. He doesn't leave until I come out the next morning.

CHAPTER 33
JADE

 step around Roan's sleeping body, and make my way out of the house. I need to get to the shop and away from this place.

I cross over into my town and I can sense something is off. There's a strange smell in the air, one not usually found this time of year. My chest tightens as the smoke creeps its way into my lungs. I move quickly around the buildings until I can see the billow of light grey rising from a few streets over.

Running, I make my way to the source of the flames and discover the shop on fire. It's early and hardly anyone is awake but I shout as loud as I can, hoping to alert someone that can help.

Flames engulf the top of the building and smoke pours from the holes in the roof. Making my way toward the shop, I attempt to look in the windows.

Fear paralyzes me as I confirm my worst fear. Mr. Eroh is inside.

The door is locked, preventing me from entering. Franticly I search for something to break a window with. A crowd begins to gather outside, crying for me to come away.

Smashing the window, I try to clear it of the glass before crawling in. I hear my name being called behind me but I ignore it. I know at least two of the men who came to help have gone to the back, looking for an alternative route inside.

The air is so thick I can barely breath inside the shop. Mr. Eroh is unconscious, clearly having been struck before the fire was set. In his hand sits a small toy that was obviously placed there after he was knocked out.

As I turn him over to check on him, the toy falls out of his hand, revealing a green wind-up toy. The one Mr. Eroh gave Roan to remind him of me.

The Commander.

This fire is to punish me; probably for running away yesterday at lunch.

I pocket the toy and do my best to lift Mr. Eroh up from the floor. He starts to stir as I move him. I shout his name until he regains awareness. He watches his shop burn around us, embers flying through the air. One lands on my shirt and I beat it out as a little hole forms in the material.

The entire shop is lit up, dancing with an orange glow. Thick smoke blankets the top and I bend low to keep from breathing in too much. In horror, I notice the clock burning, trinkets melting, and pieces of the ceiling falling around us.

I cough, though not as viciously as Mr. Eroh does. He's been inhaling the smoke much longer than I have.

Dark shadows bounce along the floor as the fire continues to spread out. The heat is so intense I'm worried my hair might melt. It's sweltering in the room and it makes it hard to think.

We make it to the door together, and I try to push it open. When it won't move, I try kicking at it. Just as I'm about to move us to the window to climb out, the door flies open and Lucas steps in.

He rushes to Mr. Eroh's other side and ducks under his shoulder. Looking like a perfect fairytale knight, he drags us both out. Outside we set Mr. Eroh in the grass and we fight the coughing that wracks our entire bodies.

"What happened?" Lucas hisses at me.

"The Commander," I whisper back.

"You're sure?"

"He left a sign," I confirm.

"I have to go take care of this. Go home. I'll be there later, don't talk to anyone else," he says as he spins to face the crowd.

I hear him making a speech about how brave it was

for me to rescue my boss and how lucky we were that he had shown up when he did. I knew he didn't actually want the credit for himself, but he had to play the role of appreciative politician for the public. He made sure my name was a part of the rescue efforts as well, knowing I needed the publicity. The fire would be played off as an accident, though, had the Commander gotten his way, it would have ended in tragedy for both Mr. Eroh and me.

I sit with Mr. Eroh and he eyes me, waiting for answers. When I feel safe enough, I slip the toy from my pocket just enough that he can see it. His nod confirms my initial thoughts: that the Commander had done this to punish me.

Lucas keeps away from us the rest of the time he is at the fire. Eventually people arrive to put it out, but most of the shop is already lost.

"Are you all right, Jade?" Mr. Eroh coughs next to me.

"I can't believe he would do something like this," I mutter next to him.

"He's planning to kill you, Jade, why would *this* surprise you?"

"I suppose it shouldn't."

"Where's your husband today? Isn't he supposed to be watching you?"

"I snuck out," I admit, regretting that choice.

"Jade!" an angry voice pierces through the noise of the crowd and the fire.

"I'm sorry," I say, flying to my feet.

"What were you thinking?" Roan hisses at me. "You could have died in there."

Panic fills his voice and I can see the desperation pleading with me to stop making choices without him. I raise my arms and pull his around me. With my hands on his shoulders, I try to calm him.

"Roan, please, people are staring," I say quietly.

"Then they'll think I'm a husband who's terrified that his wife was just in a fire," he replies.

His eyes flit down to the ground and he catches sight of Mr. Eroh.

"Are you all right, sir?" he bends down, one hand still against me for balance.

"I'm fine, son," Mr. Eroh replies calmly. He holds the toy up in his hand, careful to keep it hidden from the view of others.

Roan straightens to face me again. His face has fallen even more so than before.

"Lucas helped us out," I manage to squeak out before Roan can speak. I can tell he is livid over his father's actions, but I can't decipher his reaction to news of Lucas' involvement.

"Take her home, son," Mr. Eroh instructs, disrupting my thoughts.

"Will you be all right?" Roan waits for an answer.

"I'll be fine. I made it out publicly, I'll be safe for a

while," he confirms, showing his knowledge of the way the Commander works.

Roan nods and we weave our way through the crowd. It takes twice as long as normal to get out of town because we're stopped every few feet. Being well known in town makes for a lot of concerned friends.

Lucas is waiting inside our house when we return home, scaring us half to death.

"How did you get in here?" I yelp when I see him.

"It's not as difficult as you might think," he smirks. "Now, tell me what happened."

We take a seat in the living room, Lucas on one of the chairs and Roan wrapped around my shoulder on the couch.

"I went to work early; the place was already in flames. I saw Mr. Eroh through the window and went in. The door was stuck."

"And just how do we know it was the Commander?"

"He sent us—or Jade, rather—a message. Mr. Eroh had given me a windup toy the first time I met him; a little green gem to remind me of Jade. Somehow my father got it and left it with Mr. Eroh in the fire."

"Where was it that he got it?"

"Here…in the house," he closes his eyes, "In my room…my *separate room.*"

He throws his hand up in dismay at the realization that his father knows we aren't sharing a room.

Lucas seems intrigued by the idea, but I don't comment. I partly feel the need to slap the look off his face as he turns toward me, giving me a knowing look.

"Let me see it," Lucas says, holding out his hand for the toy.

Roan hands it to him and he inspects it. The toy catches my eye as he rolls it over. If the Commander had access to the house, he had access to everything. It also means he's now aware that Roan isn't playing by the rules anymore.

My world starts unraveling around me; the world I thought was already as unraveled as it could get.

He knows about Roan betraying him, Sophie, my Dad, maybe even Lucas. He already attacked Mr. Eroh and nearly killed him. He's threatened an entire town to ensure my father's cooperation. There are no limits to what the Commander is willing to do for revenge.

While everyone in my life is insistent that I live, I know I must die. Which means I have to work against their plans without them knowing it.

The boys discuss our options, but I'm lost in my own thoughts. I have to get away from them, but I have to do it at the right time. Without contacting the Commander, I don't know how or when to sever our ties.

Leaning forward, I pick up the windup toy where Lucas left it on the coffee table. I pause for a few moments, playing with it in my fingers before standing up.

"I think I need to lay down for a bit," I announce.

Roan and Lucas look concerned.

"Are you okay, Jade?" Roan stands.

"I'm fine," I wave him back down. "I just need a break I think."

They nod and watch me walk away. Closing the door behind me, I let my gaze sweep around the room. Wedging the chair under the doorknob, I change out of my smoke-covered clothes and into something new. I tie my hair back in an effort to keep from breathing in the smoky scent. My fingers slam into the hair comb still tucked in my tresses. I take it out, forcing it back into my hair once the tie is secure. I know I can't use it, but it's from my father and I want something that is *mine* with me when it's time.

One look back over my shoulder and I walk to the dresser where I have writing paper. I scratch out a note.

I'm sorry. I have to.

Setting it on the pillow, I allow my eyes to water for a

moment. I've made my peace with my father already and it was the hardest thing I've ever had to do. Saying goodbye to the two men in my living room was almost as excruciating. It was as traumatic as saying goodbye to Mr. Eroh the day Roan dragged me out of the shop. I haven't known either of them very long, and yet they've been a part of my life for years.

Forcing the window open as quietly as I can, I climb outside. It will be at least an hour before I am discovered, and this will all be settled by then.

I creep around the outside of the house, making sure I'm not seen. Once I'm out of eyeline, I run. My lungs still burn from the smoke inhalation, but I order myself forward, compelling my feet to carry me toward the Command Offices.

Daniella's face registers shock as I burst through the door. Jumping out of her seat, she tries to catch me, but realizing it's me and I'm clearly upset, she lets me go.

"Commander Diamond!" she shouts, attempting to announce my presence before I enter the room.

He's on his feet as I smash his door into the wall. Slamming it behind me, I march up to him, braver than I've ever been. I hold the green windup toy in my hand in front of him, glaring as viciously as I can. I throw it to the ground and it bounces several feet away.

"I've played by your rules. I've done everything you've asked. *Why* would you try to kill him?"

"Who?" he grins in delight.

"You *know* who. Mr. Eroh," I growl venomously.

"He's a bad influence, Jade. Just like your father. A message had to be sent."

"*I'm* the message."

"Yes, you are," he continues to smile. "Why are you here?"

"To end this," I say, "Haven't we had enough?"

"I'd say no, but you've managed to turn my son against me, so I guess it's time to stop toying with you. I'll end this for Roan's sake. The sooner you're gone, the sooner he can get over you." he turns his back to me in a bold move of confidence and walks around his office. "You've really messed up my plans, Jade, but we cope when we must. I know the rebellion wasn't your fault…I *was* going to make it painless for you. After all, this is a lesson for your father, not you. But now… now that you've complicated things, I'm not feeling so generous."

"Just get it over with," I beg.

He sits at his desk and motions for me to take a seat. Refusing, I cross my arms and stare him down.

"Tonight, we'll have a ceremony," he says, appraising me. "To honor you for your courage this morning."

His grin makes my hair stand on end.

"At that ceremony, you'll keel over and die a very public death. Complications from injuries sustained in the fire. You'll die a hero, Jade, just what you wanted.

You're so noble...*dying* to save your father...your friends."

"Poison, then?" I comment. "Seems to be the way you operate."

"It's efficient," he says calmly. "Your particular brand is fast working and will need to be ingested right before. We'll have water for you on stage, of course. You must be so parched after being in that fire."

He leans forward and folds his hands menacingly on his desk as his eyes glitter in delight.

"You'll drink it, Jade. You'll ask for it and when it's handed to you, you won't hesitate. You'll have a few more moments to accept our praise and then you'll die a hero. How perfectly fitting," he says, enjoying himself; reveling in my misery.

"You won't go home, Jade," he continues. "We can't have Roan getting in the way. We'll summon him right before the ceremony and he'll watch his *beloved wife* die on stage."

He rolls his eyes at the words.

"And then this time next year, we'll find him a real wife, one who can live up to expectations, one he can truly love, and you...well, you'll be forgotten completely. Except for maybe your father. Oh, we'll trot him out every so often and make him relive each precious moment of your death. It will be perfect."

"And what am I supposed to do until then?" I ask,

looking away. I can feel my lip curled in disgust. I couldn't comprehend how someone could talk so comfortably about death.

The Commander reaches into his desk and comes up with a syringe. He holds it up for me to inspect. When I don't move, he stands and pushes away from his chair.

I try not to flinch as he saunters over to me.

"See you soon, Jade," he whispers as he plunges the needle into my neck.

Everything floats away.

CHAPTER 34
ROAN

"**S**hould we check on her?" Lucas asks a few hours later.

"Maybe. I don't want to wake her if she's sleeping, though."

I walk to her door and knock gently.

"Jade?"

When she doesn't answer, I turn the doorknob to go in and check on her. It doesn't move.

"Jade?" I ask louder, getting Lucas's attention.

"What's she doing?" he asks, walking up behind me.

I try the door again.

"It's locked." I look back at him.

His worried look reflects my own. Lucas and I reach for the door, pounding and calling her name. When she doesn't answer, we both try forcing the door open. It takes several attempts but we finally break through. We nearly stumble over the chair she used to block the door.

"Where is she?" Lucas asks in a high-pitched voice, revealing the terror I feel myself.

"Oh no," I whisper.

A note sits on the bed and I already know what it means. The open window only confirms my worst fear: Jade has gone to my father.

"We have to go," I say, running out of the room to the front door. "This time of day he'll be at the office, Jade will know that. That's where she'll be."

We run through the town, making our way to the Command offices. The building looms before us and suddenly I come to my senses.

"Stop!" I command, bringing Lucas to a halt.

"What?" he looks at me frantically.

"You can't go in there. He can't know you're a part of this. If I fail, you need to save her."

He looks like he wants to protest, but he knows I'm right. Stomping his foot in the ground, he spins around.

"Fine," he says through gritted teeth. "But...*fine!*"

"Just stay close by. Listen," I instruct. "If I can get her out, I'll send her to you. You know what to do."

He nods and moves out of sight, creeping as close to the building as he dares.

There are no pretenses now. My father knows every-thing, so there's no need for me to hide.

I walk confidently into the building so as not to alarm

Daniella. She's not at her desk when I walk in, so I go straight to my father's office. He glances up as I walk in.

"I heard about this morning," he says glancing back down at his paperwork. "We'll have a ceremony tonight for her, to honor her bravery. Really, this is working out perfectly for us… more public exposure."

"Knock it off, Dad. I know you started the fire," I cut him off.

He raises an eyebrow at me. "Whatever gave you that idea, son?"

"Your calling card." When he stares at me blankly, I break. "The toy. You were in my house. You took it and you left it there for her to find."

"And suddenly you care so much about this girl?" he sets his papers down and faces me.

"She doesn't deserve to die for something as petty as this. She doesn't deserve to die at all."

"So, she got to you then. I was afraid this would happen."

"*Morality* got to me. *Human decency* got to me. *Not wanting to be a murderer* got to me, Dad," I shout.

"Keep your voice down, Roan," he warns.

"No. Not anymore. If you touch her—"

"You'll *what?*" he challenges me, standing behind his desk.

"Where is she?" I say, refusing to finish the thought.

"Preparing for tonight," he answers, "and she doesn't

want to see you. I'm sure she has to get herself in order after such a long morning. If you want to see her, come to the ceremony tonight."

Folding his arms over his chest, he provokes me to defy him. But I don't know where she is, I can't possibly hope to find her on my own... she could be anywhere in the country.

"Just tell me where she is. I want to be with her for this," I silently pray he believes I just want to see her on her last day.

"Like I said, she doesn't want to see anyone. She'll be at the ceremony tonight."

"What are you going to do to her?" I ask desperately, feeling my insides being torn apart.

"We're going to honor her, of course," he says, as if he wasn't planning an assassination.

"Please, just let me go to her," I plead, letting the tears force their way into my voice, hoping some shred of humanity in my father realizes I care for this girl and that it will end me if she's hurt.

"Go home, Roan, or better yet, go back to work. You've already missed all morning and we're getting behind."

There's nothing more I can do, so I leave, walking out the front of the building, knowing I can never go back. I don't even wait for Lucas; I know he'll find me.

Somehow, he manages to arrive at my house before I do. He already knows I have no answers.

"There's going to be a ceremony tonight, to honor how brave she was this morning. It's going to happen then. I don't know how," I say, my voice lacking any emotion. I tell Lucas about trying to find her, begging to be with her.

"Do you have any idea where your father might keep her?" he asks.

"No. It would have to be nearby, wouldn't it? He can't have her too far away if she needs to be here tonight. Oh!" I freeze. "Her father."

"He'll know what it means as soon as he hears about the ceremony," Lucas says, convincing me not to find my father-in-law. "Right now, our best bet is to find out as much as we can about this ceremony."

"Everyone will be there. It will probably be out in front of the offices, that's where they always do these things."

"So, what do we know about the offices?" Lucas says. "You work there: have you learned any tricks about the place or things outsiders might not know?"

"Nothing that I can think of. I mean, I know my way around the building, but nothing out of the ordinary."

"And you know the landscape around it. If we can get her out, we can get her away."

"Away to *where?*"

"I know a place…where I was going to hide her to begin with."

"Which is?"

"Let me worry about that. You need to focus on getting her out of there in one piece."

We discuss our options, but the entire plan hinges on what form of death my father chooses to inflict. Nothing about this will be easy.

CHAPTER 35
JADE

ell, look who's up." A voice brings me out of my fogginess. "Hello, Jade."

I sit up as fast as I can, causing the room to spin. I collapse back down on what I discover to be a small couch.

"Where am I?" I croak, my voice betraying me.

"It doesn't matter. It's almost time for the ceremony. You need to get ready." The Commander turns to face me, handing me a small glass of water. "Don't worry… It's not a test run."

He grins as I accept the water. It doesn't matter really; I'm going to die very soon anyway.

"Your adoring public is here. They're all waiting outside. Your father is in the front row." His elation radiates in his chuckle.

"Now, there are a few things we need to go over. Once we get on stage, you smile and you act gracious. You do not communicate with *anyone*. You look at me, you look at your award, you smile. Once I present you with your award, you'll be invited to give a small speech. You walk to the podium, you smile, you ask for water. It will appear as if you aren't feeling well from this morning. When it comes, you drink it and you thank all the people for coming. You've already made a show of not feeling well, so when the drugs kick in, it's understandable. The autopsy will reveal complications from the trauma you experienced this morning. And just like that, a hero is born.

"Do I make myself clear, Jade?" he asks. "Smile, pain, death. No talking, no communicating, no goodbyes."

When I don't answer, he slams his foot into the ground making me jump. "Do I make myself clear?"

"Yes," I answer to prevent him from coming closer to me. "Eyes down, gracious smile. I understand."

"Good," he backs away toward the door. "Now get dressed. Someone will come for you momentarily. Not a word to them. If they must know, you weren't feeling well and you came in here to lay down and rest."

He retreats, leaving me in the small closet-of-a-room, alone.

A dress sits on the far arm of the couch. It's a simple frock; a black colored, long dress. It will be as if I knew the end was coming and I had prepared for my funeral. In fact, it probably *is* for my funeral. *The dead hero buried in the last dress she ever wore.*

I shrug out of my clothes and shift into the dress. It really was stunning; I wish I could enjoy it more. I step into the shoes left for me and comb my hair out with my fingers. I position my hair comb over my ear where I'm sure it can be seen. I want my father to know it's there.

Answering the knock at the door, I find an older man waiting to escort me to the ceremony. I explain that I wasn't feeling well and the Commander had allowed me to rest here. He doesn't question my story.

The walk is short. Apparently, I had been kept in the Command offices the whole time. Each step brings me closer to my end. Each step brings me closer to seeing the people I love. Each step I make the choice to let go to save them. Each step only serves to solidify my choice. I will be the final piece of the game.

Stepping outside, the sunlight burst brilliantly against my face. It blinds me and I follow where I'm led. At the front of the makeshift stage, the sun finally maneuvers its way out of my eyes and I see my world before me.

CHAPTER 36
ROAN

he's even more lovely than she was the day of the Command party when she shredded her wedding gown to make a point. The black is stunning against her hair that flows wild and free down her back and shoulders and chest. The wind picks up and tosses it in the air as the sunlight catches it and makes it sparkle.

She is the image of perfection.

Somehow, she is composed as she is led to the front of the stage. My eyes dart back and forth, looking for how my father will make his plan happen. Lucas is on the other side of the stage, hoping to figure it out as well.

We chose to separate and whichever of us could get to her first, we'd take the fall. I knew that destroying my father's plans would cost me, but Lucas would probably die if he is discovered to be involved. It was a miracle he chose to invest his life in Jade's when he didn't have to.

My unending gratefulness doesn't even begin to cover the debut I owed him.

"Jade," I yell, trying to force my way to the stage.

She hears me call, but she's still blinded by the golden sunlight.

"Jade!" I shout again, only to find myself being held back.

"I'm sorry sir, no one is allowed on the stage," a man says.

"She's my wife, let me go." I struggle to free myself.

My father begins his litany of praise for the Command, but I don't hear a word.

"Please, you have to let me go, she needs me."

The men force me back as I fight against them.

"We have very specific orders from the Commander," they insist.

"I'm the Commander's *son*," I plead.

"I'm sorry, sir."

"But she's in danger, please!"

The man to my right falls, releasing his grip on me. I look back into the face of the bakery owner, the one who always brings Jade exactly what she wants. She looks into my eyes and I know what it is she cannot say. *Go.*

Slamming my fist into the man holding my left arm, I free myself and bolt for the stage.

"Thank you, everyone"—Jade coughs—"for having me here."

Her eyes are locked on her father's. He's sobbing as he watches his daughter at the podium. Men are positioned at either side of him, ready to hold him back if necessary. They look like part of the crowd, but I know they work for my father. James mumbles her name over and over again as he struggles with letting his daughter die to protect the entire town. He forces himself to stay in place, yielding to her will.

I leap onto the stage, surprising Jade and my father as she is handed a cup of water.

"She's in danger," I yell loudly enough for the crowd to hear. "Someone is trying to hurt Jade."

"No, I'm fine, Roan," she says, trying to hold me off.

"Someone is trying to kill my *wife*," I shout louder, directing the last word to her, hoping it would change things.

Had I been anyone else, my father would have strangled me on the spot for ruining his plan.

"Please don't worry," Jade says into the microphone on the podium. "He's just a little worried after the fire this morning."

She coughs again and raises the glass to her lips.

"Don't drink that," I yell, reaching for it.

"It's...fine...Roan," she coughs as if she badly needs a drink. But I know her, and I know she's going forward with this plan and she won't let me stop her.

I struggle with her for the cup, spilling half of it in the

process. The bottom of her dress soaks up the water, disappearing into the black fabric. We grapple for it and she glares at me, pleading with me to let her go.

"I can't," I whisper to her.

"You *can*," she replies.

"No," I give one final pull on the cup, tearing it out of her grasp.

She reaches for it, but I can't let her have it. My first instinct is to drop it on the ground, but if I do, this will never end. She steps toward me and I whip my head toward my father.

CHAPTER 37
JADE

oan falls so fast I can't even catch him. I can barely see him through my tears as I throw myself on his body. His whole body shakes, seizing on the ground.

"I had to," he manages to whisper as he pulls my head close to his lips.

"Roan, please, don't," I cry. "Don't leave me. I'm so sorry. I'm so sorry."

I'm shaking almost as hard as he is.

The Commander rushes to his son's side, opposite me. I look up and catch sight of him, holding his son's hand.

He's the reason Roan drank the poisoned water. He's the reason his son is dying.

I launch myself at him, but my scream is cut off as my father's hands reach around me, clamping over my mouth and forcing me back.

"Get him inside," my father commands.

Lucas appears out of nowhere and helps the Commander lift Roan into the office building. Inside the Commander's office, they set him on the floor.

"What did you give him?" my father asks briskly.

"I..." the Commander stammers.

"What. Did. You. Give. Him?"

Knowing there's no point in holding it back, the Commander tells him. My father looks around, thinking. They quickly discuss how much he ingested and what damage it was doing to his body.

Lucas and I hover over Roan's body as the convulsing slows and stops.

"Jade," Roan whispers, opening his eyes enough to lock on to mine.

"I love you," I rush to say, bringing his hand to my cheek. "I'm so sorry. I love you. Why would you do that? Why?" I choke through my tears. I'm losing the man I love.

Lucas retreats enough to give us some space.

"I couldn't lose you," Roan admits, eyes fluttering closed only to snap back open. His body continues to still.

"So instead I have to lose you?"

"He can't touch you now. Tell them it was him," he brushes my hair back weakly. "Lucas will take care of you."

Our fathers are out of hearing range, but he still lowers his voice. Lucas is in the room. Even if the Commander thought he didn't know before, he would know now that the Commander admitted it.

"Stay strong, Jade. Don't go out without a fight. You have too much to live for."

"So do you," I try insisting.

"I had *you*. And now you're safe," he says smiling.

"You have the people. You have to lead them," I insist.

"No, Jade. *You* have to lead them," he smiles. "You're technically next in line now. And besides, you've been taking care of them for over a decade now. They'll want you."

"Roan, please," I sputter as I feel him slipping away from me.

"Get out of the way, Jade," I hear Lucas demand as he wraps his arms around my waist and pulls me back. My dress trails after me, brushing over Roan's legs before I'm pulled far enough away.

I struggle against him to get back to Roan until I see my father run past us and kneel by the man I married only a few short months ago.

"Look at me," Lucas says, spinning me around to face him. "Jade, focus on me. Whatever is going on back there, you don't need to see."

He holds my gaze, refusing to let me turn back as my father works to save Roan.

"Jade, listen to me. I have to get you out of here, now. It's too dangerous to leave you here."

"I'm not going anywhere, Lucas. I'm not leaving him," I refuse. "He can't hurt me now anyway, they all know."

"No Jade, they don't. They know someone is trying to hurt you. They know Roan had knowledge of that. He chose to protect his father when he stopped you, so no one knows it was him.

"I did not spend my entire life watching out for you to have you mess it up now.

"Anything could happen in this room. He could kill us all and say the people who tried to hurt you broke in and finished us all off to make a point."

"Well, we're not leaving my father here with him then. He can't take all of us on all by himself."

When he can't move me, he gives in, letting me stay. I try turning, but his grip on my arm is so tight that I can't.

"Thank you, Lucas, for protecting me all these years," I say, not knowing what else to do. I can't bear to listen to them work on Roan. "I wish I had known. We would have been… good friends."

"Friends," he contemplates. "Yes, I'm sure we would have been."

For the first time since I've met the man, he doesn't look charming. He looks worried and sad. He looks like the most dependable person in my world. *This* is the man

I would have known had he not been in the shadows all of my life.

"Jade," Roan's voice says softly.

Lucas lets me break free, and I run to Roan as my father backs away. A moment later I hear my father struggling with the Commander as he throws him against a wall. Lucas works to break up the fight, but the yelling continues.

My fingers brush over Roan's cheek.

"I don't know what they did," he struggles to breathe. "But your dad says I'm going to be okay."

I'm so overjoyed that I kiss him. He can't breathe, can't move, but somehow, he finds it in him to wrap his arm around me and kiss me back.

"I love you, Jade Jareau Diamond," he whispers.

"I love you, too, Roan Diamond." I smile and kiss him again.

"Enough!" Lucas shouts, finally pulling the dueling men apart.

"This is treason!" the Commander shouts. "You will hang for this!"

"For what?" my father challenges.

"For trying to kill the Commander!"

"You tried to kill my daughter! You've killed others! Once the people find out about this…"

"But they won't," the Commander grins. "Roan will never turn on me. And he's the only one they *might* believe. And the entire rest of the Command obeys *me*. Besides, there were people with me this whole time… I *couldn't* have done anything."

"But you did," Roan's voice cracks as he struggles to sit up. I push him back, catching his head in my hand and cradling it there. "You're done. Jade is free. This feud is over."

The Commander examines his son with his hand wrapped around my arm, calculating his next move.

"All right," he agrees after several moments.

"All right?" my father questions.

"We're done. I won't try to kill her anymore."

"She's free. She can see me whenever she wants. She does not answer to you and you will stay away from her," my father clarifies the terms.

"She's free to see you. But if there's any rebellious action," he glares at my father, "you both will be held accountable."

"If you want retribution, Robert, call me out publicly. Do not threaten my daughter or me again. And if you threaten the town again, so help me, I'll make sure the entire country knows about this. There are four witnesses in this room, not to mention witnesses to your terror outside of this building. They can't ignore us all. There are more of us than there are of you. We can overtake you," my father's words quicken as he speaks and I see the spark from when I was five jump back into his eyes.

"Careful, James, that sounds rather treasonous," Robert warns in a terrifying voice.

"Enough," Lucas says. "We're leaving. Now. You will not stop us and you won't go after them again."

"Ahh, yes, Lucas. I nearly forgot about you," the Commander growls as his lips curl, cutting Lucas off. "What would your father think if he could see you now?"

"He'd be proud," my father interjects. "Robert, *you fool.* Who else do you think *led* that rebellion?"

"*Asher...?*"

Realization washes over the Commander's face. He hadn't known he had missed a leader. I can see the anger building inside of him. That same hatred he radiated the day he married me to his son pulsed out of him as he moved toward Lucas.

"It's a good thing I *didn't* know, Lucas, because I would have—"

"What? Killed me like you tried to kill Jade? Only my death would have been a lot earlier, wouldn't it have been? Probably more traumatic too. At least you had the pleasure of watching James in terror all these years. My death would have had to have been horrific in order to inflict the same torment on my father."

"That's right. You've always been a smart boy. *Too* smart, apparently. It's a shame, Lucas; you could have had a nice life if you had just let go of your father's trivial ideals." The Commander's taunting turned to shouts.

"And now what…?" Lucas challenges.

I help Roan sit up as we watch the scene unfold. My eyes dart around the room. I search for anything we can use to defend ourselves. The argument escalates with every word as the men challenge each other.

My hand flits up to my hair. The poison.

I attempt to untangle it from my hair, ripping out strands in the process.

"And now you pay," the Commander answers.

He charges toward Lucas, knocking them both down. The door bursts open and Daniella fights her way inside, screaming at Lucas to stop.

On their feet again, Lucas swings at the Commander. They are in an all-out brawl by the time I finally get the hair comb free of my wild hair.

"Stop!" I shout.

"Jade, what are you doing?" Roan asks.

"It's poison, I'm going to threaten him to make him back off," I reply looking back at Roan. His eyes are wide, realizing what I'd been carrying with me all this time.

Somehow, the Commander manages to reveal a knife he had hidden in his jacket pocket as the blows become worse. I scream as he stabs Lucas.

He stumbles backward, landing against the wall. Blood pours from the wound in his abdomen. He fixes his eyes on the Commander.

"Get her out of here!" he shouts to my father who is trying to protect Daniella from the fight.

She pushes past him, lunging at the Commander. She attempts to pull him away but he shoves her off as he moves in to attack Lucas again.

"No!" I shout, but as I attempt to stand to my feet, Roan rips the poison from my hand.

Terrified, I look down at him, still sitting on the floor. I know I have to get it back if I'm going to stop this madness. But before I can turn on him, he throws the hair comb across the room.

"Lucas!" he shouts, knowing it's the only way. "It's poison!"

Roan gives Lucas permission to save himself, even if it costs his father his life. He loves his father and I can see the anguish in his eyes as he protects Lucas, but he can't let his father hurt the man. He will protect others, no matter the cost. Given his father's murderous rampage, he has no choice. It's the only way.

Lucas manages to scoop it up and fumbles to get it open. The Commander falls to his knees and wrestles it away, ripping it free and exposing the dangerous piece that contains the toxin.

Daniella screams, pulling as hard as she can. Her job has always been to protect the Commander. She worships the man, as many in the Command do. Her attempts to save him are of no use. The Commander will not be deterred.

As he elbows her back, she slips, falling in between Lucas and the Commander. Her hands grip his shoulder, arching her into the Commander's chest in an attempt to catch herself.

Her eyes lock on to the Commander's as the life slips out of them. He breathes in, realizing what happened. It's as if a switch goes off in him and he crumples. Pulling his secretary into his arms, he fights to wake her up. She remains lifeless.

"Save her," he begs, holding the woman to my father.

"I can't, Robert," my father shakes his head mournfully. "She's gone."

Lucas scrambles for the poison, ripping it away from the reach of the Commander. He closes it and throws it back to me. I hand it to Roan, trusting him to take care of it. He looks so relieved that his father is alive and so heartbroken over Daniella all at the same time.

My father takes the knife away from the Commander and helps Lucas move away from the man. I scramble to his side and use my father's jacket to apply pressure to the wound until my father can look at it. Over the years, and even before the rebellion as my father was preparing for it, he learned a great deal of medical procedures. He made sure all of his people were well trained before the takeover took place.

Roan cautiously moves toward us, still uneasy from his own bout with poison. He sits in front of me, blocking me from his father who is still crashing down from the high of his rage.

Lucas attempts to sit up, but I force him to lay still. Gathering everything he has, he addresses us.

"Your secretary is dead, Robert. There's no going back now."

The Commander glances up, looking around at us all. He nods, connecting the dots.

"It was Daniella," the Commander slowly says. "She tried to poison Jade. When Roan found out and it failed, she came in here to finish the job. Daniella has no family; no one to say she wasn't plotting this.

"In a heroic turn of events, Lucas tried to stop her, at which point he was stabbed," he says, taking out the knife and wiping the handle clean. He places it in Daniella's hand. "Lucas fought her off, but in the struggle, the knife found its way into her. She bled out before we could do anything."

He lifts his secretary's hand and plunges the knife into her abdomen, creating a large cut. Blood pools out, but not enough. He moves her body to the stains left by Lucas.

"We now have our person who attempted to hurt Jade. We have a hero in Lucas. Roan is still alive, the poison clearly not working the way it should have," he directs.

"And you have a narrative in which you didn't murder anyone," my father concludes.

"And you will not contradict me," the Commander rises to his feet, lifting himself as high as he can. "Because all those people are still loyal to me. And this can still have a *very* different ending."

My father considers his words, but it's Roan that speaks.

"We will not contradict you, Father. But, like we said… Jade is free now. And if you ever do anything to change that, there are four witnesses in this room who will tell the people what really happened here today: You killed Daniella, you nearly killed me, and you stabbed Lucas."

Roan struggles to his feet. My father moves to Roan's side but when he sees Lucas, he turns to him. I move back, standing to take my place beside my husband.

"You are done. You no longer have control over me or Jade. I will continue to work here, but I will do it on my terms. When the time comes, *and it's coming sooner than you think*, I will take over as Commander and you will step down. You'll be able to enjoy the rest of your life at home, instead of in a cell. You will endorse whatever I choose to do.

"Jade is free to live her life however she wants. You will not interfere. If she chooses to stay with me, she will be the next Commander's wife and she will handle those responsibilities as she sees fit."

Without backing down, Roan makes his list of demands. I slip my arm through his, both to steady him and to let him know how proud I am of him.

"She can't stay," the Commander says.

"Yes, she can. If she'll have me, she can stay and do whatever she wants." Roan looks to me and I smile.

"She has obligations as a Commander's wife, even one that isn't Commander yet," the Commander insists.

"And she's aware of that. She will do what she has to do."

I nod, confirming that I understand.

"And James and Lucas will be left alone, too. They are, after all, heroes now."

I beam as Roan says this. I'm enjoying commanding the Commander now.

People pound on the door, trying to get in. They heard all the shouting, but the door remained locked in an effort to save the lives of anyone else that might suffer Daniella's fate.

"Now or never, Dad. Agree and we open that door

and let you do the talking. Don't agree and I'll be the one that greets them at the door," he threatens.

"Fine."

"You step down this year, Dad. Just enough time for you to wrap things up and publicly put your trust in me."

The Commander looks panicked, but he doesn't have a choice. The people are forcing their way in the door.

"Fine."

"And you don't touch *my wife* ever again."

"Fine," he snaps.

"Jade, get the door," Roan says quietly to me.

I rush to the door and open it just before they try breaking in.

"We're safe," I say as they push past me.

The Commander holds up his hand and waves them off.

"Daniella was the one who tried to hurt Jade. She came back to finish what she started. Thankfully, Lucas was quick on his feet and fought her off. He was injured in the process but James was here helping Roan and was able to take care of them both. It's a miracle James remembers so much of what his wife taught him."

Of course, he would drag my mother into this. But... how did he know my mother used to be a nurse? I suppose he might remember her mentioning it at a Command Party before she died but that was so long ago.

The people gathered around us, flustering over each

of us. A doctor races in. Assessing that Lucas was the one in need of the most attention, he kneels to work on him first. Roan tucks the hair comb back in my hair when no one is looking, keeping it far from prying eyes that might question the Commander's story.

A few hours later, we are on the stage again, listening to the Commander repeat his story for the public. Lucas is in the hospital, recovering from his wounds. Roan stands by me, his arm wrapped around my shoulder for support. My father stands guard over us on my other side.

Daniella is painted as a villain. I nearly cry as I listen to the Commander destroy that beautiful woman's life. She gave everything she had to the Command and she died trying to protect the Commander. She didn't deserve this.

After the speech, we all went home, safe for the first time in over a decade.

CHAPTER 38
JADE

I stand in front of the Command office buildings in my hometown. The Commander went through with his plan to destroy my beautiful library. Roan holds my hand, silently comforting me.

Lucas walks to the podium as the Commander returns to his seat. He has a nasty scar where he was stabbed, but in the two months since our liberation, he's recovered quickly and gone back to work.

He gives a speech about the new building and how helpful it will be to the Command employees and the town as a whole. He also promises to find a way to give back to the community since the library is no longer available.

Mr. Eroh's shop has been rebuilt and part of the store will be turned into a small library for people to borrow books from until a new building can be constructed. I love going to work every day and helping people find something to read.

At the end of the speeches, we all wander inside to tour the new offices. My father has the largest office. He let me decorate it for him. My drawing of the pond sits proudly on his desk. The portrait Roan painted of me sits on one wall.

Lucas' office is spacious and perfectly suited to him. Roan and I linger behind to talk with him. We chat for a moment before Lucas and Roan are called out for a brief meeting.

I sit perched on his desk, awaiting their return. Now that Lucas is free to live his life without watching over me, I plan on finding him a nice girlfriend.

I don't bother looking up as I hear someone slip in the door. The footsteps are heavy, clearly one of the men in my life.

"Do you like the new offices, Jade?"

My head whips up as I realize the Commander is in the room with me. I haven't spoken to him since the day Daniella died, other than what I was forced to do in public.

He sneers at me.

"Oh, you didn't think it would be that easy to be rid of me, now did you?" he taunts. "Don't worry, the boys are still in their meeting. I wanted to catch you alone, my *ever-so-practical* daughter-in-law."

I look around for a weapon, just in case. His presence makes my hair stand on end and I know his being here isn't a coincidence. He has something planned.

"We need to talk, Jade," he pauses, smiling triumphantly.

"We're not done yet," he opens his hand to reveal a necklace. *My mother's necklace.* The one *Aunt Sophie* has worn since the day my mother died.

I look up into his eyes and find murder written there.

Read the first chapter of RISEN after the Acknowledgements

ACKNOWLEDGMENTS

Well, we've survived the start to another series. Don't say I didn't warn you—*I totally warned you.*

I absolutely love Jade's story. I liked it from the start, fell completely in love with it halfway through, and now, all these years later, I love it even more. Her story is so special to me and her integrity is inspiring.

Thank you to the amazing people in my own life who have shown that kind of integrity. It isn't easy to suffer to protect others.

To my sister, who actually lived the butterfly scene with me. That was one of the defining horrifying moments of our young adulthood...I know this is horrible, but I'm glad I wasn't sobbing alone. (*I bet you don't even remember that!*)

Special thanks, from all of us, to my darling beta readers who rallied around Smarmy (Lucas) and forced me not to write him out of the book. I know you're all really attached to him, so thanks for making me keep him and let him have his important role in the story. I know you all thought it was hilarious when I was complaining about him as I was writing. *You win; he can stay.*

Thank you, thank you, thank you to Alexis and Elissa. You kept me sane and you saved my life. I cannot tell you how grateful I am to you both!

Thanks to Claerie for your help and support!

To Awnna Marie Evans, you saved me and you're amazing. I am so grateful to you! I love that I got to work with you on this project. I appreciate you so much and I'm so glad to call you friend!

Alexis, thank you for the beautiful artwork that you created once again for my book. I'd be lost without you! Your work is spectacular and you amaze me every single time!

Thank you to my amazing fans! You made *Golden* such a success and now you've done it again for *Jaded*! I love you guys! You're the best!

Special shout out to Yentl for all of your hard work and amazing support! I truly appreciate you being a part of my author life!

Now I know you have questions and I promise I'm going to answer them. I know exactly how this duology ends, and I have known since only a few chapters into *Jaded*. There is a plan. I'm dying to share *Risen* with you, and rest assured, it is coming. But don't say I didn't warn you.

Keep reading for a first look at the sequel, Risen, as well as find out how to get bonus scenes, play an interactive game to help Mr. Eroh as he tries to SAVE JADE behind the scenes of the story and then see how your actions played into the book—no really, if you read Jaded again, you can see what you did to move the story forward—and more!

Stay inspired,

-K.M. Robinson

RISEN: BOOK TWO OF THE JADED DUOLOGY

If the only way to save everything you've gained was to sacrifice yourself, would you be able to do it?

Jade is the only one who knows the Commander has one last trick up his sleeve and now she has to make a deal with the devil to protect the people she loves. Distancing herself from Roan, her father, and friends isn't easy, but if it means they get to live, she'll do whatever it takes.

Roan is blissfully unaware that anything is wrong as he takes over as Commander now that his father has been defeated, but as he works to better the country, he starts to discover something isn't right. Teaming up with Lucas and the rest of the people that love Jade, he's ready to fight for her life and turn his back on his family to do it.

With an out-of-control villain trying to enact his final endgame move, it's a devastating fight to see who will survive.

One will be lost. One will be found. In the midst of heartbreak, only one will survive.

Now available!

Learn more about riseninfo.kmrobinsonbooks.com

"Where did you get that?" I launch myself at the Commander's hand, attempting to snatch away my mother's necklace. My Aunt Sophie has worn that necklace since my mother died when I was five. He pulls it out of my reach.

"You know where I got it." The Commander sneers at me, allowing me to take the necklace from him. I intentionally dig my nails into his palm, making him wince.

"I told you, Jade, it's not that easy to be rid of me. Now, you and I had a deal and we're not done yet."

"What do you want?" I growl, praying Roan, Lucas, or my father would walk into the office, even though I know they are still in the meeting.

"I want you to hold up your end of the deal. Someone needs to pay for that rebellion, and it's going to be you."

I have a feeling it's also about the fact that I survived and this is payback.

"In case you've forgotten," I challenge my husband's father, *"you're* the one who killed Daniella in your office after you poisoned *your own son* in an attempt to poison *me.* You're not the one with leverage here."

"Oh, but, Jade, I am. As you can see by the necklace in your hand, I have Sophie. You say or do anything other than *exactly* what I tell you to say, and Sophie dies... and then I'll take your father out." He grins at me.

When I was five years old, my father, along with Lucas's father and several other political leaders, led a rebellion against the Commander and the Command. The goal was to reestablish a democracy in the country instead of the dictatorship we suffer under now. When it failed, the Commander found out my father was behind it. He couldn't do anything against my father publicly, but my life was fair game.

I was committed to marrying the Commander's son, Roan. His job was to gain my trust and kill me. Somewhere along the line, Roan decided he couldn't go through with it. With Lucas' help, we all managed to stay alive well past the point of intended internment.

Unlike my father, Lucas' father wasn't caught after the

rebellion ended and he charged Lucas with protecting me when we were children. I never knew him, but he was always looking out for me. When I nearly died, he inserted himself into my life once again to take care of me. He even went as far as to pretend to be friends with Roan so he could watch out for me from the inside. Now that the truth is out, they are working on becoming friends for real.

My father and Lucas work together in my hometown. Their new offices are being revealed today. I'm positive Lucas has weapons hidden around the room, but I try to keep my eyes from darting back and forth to look for them as the Commander stands before me.

"And what if I go public with this?" I ask.

"You might be able to protect your father, but you'll never get to Sophie in time." He shrugs carelessly. "But you should be aware that I also have people strategically placed to watch your father too."

"What do you want?" I ask again.

"I told you—you're going to die. I don't care how, really, as long as you're dead. You've destroyed my plans long enough, and I want my son to be rid of you. I never should have trusted him to be a part of this. But I got him *into* this mess, and now I'm going to get him *out* of it. You won't bewitch him any longer, Jade."

"He came to the conclusion that you were a *monster* all

on his own, *Robert.*" It was the first time I had referred to him as anything other than his title. He no longer holds power over me...although at this point, he apparently *does.*

"Make a choice, Jade. You or Sophie."

The commander reaches out, taking the necklace back from my limp hand. He dangles it, swinging it back and forth like the pendulum on one of the grandfather clocks in Mr. Eroh's shop where I work.

"Tick tock, my dear," he sings at me.

I watch as it sways back and forth, weighing my options.

I want to run to Roan and tell him what his father is doing. I have three men in this building who would put a stop to the Commander this instant, if only I could reach them.

"Don't even think about it, Jade," the Commander says, as if reading my mind. "You have precisely one minute to answer me. One of my people is waiting for your answer. If they don't hear from me in the next few moments, they execute Sophie on the spot."

"So what exactly is your master plan *this* time?" I bite.

"Same as before." He smiles. "We make believe we like each other for the public. You don't tell Roan or Lucas or your father. You leave your people out of this. You back me on absolutely everything I say, *publicly,* and sing my praises. In a little while, you'll be in an accident. Not even your father will be able to pin it on me. And this time, Roan doesn't get hurt."

"He'll know it was you if I die. You won't fool him."

"Maybe not, but he'll never give me up. And he'll move on, you'll see. Well, *no*, actually, I don't suppose you will." He laughs. "You've caused me more trouble than your father has, Jade, and that's surprising. I should have just killed you when you were a child and spared myself all this grief."

"Clearly you should have," I agree sarcastically.

"Last chance, Jade. Agree to stand by me and die when the time is right in exactly one month from now, or say goodbye to Sophie right here and now."

Laughter erupts outside the door, down the hall. The men were coming back.

"Now or never," he says quietly.

I can't let Sophie die. I have a month until my execution date, apparently, which gives me time to figure things out.

"Tick tock."

The laughter gets closer and the Commander moves to slip out the door. He shrugs.

"Fine by me," my father-in-law says at my silence.

"Wait!" I call. He turns and I give him a short nod.

The Commander smiles as he tosses the necklace to me.

"Now be a good girl and keep your mouth shut...I'll

know if you don't—I have people everywhere" he adds and darts out the door, giving him just enough time to slip away before the men turn the corner and approach.

"Are you okay, Jade?" Roan frowns as he follows Lucas into the room.

I have one month to live... yeah, I'm great.

I give him a small smile, trying to recover from my conversation with his father.

"Is your meeting done?" I ask.

"Yes, are you ready to go home?"

Yes, I have to get out of here and figure out what to do.

"Sure," I nod.

"Lucas, you want to come over? We can hang out and have dinner," Roan suggests.

He forgave Lucas awfully fast for having learned their entire friendship was a farce. But who am I to judge?

"Yeah, sure," he shrugs. Reaching around me, he grabs his jacket and tosses it over his arm. It's far too warm for jackets, but I have a feeling it's for appearance's sake.

We stop in my father's office. He smiles when I step inside.

"Headed home?" he wraps an arm around my shoulder.

"Yeah, Lucas is coming over for dinner, want to come?"

"I wish I could," he says sadly. "Unfortunately, now

that the offices are up and running, they've got me swamped. Maybe tomorrow we could have lunch?"

Now that I was finally free to see my father publicly, we've been spending a lot of time together when I'm in town to work. Whenever he can sneak away for lunch, we meet at the bakery. If he can catch a few spare minutes, he'll pop into Mr. Eroh's store to say hello. Now that he's settled into his new workspace, I plan on visiting him at work more often too.

"Sure, that would be great."

"See you tomorrow." He kisses the top of my head and waves to Roan and Lucas as we all retreat into the hallway.

My ultimate goal is to get my father and Roan to spend more time together. Their relationship is still pretty rocky after the whole *Roan-is-trying-to-kill-me* incident.

We chat on the way back to the house. I let the boys go out to the garden while I poke around the kitchen looking for something to feed them a bit later. I've been trying to give them a little extra space in hopes that it will make the coconspirators-to-*actual*-friends transition faster.

As soon as they are out of sight, I pull the necklace out of my pocket where I hid it when they walked in. It sparkles in the same way it used to when my Aunt Sophie wore it when I was little...before she started keeping her distance. Once the marriage mandate was made public, Sophie kept far away so she wouldn't be connected to us when the time came for me to be killed. The plan was for her to work behind the scenes to help me, but it wouldn't work if people knew about her being a part of my life.

I examine every inch of the necklace, hoping Sophie left some kind of clue. Finding nothing, I open the locket. A piece of paper floats out and I catch it in mid-air.

Tonight. 11pm.

My eyes tear as I realize it's not a note from Sophie, but from the Commander. As if he didn't have enough of a say earlier. Now I have to sneak out of my own home to go and meet him.

For two months I had been free of the man and now I am right back under his control.

I wish I could tuck my hair clip back into my long tresses, but that bit of safety was revealed during my last meeting with the Commander, when he used it to accidentally kill his secretary, Daniella. The poison inside had killed her almost instantly, providing the perfect scapegoat for the Commander to avoid being blamed for attempting to kill me, nearly killing his son, and trying to get revenge on my father. Now I have no safety net as I go to meet the monstrous leader of our tiny country.

I destroy the note, ripping it into tiny pieces. Disposing of it, I wish I were banishing the Commander instead of just his note.

Dinner goes by quickly. It's nice spending time with Roan and Lucas. They've really become my best friends over these past few months. I've come to rely on their friendship.

Lucas says goodnight and heads home as darkness draws in.

"So, are you really doing okay? I know today was hard for you." Roan asks, guiding me to the couch.

I lean against his shoulder, resting my head on him.

"I hated seeing the library gone," I admit, "but the offices are nice."

"You did a great job on your father's office," he compliments me.

I smile as I stare across the room. He can feel it against his shoulder, and he grins too, his cheek moving my hair as he does.

"This is nice," he finally says.

I can't say I disagree. Being with Roan is *more* than nice.

We sit for a few more minutes before I announce I'm going to bed. He watches me walk away before I hear him get up to go to his own room. Even though we've decided to start a real relationship, we've kept our boundaries. We may be married *technically*, but we're taking things slow and getting to know each other.

Once I'm sure he's in for the night, I prop open my window and climb out. It eerily reminds me of the day I snuck out two months ago to meet the Commander... *also to make a deal for my death.* This was becoming a habit.

It's strange walking through the town at night on my own. It's never been safe for me to be alone, but even with my newfound freedom, I had yet to venture outside by myself at night.

The stars shimmer as I walk. Only a few clouds skim past the moon, hardly blocking my only source of light. It's starting to get cooler in the evenings now and I shiver as I walk. I wish I had thought to dress warmer.

The guards let me in when I reach the gate of the Commander's home. I don't even have to ask where to go; I know where he'll be waiting.

Since his first plan failed disastrously, he'll be keeping things close to the vest this time. I doubt even his wife, Alice, will know. The soft glow from the pool house tells me I'm right.

Inside, the dim light reflects off of the water, fluid white lines dancing across the walls. The last time I was here was when Roan kissed me for the first time. How I wish we were back in that drying box, air flying all around us, with Roan's arms wrapped around me, pulling me closer as our lips pulsed together.

"Surprised to see me?" I ask as I stand by the door. I leave it open with my hand between it and the doorframe in case I need to escape.

"You're a smart girl, Jade. I figured you'd find my note." He takes a step toward me and I tense. "Like I said, Jade, you have a month. Now sit down."

When I refuse, he continues.

"The good news is, I have a plan, Jade. Better than the last one. This time, I don't even have to lift a finger."

"And how is that?" I ask.

"Because, Jade, when I'm done, the entire country is going to hate you. You see, my dear, I'm turning *you* into the villain this time. No more hero status for you. You're going down, but not in a blaze of glory; *you're* going down in *flames*."

"A villain?" I smirk. He can't turn the people against me.

"They'll hate you when I'm done." He seems so proud of himself. "Like I said, you're going to agree with everything I tell you to do, so when I start letting you make public choices that the people don't like… well, they'll be angry with you—angry enough to kill."

And suddenly I understand. He *does* have the power to do that. I have to say and do everything he tells me to, and if he makes me hurt the people, they'll eventually turn on me. If he's giving me a month for a time limit, whatever I'm going to do publicly must be big…and truly terrible.

"What—?" I start but get cut off.

"You're going to destroy this country, one piece at a

time. You'll stand for everything your father hated all those years ago. You'll publicly side with me and do things even *I* wouldn't dream of doing. Now that I *trust you*— at least as far as the public is concerned—and I start giving you responsibilities and power, you're going to go a little mad, my dear. This is going to be so fun to watch." He grins. "And the people—*even Roan*—will think the power has gone to your head and you're getting carried away. They'll never even question it."

"You expect all this to happen in a month?"

"Oh, yes, Jade, I do." He smiles, flashing his teeth at me. "Because I seem to be *falling ill*. You know it's going to happen anyway because of Roan's mandate. He'll simply think I'm playing nice. And while *he* steps up, so will *you*. But, *of course*, we have *so* much faith in you that we give *you* more power than *any* Commander's wife has been given; we'll give you *real* power. And when your decisions come out shaky...well, *I'm too sick to handle it* until after the fact. And we all know Roan can't control you. Someone will step up to fix the problem, I'm sure of that."

"Meaning you'll *make sure* someone does," I comment angrily.

He touches his chest as if genuinely concerned.

"Meaning I have to keep in touch with my people. If they are unhappy, I need to know about it. I may not be able to do anything other than advise, but, my dear," he sneers gleefully at me, "I'll be careful to make sure they know they *aren't allowed to hurt you in order to stop you.* That should do the trick."

He really *does* have it all figured out. It's truly the perfect plan—much better than his first plan. Or second. And this time, his hands would be clean as far as anyone could prove.

"So, Jade, time to strike a deal," he says arrogantly.

"Fine," I whisper, unable to look at him.

"What was that, dear?" he taunts me.

"Fine," I shout, despising him with everything in me.

"Good. Then Sophie can live another day. She'll be so pleased." He drops the happy act and his usual hatred spews out. "One word—to anyone—and she dies. Push me, and your father dies. I will no longer care about public image; I'll kill him and make sure everyone knows and that is how I will lead from now on.

"Furthermore, if Roan even comes *close* to finding out, you have no idea how sorry you'll be. Now, run along, Jade. I'll be *unable* to be in the office tomorrow. I expect *you* here the day after, *with* Roan, when I tell him he's temporarily taking over. Play nice and this will all go a lot easier. Understood?"

I nod and he raises an eyebrow, waiting for me to speak.

"Fine," I agree to his sick game.

Taking a step toward me, he runs his hand down my

arm slowly, as he once did several months ago to upset my father. I wrench away from him and fling the door open. Running, I hear him laughing after me.

I signed a deal with a monster tonight.

Again.

BONUS SCENES

Want to read a bonus scene from Jaded? We're giving out an exclusive bonus scene over on the K.M. Robinson Facebook page where you can read a scene from before Jade's wedding that motivated Jade to dye her wedding dress in rebellion.

Get them by sending the page a direct message
at
www.facebook.com/kmrobinsonbooks

We're constantly giving out additional bonus scenes for

preorder swag, giveaways, and more, so watch the social media pages carefully for the next scene giveaway.

K.M. Robinson also has bonus scenes and extras from all of her books on
newsletter.kmrobinsonbooks.com

Sign up now for weekly emails with special bonuses, extras, live broadcasts replays and upcoming dates, events, coloring pages, games, introductions to new authors+live broadcasts with them, and more.

WORLD PORTALS

Ready to learn exclusive facts about The Jaded Duology and other K.M. Robinson Series?

World Portals are now available on
www.kmrobinsonbooks.com

Learn behind the scenes facts, watch videos, play games, check out our book filters, find out where to get bonus scenes, view fan art, and get access to other secrets we've hidden away inside the World Portals on the website.

The World Portals are constantly changing and information is being taken away and added all the time, so check back frequently for new content!

SAVE JADE GAME

Join Mr. Eroh on his mission to save Jade from Commander Diamond, his son, Roan, and their revenge mission to murder an innocent woman.

Join the battle for Jade's life and go on a mission for her mentor to help save Jade.

This interactive, choose-your-own-adventure game is played through Facebook messenger so you never miss a mission. Played over the course of two-three days, Mr. Eroh will send several missions which you can then go back into the story to see how your choices affected Jade's journey.

PLAY THE GAME

at

savejadegame.kmrobinsonbooks.com

Mr. Eroh will send a series of missions over the course of a few days, with gaps of time in between so you can "complete the missions" and report back. He will be in touch!

Have fun running missions to help save Jade and then go back in the story to see how your choices directly affect Jade in the story.

Want to get your hands on some incredible Facebook filters for Jaded? Now you have the ability to get filters for the story, characters, etc right inside your phone.

You can use these on your photos, profile pictures,

videos, and live broadcasts. All you have to do is like my author page and they will automatically show up in your filters!

I've even taken these clips and put them on Instagram Stories by saving them to my phone and uploading them to Instagram.

Visit www.facebook.com/kmrobinsonbooks to grab these filters for your photos, videos, and broadcasts! Bonus points for tagging me @kmrobinsonbooks so I can see how you're supporting The Jaded Duology.

ABOUT THE AUTHOR

K.M. Robinson is a storyteller who creates new worlds both in her writing and in her fine arts conceptual photography. She is a marketing, branding and social media strategy educator who is recognized at first sight by her very long hair. She is a creative who focuses on photography, videography, couture dress making, and writing to express the stories she needs to tell. She almost always has a camera within reach. Visit her at her website: www.kmrobinsonbooks.com

CONNECT ON SOCIAL MEDIA

facebook.com/kmrobinsonbooks

instagram.com/kmrobinsonbooks

twitter.com/kmrobinsonbooks

Get free excerpts and full novels from K.M. Robinson at
excerpt.kmrobinsonbooks.com

ALSO BY K.M. ROBINSON

The Golden Trilogy

Book One: Golden

Forged: A Golden Novella

Book Two: Locked

Book Three: Edge

The Complete Series Boxset/Omnibus with Tempered: an exclusive bonus novella

The Jaded Duology

Book One: Jaded

Book Two: Risen

The Complete Series Boxset/Omnibus with exclusive epilogue

The Siren Wars Saga

Book One: The Siren Wars

Book Two: Darker Depths

Book Three: Beyond The Shores

Origins of the Siren Wars: Prequel Novella

Book Four: Forbidden Waters (coming soon)

The Legends Chronicles

Along Came A Spider: A Prequel Novelette

And They'll Come Home: A Prequel Novelette

The Archives of Jack Frost Series

The Revolution of Jack Frost

The Redemption of Jack Frost (coming soon)

Stealing Steam Series

Book One: Lions and Lamps

Book Two: Pistons and Prisoners

Book Three: Railcars and Rulers

Top Hats and Telegraphs: A Prequel Novella

The Complete Series Boxset/Omnibus with Vambraces and Victories: an exclusive bonus novella

Virtually Sleeping Beauty: A Novella Retelling

The Goose Girl and The Artificial: A Novella Retelling

The Sinking: A Little Mermaid Novella Retelling

Cindrill: A Cinderella Assassin Novella Retelling

Sugarcoated: A Hansel and Gretel's Witch Novella Retelling

GOLDEN: BOOK ONE OF THE GOLDEN TRILOGY

Goldilocks wasn't naive. She was sent on a mission and Dov Baer is her new target.

When Auluria tricks the Baers into letting her into their home, they have no idea she's actually been sent by the enemy to destroy them. Intent on gathering information for her cousin to hand over to the Society seeking to destroy all of the rebel factions—including her own—she's willing to sacrifice Dov Baer to save her people... until she realizes her cousin lied to her.

Now that she's seen who Dov truly is, she has to decide between staying loyal to her only remaining family or protecting the man she's falling for. If her allegiances are discovered, either side could destroy her—assuming the Society doesn't get her first

Available now!

Learn more about The Golden Trilogy at goldeninfo. kmrobinsonbooks.com

THE SIREN WARS: BOOK ONE OF THE SIREN WARS SAGA

War has hovered around the kingdom of Scylla for generations ever since the original sirens left the mer collection generations ago after nearly drowning the human prince. Over the years, select mermaids from the royal bloodline have been trained as spies to work for the reigning kings and queens, keeping the collection safe from sirens and humans.

Celena and her partner, Merrick, work covertly for the royals—not even her twin brother knows. When they discover the sirens have broken through the barriers the mer set up to keep the sirens out, Celena and her friends must race to the old kingdom of Metten to stop them from starting a war within their borders.

When she's dragged to the surface, Celena realizes that the war above the waters is as deadly as the one below the waves—and sacrificing herself may be the only way to protect her family.

The Siren Wars have only just begun.

Available now!
Learn more about The Siren Wars Saga at sirenwarsinfo.
kmrobinsonbooks.com

deadlier, and he knows he can't trust the girl who snuck into the competition this year...but Cyra might not survive his ruthlessness either in a game where only the lion's heart can win.

All wishes require sacrifice, and someone is going to pay the price for the Stourbridge.

Available now!
Learn more about The Stealing Steam Series at
lionsandlampsinfo.kmrobinsonbooks.com

ALONG CAME A SPIDER: THE FIRST PREQUEL NOVELETTE TO THE LEGENDS CHRONICLES

Little Hacker Muffet
sat on her tuffet
destroying her cords and Way.
Along came a hacker named Spider,
who sat down beside her
and frightened his opponent away.

When Fet, one of the most skilled hackers in the Legends, discovers her best friend and leader of her group has been abducted and held for ransom, she must escape unnoticed and find Peep before it's too late.

When Spider, a new recruit training to join her hacker

ring, slips out with her and claims to have a plan to save her friend, Fet is forced to bring him along. As she discovers he's not who he claims to be, she faces grave danger and learns just how deadly a spider bite can be.

Now available!
Learn more about The Legends Chronicles at
acasinfo.kmrobinsonbooks.com

VIRTUALLY SLEEPING BEAUTY

o wake her up, he has to enter the game and help her beat it...

Surely the class president wouldn't illegally over-juice to stay in the virtual reality game citizens are allowed to play for four hours a day, but when Royce's aunt calls in a panic because her goddaughter hasn't left the game yet, his only option is to go inside the game and drag the girl out.

The golden knight quickly discovers the princess' absence in the real world isn't of her own doing—*she's trapped inside the game by unknown forces*—and if she can't escape soon, she could die for real outside of the game. He's even more shocked to discover that Rora outranks him inside of the game, which means she'll have to fight to *protect herself* from the evils locking her inside a dangerous world.

Can Rora and Royce work together to outsmart a vicious queen and evil magician, and defeat digital dragons, or will Rora slowly fade away until there's nothing left but an empty shell and the game ranking she will leave behind?

Now available!

Learn more about Virtually Sleeping Beauty at
vsbinfo.kmrobinsonbooks.com

THE REVOLUTION OF JACK FROST

No one inside the snow globe knows that Morozoko Industries is controlling their weather, testing them to form a stronger race that can survive the fall out from the bombs being dropped in the outside world—all they know is that they must survive the harsh Winter that lasts a month and use the few days of Spring, Summer, and Fall to gather enough supplies to survive.

When the seasons start shifting, Genesis and Jack know something is going on. As their team begins to find technology that they don't have access to inside their snow globe of a world, it begins to look more and more like one of their own is working against them.

. . .

Genesis soon discovers Morozoko Industries, but when a foreign enemy tries to destroy their weather program to make sure their destructive life-altering bombs succeed in destroying the outside world, only one person can shut down the machine that is spinning out of control and save the lives of everyone inside the bunker—Jack.

Now available!
Learn more about The Revolution of Jack Frost at
jackfrostinfo.kmrobinsonbooks.com

THE GOOSE GIRL AND THE ARTIFICIAL

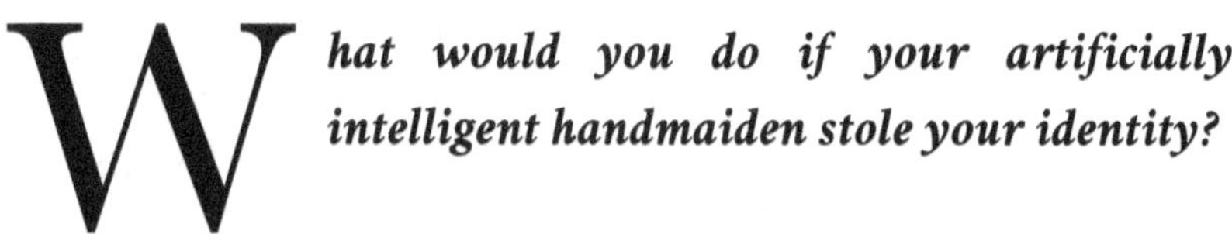

Threatened by her Artificial, Arta, Princess Goselyn is forced to switch places and pretend she isn't human when she reaches Prince Corinth to negotiate a treaty they both need to be able to take their respective crowns one day. If she doesn't comply, her Artificial, controlled by her evil cousin, will not only kill Goselyn's mother, but Prince Corinth and his father as well.

Can the quiet princess outsmart a machine created to be more intelligent than she is, all while surviving the other

Artificials and robots working against her in the foreign palace, or will Corinth and his father find out and destroy her chance to save them all?

356

Learn more about The Goose Girl and The Artificial at
goosegirlinfo.kmrobinsonbooks.com

THE SINKING

The sea witch wants to silence her, but not for the reason you think.

When a quirky older woman pawns a fancy seashell necklace at her mother's antique shop on the pier, Cara doesn't think much about the story the woman spins about the wearer turning into a mermaid.

On her way home, she accidentally drops the necklace into the ocean and is swept out to sea where she meets— a merman who volunteers to take her to his mother, the sea queen, to help her get her legs back.

· · ·

Cara soon learns that it's Quay's eighteen birthday—a day that has been a curse for his family—and is meant to be one for her too. Now she must fight to survive the sea with Quay at her side.

Fans of The Little Mermaid will love this twisted take on the beloved story.

Now available!
Learn more about The Sinking at
thesinkinginfo.kmrobinsonbooks.com

CINDRILL

inderella is an assassin out to murder the prince...*but he's hunting her too.*

The nanobots Cindrill's master gives her to use as a mask allow her to slip into the ball wearing a face that isn't hers, but when the assassination attempt goes sideways, Prince Davin doesn't understand why her face changes when he injures her, slicing her foot open around a unique pair of shoes as she runs away.

When Cindrill runs into the prince the next day without her nanobot mask on, he doesn't recognize her, but immediately decides her skills will be useful on his hunt for the would-be-assassin woman who nearly killed his father and his fiancée the night before.

Both are tasked with the job of murdering the other, but things don't quite go as they had planned when Cindrill's master and Davian's fiancée interfere as the two try to decide whether or not to kill the other.

It's hard to recognize a woman when she uses technology to change her appearance, but Cindrill is going to use that to her full advantage as she destroys the prince. **Will either survive?**

Now available!

Learn more about Cindrill at
cindrillinfo.kmrobinsonbooks.com

SUGARCOATED

Hansel and Gretel's witch was actually on their side...

Annika's job is to create a cake to match the candy-colored rooftops, nightly firework shows, and daily parades ending in unexpected executions for the mad king's ball, but her true mission is to sneak a thirteen-year-old assassin into the palace using her gift of illusions.

Hansel's job is to protect his little sister, Gretel, once she assassinates King Levin and ends the destruction in Candestrachen, using his power over light to rescue the young girl from the chaos her influence over life and death will create.

· · ·

When the entire forest reconstructs itself under Gretel's command while trying to save herself from a king's guard, Hansel and Annika must put their feelings aside and ensure their plan holds true—even if it means one of them has to sacrifice themselves to protect the mission.

Her illusions were meant to save her....but not everyone will survive the assassination attempt.

Learn more about Sugarcoated at
sugarcoatedinfo.kmrobinsonbooks.com

BLOOD IS SILENT

R ed Riding Hood is a circus aerialist and the wolf is ready to cage her.

Sienna has grown up working for the circus, dangling off her signature red silks every night. Her grandmother has been known to wander off to train new acts for their boss, but when Sienna tries to find her to bring her back to the show, she doesn't expect the dashing and dangerous Elijah to join her.

When they finally find Grandma Ida has been transformed deep in the heart of the woods, Sienna will stop at nothing to save her—but the wolf has her right where he wants her, and she won't be able to escape his claws.

She was told not to go into the woods alone.

Now available!

Learn more about Blood Is Silent at
bloodissilentinfo.kmrobinsonbooks.com